TWO FOR THE DOUGH

BY JANET EVANOVICH

THE STEPHANIE PLUM NOVELS

One for the Money	*Finger Lickin' Fifteen*
Two for the Dough	*Sizzling Sixteen*
Three to Get Deadly	*Smokin' Seventeen*
Four to Score	*Explosive Eighteen*
High Five	*Notorious Nineteen*
Hot Six	*Takedown Twenty*
Seven Up	*Top Secret Twenty-One*
Hard Eight	*Tricky Twenty-Two*
To the Nines	*Turbo Twenty-Three*
Ten Big Ones	*Hardcore Twenty-Four*
Eleven on Top	*Look Alive Twenty-Five*
Twelve Sharp	*Twisted Twenty-Six*
Lean Mean Thirteen	*Fortune and Glory*
Fearless Fourteen	

THE FOX AND O'HARE NOVELS WITH LEE GOLDBERG

The Heist	*The Pursuit*
The Chase	*The Big Kahuna*
The Job	(with Peter Evanovich)
The Scam	

KNIGHT AND MOON

Curious Minds	*Dangerous Minds*
(with Phoef Sutton)	

THE LIZZY AND DIESEL NOVELS

Wicked Appetite	*Wicked Charms*
Wicked Business	(with Phoef Sutton)

THE BETWEEN THE NUMBERS STORIES

Visions of Sugar Plums	*Plum Lucky*
Plum Lovin'	*Plum Spooky*

THE ALEXANDRA BARNABY NOVELS

Metro Girl	*Troublemaker*
Motor Mouth	(graphic novel)

JANET EVANOVICH

TWO FOR THE DOUGH

A STEPHANIE PLUM NOVEL

POCKET BOOKS

New York   London   Toronto   Sydney   New Delhi

Pocket Books
An Imprint of Simon & Schuster, Inc.
1230 Avenue of the Americas
New York, NY 10020

This book is a work of fiction. Any references to historical events, real people, or real places are used fictitiously. Other names, characters, places, and events are products of the author's imagination, and any resemblance to actual events or places or persons, living or dead, is entirely coincidental.

This Pocket Books paperback edition March 2021

POCKET and colophon are registered trademarks of Simon & Schuster, Inc.

For information about special discounts for bulk purchases, please contact Simon & Schuster Special Sales at 1-866-506-1949 or business@simonandschuster.com.

The Simon & Schuster Speakers Bureau can bring authors to your live event. For more information or to book an event, contact the Simon & Schuster Speakers Bureau at 1-866-248-3049 or visit our website at www.simonspeakers.com.

Manufactured in the United States of America

10 9 8 7 6 5 4 3 2 1

ISBN 978-1-9821-5390-8
ISBN 978-0-684-86853-0 (ebook)

To Alex and Peter

*Because they've always
had more faith
than common sense—
and are careful not to step
on a dream*

CHAPTER
1

I knew Ranger was beside me because I could see his earring gleaming in the moonlight. Everything else about him—his T-shirt, his flack vest, his slicked-back hair, and 9mm Glock—was as black as the night. Even his skin tone seemed to darken in shade. Ricardo Carlos Mañoso, the Cuban-American chameleon.

I, on the other hand, was the blue-eyed, fair-skinned product of a Hungarian-Italian union and was not nearly so cleverly camouflaged for clandestine evening activities.

It was late October, and Trenton was enjoying the death throes of Indian summer. Ranger and I were squatting behind a hydrangea bush at the corner of Paterson and Wycliff, and we weren't enjoying Indian summer, each other's company, or much of anything else. We'd been squatting there for three hours, and squatting was taking its toll on our good humor.

We were watching the small clapboard Cape Cod at 5023 Paterson, following a tip that Kenny Mancuso was scheduled to visit his girlfriend, Julia Cenetta. Kenny Mancuso had recently been charged with shooting a gas station attendant (who also happened to be his former best friend) in the knee.

Mancuso had posted a bail bond via the Vincent Plum Bail Bonding Company, insuring his release from jail and returning him to the bosom of polite society. After his release he'd promptly disappeared and three days later failed to show face at a preliminary hearing. This did not make Vincent Plum happy.

Since Vincent Plum's losses were my windfalls, I saw Mancuso's disappearance from a more opportunistic perspective. Vincent Plum is my cousin and my employer. I work for Vinnie as a bounty hunter, dragging felons who are beyond the long arm of the law back into the system. Dragging Kenny back was going to net me 10 percent of his $50,000 bond. A portion of that would go to Ranger for assisting with the takedown, and the rest would pay off my car loan.

Ranger and I had a sort of loose partnership. Ranger was a genuine, cool-ass, numero-uno bounty hunter. I asked him to help me because I was still learning the trade and needed all the help I could get. His participation was in the ballpark of a pity fuck.

"Don't think this is gonna happen," Ranger said.

I'd done the intel and was feeling defensive that maybe I'd had my chain yanked. "I spoke to Julia this morning. Explained to her that she could be considered an accessory."

"And that made her decide to cooperate?"

"Not exactly. She decided to cooperate when I told her how before the shooting Kenny had been sometimes seeing Denise Barkolowski."

Ranger was smiling in the dark. "You lie about Denise?"

"Yeah."

"Proud of you, babe."

I didn't feel bad about the lie since Kenny was a scumbag felon, and Julia should be setting her sights higher anyway.

"Looks like maybe she thought twice about reaping the rewards of revenge and waved Kenny away. You find out where he's living?"

"He's moving around. Julia doesn't have a phone number for him. She says he's being careful."

"He a first-time offender?"

"Yeah."

"Probably nervous about checking into the big house. Heard all those stories about date rape."

We turned silent as a pickup approached. It was a new Toyota 4x4 fresh off the showroom floor. Dark color. Temporary plates. Extra antennae for a car phone. The Toyota eased up at the Cape Cod and pulled into the driveway. The driver got out and walked to the front door. His back was to us and the lighting was poor.

"What do you think?" Ranger asked. "Is that Mancuso?"

I couldn't tell from this distance. The man was the right height and weight. Mancuso was twenty-one years old, six feet tall, 175 pounds, dark brown hair. He'd been discharged from the army four months ago, and he was in good shape. I had several pictures that were obtained when the bond had been posted, but they didn't do me any good from this angle.

"Could be him, but I can't swear to it without seeing his face," I said.

The front door of the house opened and the man disappeared inside. The door closed shut.

"We could go knock on the door nice and polite and ask if he's the man," Ranger said.

I nodded in agreement. "That might work."

We stood and adjusted our gun belts.

I was dressed in dark jeans, long-sleeved black turtleneck, navy Kevlar vest, and red Keds. I had my curly, shoulder-length brown hair tied in a ponytail, tucked under a navy ball cap. I wore my five-shot .38 Smith & Wesson Chief's Special in a black nylon webbed hip holster with cuffs and a defense spray wedged into the back of the belt.

We walked across the lawn and Ranger rapped on the front door to the house with a flashlight that was eighteen inches long and eight inches round at the reflector. It gave good light, and Ranger said it was excellent for making serious head dents. Fortunately, I've never had to witness any bludgeoning. I'd fainted flat out watching *Reservoir Dogs* and had no illusions about my blood-and-guts comfort level. If Ranger ever had to use the flashlight to crack skulls while I was around, I intended to close my eyes . . . and then maybe I'd take up another profession.

When no one answered I stepped to the side and unholstered my revolver. Standard procedure for the backup partner. In my case, it was more or less an empty gesture. I religiously went to the range to practice, but truth is I'm hopelessly unmechanical. I harbor an irrational fear of guns, and most of the time keep my little S & W empty of bullets so I won't accidentally blast the toes off my foot. On the one occasion I'd had to shoot somebody I'd been so flustered I'd forgotten to take my gun out of my pocketbook before pulling the trigger. I wasn't eager to repeat the performance.

Ranger rapped again, with more force. "Fugitive apprehension agent," he called out. "Open the door."

This drew a response, and the door was opened, not by Julia Cenetta or Kenny Mancuso, but by Joe Morelli, a Trenton Police Department plainclothesman.

We all stood silent for a moment, everyone surprised to see everyone else.

"That your truck in the driveway?" Ranger finally asked Morelli.

"Yeah," Morelli said. "Just got it."

Ranger nodded. "Good-looking vehicle."

Morelli and I were both from the burg, a blue-collar chunk of Trenton where dysfunctional drunks were still called bums and only pansies went to Jiffy Lube for an oil change. Morelli had a long history of taking advantage of my naiveté. I'd recently had the opportunity to even the score, and now we were in a period of reevaluation, both of us jockeying around for position.

Julia peeked at us from behind Morelli.

"So what happened?" I said to Julia. "I thought Kenny was supposed to stop around tonight?"

"Yeah, right," she said. "Like he ever does anything he says."

"Did he call?"

"Nothing. No call. Nothing. He's probably with Denise Barkolowski. Why don't you go knock on her stupid door?"

Ranger stayed stoic, but I knew he was smiling inside. "I'm out of here," he said. "Don't like to get involved in these domestic unpleasantries."

Morelli had been watching me. "What happened to your hair?" he asked.

"It's under my hat."

He had his hands shoved into his jeans pockets. "Very sexy."

Morelli thought everything was sexy.

"It's late," Julia said. "I gotta go to work tomorrow."

I looked at my watch. It was ten-thirty. "You'll let me know if you hear from Kenny?"

"Yeah, sure."

Morelli followed me out. We walked to his truck and stared at it in silence for a while, thinking our own thoughts. His last car had been a Jeep Cherokee. It had been bombed and blown to smithereens. Fortunately for Morelli, he hadn't been in the car at the time.

"What are you doing here?" I finally asked.

"Same as you. Looking for Kenny."

"I didn't think you were in the bond enforcement business."

"Mancuso's mother was a Morelli, and the family asked if I'd look for Kenny and talk to him before he got himself into any more trouble."

"Jesus. Are you telling me you're related to Kenny Mancuso?"

"I'm related to everyone."

"You're not related to me."

"You have any leads besides Julia?"

"Nothing exciting."

He gave that some thought. "We could work together on this."

I raised an eyebrow. Last time I worked with Morelli I'd gotten shot in the ass. "What would you contribute to the cause?"

"Family."

Kenny might be dumb enough to turn to family. "How do I know you won't cut me out at the end?" As he was sometimes prone to do.

His face was all hard planes. The sort of face that started off handsome and gained character as it aged. A paper-thin scar sliced through his left eyebrow. Mute testimony to a life lived outside the normal range of caution. He was thirty-two. Two years older than me. He was single. And he was a good cop. The jury was still out on its assessment of him as a human being.

"Guess you'll just have to trust me," he said, grinning, rocking back on his heels.

"Oh boy."

He opened the door to the Toyota and new-car aroma washed over us. He hitched himself up behind the wheel and cranked the engine over. "Don't suppose Kenny will show up this late," he said.

"Not likely. Julia lives with her mother. Her mother's a nurse on the night shift at St. Francis. She'll be home in half an hour, and I can't picture Kenny waltzing in when Momma's here."

Morelli nodded agreement and drove off. When his taillights disappeared in the distance I walked to the far corner of the block where I'd parked my Jeep Wrangler. I'd gotten the Wrangler second-hand from Skoogie Krienski. Skoogie had used it to deliver pizza from Pino's Pizzeria, and when the car got warm it smelled like baking bread and marinara sauce. It was the Sahara model, painted camouflage beige. Very handy in case I wanted to join an army convoy.

Probably I was right about it being too late for Kenny to show, but I figured it wouldn't hurt to hang out a little longer and make sure. I snapped the top on the Jeep so I wouldn't be so visible, and slouched back to wait. It wasn't nearly as good a vantage point as the hydrangea bush, but it was okay for my purposes. If Kenny appeared, I'd call Ranger on my cellular phone. I wasn't anxious to do a single-handed capture of a guy going down for grievous wounding.

After ten minutes a small hatchback passed by the Cenetta house. I slunk down in my seat and the car continued on. A few minutes later, it reappeared. It stopped in front of the Cape Cod. The driver beeped the horn. Julia Cenetta ran out and jumped into the passenger seat.

I rolled my engine over when they were half a block away, but waited for them to turn the corner before I hit the lights. We were on the edge of the burg, in a residential pocket of moderately priced single-family houses. There was no traffic, making it easier to spot a tail, so I stayed far behind. The hatchback connected with Hamilton and headed east. I hung tight, closing the gap now that the road was more traveled. I held this position until Julia and friend pulled into a mall lot and parked on the dark fringe.

The lot was empty at this time of night. No place for a nosy bounty hunter to hide. I cut my lights and eased into a parking place at the opposite end. I retrieved binoculars from the backseat and trained them on the car.

I almost jumped out of my shoes when someone rapped on my driver-side door.

It was Joe Morelli, enjoying the fact that he'd been able to catch me by surprise and scare the heck out of me.

"You need a night scope," he said affably.

"You're not going to see anything at this distance in the dark."

"I haven't got a night scope, and what are you doing here anyway?"

"I followed you. Figured you'd watch for Kenny a while longer. You're not very good at this law enforcement stuff, but you're freaking lucky, and you've got the temperament of a pit bull with a soup bone when you're on a case."

Not a flattering assessment, but dead accurate. "You on good terms with Kenny?"

Morelli shrugged. "Don't know him all that well."

"So you wouldn't want to drive over there and say hello."

"Hate to ruin Julia's good time if it isn't Kenny."

We were both staring at the truck, and even without a night scope we could see it had begun to rock. Rhythmic grunting sounds and whimpers carried across the empty lot.

I resisted the urge to squirm in my seat.

"Damn," Morelli said. "If they don't pace themselves, they're going to kill the shocks on that little car."

The car stopped rocking, the motor caught, and the lights flashed on.

"Jeez," I said. "That didn't take long."

Morelli hustled around to the passenger seat. "Must have gotten a head start on the way over. Wait until he hits the road before you use your lights."

"That's a great idea, but I can't see without my lights."

"You're in a parking lot. What's to see besides three acres of unobstructed macadam?"

I crept forward a little.

"You're losing him," Morelli said. "Step on it."

I pushed it up to 20, squinting into the darkness, swearing at Morelli that I couldn't see jackshit.

He made chicken sounds, and I mashed the gas pedal to the floor.

There was a loud *wump,* and the Wrangler bucked out of control. I slammed my foot to the brake and the car came to a sudden stop with the left side tilted at a 30-degree angle.

Morelli got out to take a look. "You're hung up on a safety island," he said. "Back up, and you should be okay."

I eased off the island and rolled several feet. The car pulled hard to the left. Morelli did the take-a-look thing again while I thrashed around in the driver's seat, sputtering and fuming and berating myself for listening to Morelli.

"Tough break," Morelli said, leaning into the open window. "You bent your rim when you hit the curb. You got road service?"

"You did this on purpose. You didn't want me to catch your rotten cousin."

"Hey, Cupcake, don't blame me just because you made some bad driving decisions."

"You're scum, Morelli. Scum."

He grinned. "Better be nice. I could give you a ticket for reckless driving."

I yanked the phone out of my pocketbook and called Al's Auto Body. Al and Ranger were good friends. During the day Al ran a legitimate business. I suspected that at night he ran a chop shop, hacking up stolen cars. It didn't matter to me. I just wanted to get my tire fixed.

An hour later I was on my way. No sense trying to track down Kenny Mancuso. He'd be long gone. I stopped at a convenience store, bought a pint of artery-clogging coffee ice cream, and headed for home.

I live in a blocky three-story brick apartment building located a couple miles from my parents' house. The front door to the building opens to a busy street filled with little businesses, and a tidy neighborhood of single-family bungalows sprawls to the rear.

My apartment is in the back of the building, on the second floor, overlooking the parking lot. I have one bedroom, one bath, a small kitchen, and a living room that combines with the dining area. My bathroom looks like it came off the set from *The Partridge Family,* and due to temporarily strained finances my furniture could be described as eclectic—which is a snooty way of saying nothing matches.

Mrs. Bestler from the third floor was in my hall when I got off the elevator. Mrs. Bestler was eighty-three and didn't sleep well at night, so she walked the halls to get exercise.

"Hey, Mrs. Bestler," I said. "How's it going?"

"Don't do no good to complain. Looks like

you've been out working tonight. You catch any criminals?"

"Nope. Not tonight."

"That's a pity."

"There's always tomorrow," I said, unlocking my door, slipping inside.

My hamster, Rex, was running on his wheel, his feet a blur of pink. I tapped on the glass cage by way of greeting, causing him to momentarily pause, his whiskers twitching, his shiny black eyes large and alert.

"Howdy, Rex," I said.

Rex didn't say anything. He's the small, silent type.

I dumped my black shoulder bag on the kitchen counter and got a spoon from the cutlery drawer. I popped the top on the ice cream container and listened to my phone messages while I ate.

All of the messages were from my mother. She was making a nice roast chicken tomorrow, and I should come for dinner. I should be sure not to be late because Betty Szajack's brother-in-law died and Grandma Mazur wanted to make the seven o'clock viewing.

Grandma Mazur reads the obituary columns like they're part of the paper's entertainment section. Other communities have country clubs and fraternal orders. The burg has funeral parlors. If people stopped dying, the social life of the burg would come to a grinding halt.

I finished off the ice cream and put the spoon

in the dishwasher. I gave Rex a few hamster nuggets and a grape and went to bed.

I woke up to rain slapping against my bedroom window, drumming on the old-fashioned black wrought-iron fire escape that serves as my balcony. I liked the way rain sounded at night when I was snug in bed. I couldn't get excited about rain in the morning.

I needed to harass Julia Cenetta some more. And I needed to run a check on the car that had picked her up. The phone rang, and I automatically reached for the portable at bedside, thinking it was early to be getting a phone call. The digital readout on my clock said 7:15.

It was my cop friend Eddie Gazarra.

"Morning," he said. "Time to go to work."

"Is this a social call?" Gazarra and I had grown up together, and now he's married to my cousin Shirley.

"This is an information call, and I didn't make it. Are you still looking for Kenny Mancuso?"

"Yes."

"The gas station attendant he nailed in the knee got dead this morning."

This put me on my feet. "What happened?"

"A second shooting. I heard from Schmidty. He was working the desk when the call came in. A customer found the attendant, Moogey Bues, in the gas station office with a big hole in his head."

"Jesus."

"I thought you might be interested. Maybe

there's a tie-in, maybe not. Could be Mancuso decided shooting his pal in the knee wasn't enough, and he came back to blow the guy's brains out."

"I owe you."

"We could use a baby-sitter next Friday."

"I don't owe you that much."

Eddie grunted and disconnected.

I took a fast shower, blasted my hair with the hair dryer, and squashed it under a New York Rangers hat, turning the brim to the back. I was wearing button-fly Levi's, a red plaid flannel shirt over a black T-shirt, and Doc Martens in honor of the rain.

Rex was asleep in his soup can after a hard night on the wheel, so I tiptoed past him. I switched the answering machine on, grabbed my pocketbook and my black-and-purple Gore-Tex jacket, and locked up behind myself.

The gas station, Delio's Exxon, was on Hamilton, not far from my apartment. I stopped at a convenience store on the way and got a large coffee to go and a box of chocolate-covered doughnuts. I figured if you had to breathe New Jersey air, there wasn't much point in getting carried away with always eating healthy food.

There were a lot of cops and cop cars at the gas station, and an emergency rescue truck had backed itself up close to the office door. The rain had tapered off to a fine drizzle. I parked half a block away and made my way through the crowd, taking my coffee and doughnuts with me, looking to spot a familiar face.

The only familiar face I saw belonged to Joe Morelli.

I sidled up to him and opened the doughnut box.

Morelli took a doughnut and shoved half in his mouth.

"No breakfast?" I asked.

"Got yanked out of bed for this."

"I thought you were working vice."

"I am. Walt Becker is the primary here. He knew I was looking for Kenny, and thought I'd want to be included."

We both chewed some doughnut.

"So what happened?" I asked.

There was a crime photographer working in the office. Two paramedics stood by, waiting to zip the body into a bag and take off.

Morelli watched the action through the plate-glass window. "The M.E. estimates time of death at six-thirty. That's right about when the victim would have been opening up. Apparently someone just walked in and blew him away. Three shots to the face, close range. No indication of theft. The cash drawer was intact. No witnesses so far."

"A hit?"

"Looks like it."

"This garage selling numbers? Dealing dope?"

"Nothing I know about."

"Maybe it's personal. Maybe he was screwing someone's wife. Maybe he owed money."

"Maybe."

"Maybe Kenny came back to shut him up."

Morelli didn't move a muscle. "Maybe."

"You think Kenny'd do that?"

He shrugged. "Hard to say what Kenny'd do."

"You run the plate on that car last night?"

"Yeah. It belongs to my cousin Leo."

I raised an eyebrow.

"It's a big family," he said. "I'm not that close anymore."

"You going to talk to Leo?"

"Soon as I'm out of here."

I sipped some of the steaming coffee and watched his eyes lock onto the Styrofoam cup. "Bet you'd like to have some nice hot coffee," I said.

"I'd kill for coffee."

"I'll let you have some if you'll let me tag along when you talk to Leo."

"Deal."

I took one last sip and passed him the cup. "You check on Julia?"

"Did a drive-by. The lights were out. Didn't see the car. We can talk to her after we talk to Leo."

The photographer was finished and the paramedics went to work, trundling the body into a bag, hefting it onto a stretcher. The stretcher clattered as it rolled over the doorstep, the bag jiggling with its dead weight.

The doughnut sat heavy in my stomach. I didn't know the victim, but I felt his loss all the same. Vicarious grief.

There were two homicide detectives on the scene, looking professional in trench coats. Under the trench coats they wore suits and ties. Morelli was wearing a navy T-shirt, Levi's, a tweed sport coat, and running shoes. A fine mist had settled on his hair.

"You don't look like the other guys," I said. "Where's your suit?"

"You ever see me in a suit? I look like a casino pit boss. I have special dispensation never to wear a suit." He took his keys from his pocket and gestured to one of the detectives that he was leaving. The detective nodded acknowledgment.

Morelli was driving a city car. It was an old tan Fairlane sedan with an antenna wired from the trunk and a hula doll stuck in the back window. It looked like it couldn't do 30 going uphill. It was dented and rusted and grime-coated.

"You ever wash this thing?" I asked.

"Never. I'm afraid to see what's under the dirt."

"Trenton likes to make law enforcement a challenge."

"Yeah," he said. "Wouldn't want it to be too easy. Take all the fun out of it."

Leo Morelli lived with his parents in the burg. He was the same age as Kenny, and he worked for the Turnpike Authority, like his father.

A blue-and-white was parked in their driveway, and the whole family was outside talking to a uniform when we pulled up.

"Someone stole Leo's car," Mrs. Morelli said. "Can you imagine? What's this world coming to? These things never used to happen in the burg. Now look."

These things never happened in the burg because it was like a retirement village for the mob. Years ago when Trenton rioted no one even considered sending a squad car in to protect the burg. Every old soldier and capo was up in his attic getting out his tommy gun.

"When did you notice it gone?" Morelli asked.

"This morning," Leo said. "When I came out to go to work. It wasn't here."

"When did you see it last?"

"Last night. When I came home from work at six o'clock."

"When was the last time you saw Kenny?"

Everybody blinked.

"Kenny?" Leo's mother said. "What's Kenny got to do with this?"

Morelli was back on his heels with his hands in his pockets. "Maybe Kenny needed a car."

No one said anything.

Morelli repeated it. "So, when was the last time anybody talked to Kenny?"

"Christ," Leo's father said to Leo. "Tell me you didn't let that asshole idiot have your car."

"He promised me he'd bring it right back," Leo said. "How was I to know?"

"Shit for brains," Leo's father said. "That's what you got . . . shit for brains."

We explained to Leo how he'd been aiding and abetting a felon, and how a judge might look askance at such an activity. And then we explained how if he ever saw or heard from Kenny again he should right away rat on him to his cousin Joe or Joe's good friend Stephanie Plum.

"Do you think he'll call us if he hears from Kenny?" I asked when we were alone in the car.

Morelli stopped for a light. "No. I think Leo will beat the crap out of Kenny with a tire iron."

"It's the Morelli way."

"Something like that."

"A man thing."

"Yeah. A man thing."

"How about after he beats the crap out of him? Do you think he'll call us then?"

Morelli shook his head. "You don't know much, do you?"

"I know a lot."

This brought a smile to Morelli's lips.

"Now what?" I asked.

"Julia Cenetta."

Julia Cenetta worked in the bookstore at Trenton State College. We checked her house first. When no one answered we headed off for the college. Traffic was steady, with everyone around us rigidly obeying the speed limit. Nothing like an unmarked cop car to slow things down to a crawl.

Morelli entered through the main gate and looped around toward the single-level brick-and-cement bookstore complex. We passed by a duck pond and a few trees and expanses of lawn that hadn't yet succumbed to winter blight. The rain had picked up again and was coming down with the boring relentlessness of an all-day soaker. Students walked head down, with the hoods pulled up on raincoats and sweat-shirts.

Morelli took a look at the bookstore lot, filled to capacity with the exception of a few slots on the outermost rim, and without hesitation parked in a no-parking zone at the curb.

"Police emergency?" I asked.

"You bet your sweet ass," Morelli said.

Julia was working the register, but no one was buying, so she was standing hip against the cash drawer, picking at her fingernail polish. Little frown lines appeared between her eyebrows when she saw us.

"Looks like a slow day," Morelli said to her.

Julia nodded. "It's the rain."

"Hear anything from Kenny?"

Color crept into Julia's cheeks. "Actually, I sort of saw him last night. He called right after you left, and then he came over. I told him you wanted to talk to him. I told him he should call you. I gave him your card with your beeper numbers and everything."

"Do you think he'll come back tonight?"

"No." She shook her head for emphasis. "He said he wasn't coming back. He said he had to keep a real low profile because there were people after him."

"The police?"

"I think he meant someone else, but I don't know who."

Morelli gave her another card with instructions to call him anytime, day or night, if she heard from Kenny.

She looked noncommittal, and I didn't think we should count on much help from Julia.

We went back out into the rain and hustled to the car. Aside from Morelli, the only piece of cop equipment in the Fairlane was a recycled two-way radio. It was tuned to the police tactical channel and the dispatcher relayed calls between bursts of static. I had a similar radio in my Jeep, and I was struggling to learn the police codes. Like all other cops I knew, Morelli listened unconsciously, miraculously processing the garbled information.

He turned out of the campus, and I asked the inevitable question. "Now what?"

"You're the one with the instincts. You tell me."

"My instincts aren't doing a lot for me this morning."

"Okay, then let's run down what we have. What do we know about Kenny?"

After last night we knew he was a premature ejaculator, but that probably wasn't what Morelli wanted to hear. "Local boy, high school graduate, enlisted in the army, got out four months ago. Still unemployed, but obviously not hurting for money. For unknown reasons he decided to shoot his friend Moogey Bues in the knee. He got caught in the process by an off-duty cop. He had no priors and was released on bond. He violated his bond contract and stole a car."

"Wrong. He borrowed a car. He just hasn't gotten around to returning it yet."

"You think that's significant?"

Morelli stopped for a light. "Maybe something happened to change his plans."

"Like acing ol' Moogey."

"Julia said Kenny was afraid someone was after him."

"Leo's father?"

"You're not taking this seriously," Morelli said.

"I'm taking it very seriously. I'm just not coming up with much, and I don't notice you sharing a lot of your thoughts with me. For instance, who do you think is after Kenny?"

"When Kenny and Moogey were questioned about the shooting they both said it was over a personal issue and wouldn't discuss it. Maybe they had some bad business going on."

"And?"

"And that's it. That's what I think."

I stared at him for a moment, trying to decide if he was holding out on me. Probably he was, but there was no way to tell for sure. "Okay," I finally said on a sigh, "I have a list of Kenny's friends. I'm going to run through it."

"Where'd you get this list?"

"Privileged information."

Morelli looked pained. "You broke into his apartment and stole his little black book."

"I didn't steal it. I copied it."

"I don't want to hear any of this." He glanced down at my pocketbook. "You're not carrying concealed, are you?"

"Who, me?"

"Shit," Morelli said. "I must be crazy to team up with you."

"It was your idea!"

"Want me to help with the list?"

"No." I figured that might be like giving a lottery ticket to your neighbor and having him win the jackpot on it.

Morelli parked behind my Jeep. "There's something I need to tell you before you leave."

"Yes?"

"I hate those shoes you're wearing."

"Anything else?"

"I'm sorry about your tire last night."

Yeah, right.

By five o'clock I was cold and wet, but had gotten through the list. I'd done a combination of phone calls and face-to-faces, and had netted very little. Most of the people were from the burg and had known Kenny all of his life. No one admitted to having contact with him after his arrest, and I had no reason to suspect they were lying. No one knew of any business deals or personal problems between Kenny and Moogey. Several people testified to Kenny's volatile personality and wheeler-dealer mentality. These comments were interesting, but too general to be really helpful. A few conversations had long, pregnant pauses that made me uncomfortable, wondering what was left unsaid.

As my last effort of the day I'd decided to check Kenny's apartment again. The super had let me in two days before when he'd been temporarily confused as to my law enforcement affiliation. I'd surreptitiously lifted a spare key while admiring the kitchen, and now I could tippy-toe around whenever I wanted. The legality of this was a tad gray, but it would only be bothersome if I got caught.

Kenny lived just off Route 1 in a large apartment complex named Oak Hill. Since there were no hills or oaks in sight I can only guess they were leveled to make way for the three-story brick bunkers advertised as affordable luxury housing.

I parked in one of the slots and squinted through the dark and the rain to the lighted front entrance. I waited a moment while a couple sprinted from their car and hurried into the building. I transferred Kenny's keys and my defense spray from my big black leather purse to my jacket pocket, pulled my jacket hood over my damp hair, and lurched out of the Jeep. The temperature had dropped during the course of the day, and the chill seeped through my wet jeans. So much for Indian summer.

I walked through the lobby with my head down and hood still up and had the good fortune to get an empty elevator. I rode to the third floor and hurried down the corridor to 302. I listened at the door for a moment, and heard nothing. I knocked. I knocked again. No answer. I inserted the key and with hammering heart quickly stepped inside, immediately flicking the lights on. The apartment appeared to be empty.

I went room to room in a cursory search and decided Kenny hadn't returned since my last visit. I checked his answering machine. No messages.

Once again, I listened at the door. All was silent on the other side. I turned the lights out, took a deep breath, and propelled myself out into the hall, gasping with relief that the whole thing was over and I hadn't been seen.

When I got back to the lobby I went straight to the mailboxes and checked Kenny's. It was crammed full of stuff. Stuff that might help me find Kenny. Unfortunately, tampering with the mail is a federal offense. Stealing mail is an especially big no-no. It would be wrong, I told myself. Mail is sacred. Yes, but wait a minute. I had a *key!* Didn't that give me some rights? Again, this was a gray issue since I'd sort of stolen the key. I put my nose to the grate and looked inside. A phone bill. This might give me clues. My fingers itched with the need to get at the phone bill. I was dizzy with temptation. Temporary insanity, I thought. I was in the grip of temporary insanity. All right!

I took a deep breath, rammed the key into the tiny keyhole, opened the mailbox, and shoveled the mail into my big black bag. I clicked the little mailbox door closed and left in a sweat, trying to get to the safety of my car before sanity returned and my defense was screwed.

CHAPTER

2

I crammed myself behind the wheel, locked the doors, and furtively looked around to see if I'd been spotted committing a federal offense. I had my pocketbook pressed to my chest, and there were little black dots dancing in front of my eyes. Okay, so I wasn't the coolest, baddest bounty hunter ever. What mattered was that I was going to get my man, right?

I stuck the key into the ignition, cranked the engine over, and pulled out of the lot. I slapped Aerosmith into the tape deck and punched up the volume when I hit Route 1. It was dark and raining, with bad visibility, but this was Jersey, and we don't slow down for anything. Brake lights flashed in front of me, and I fishtailed to a stop. The traffic light turned green, and we all took off with our foot to the floor. I cut over two lanes to line up for the turnoff, beating out a

Beemer. The driver flipped me the bird and blew his horn.

I responded with some derisive Italian hand gestures and commented on his mother. Being born in Trenton carries a certain responsibility in these situations.

Traffic dragged along city streets, and I was relieved to finally cross over the train tracks and feel the burg growing closer, sucking me forward. I reached Hamilton, and the tractor beam of familial guilt locked onto my car.

My mother was peering out the storm door when I parked at the curb. "You're late," she said.

"Two minutes!"

"I heard sirens. You weren't in an accident, were you?"

"No. I wasn't in an accident. I was working."

"You should get a real job. Something steady with normal hours. Your cousin Marjorie got a nice secretarial job with J and J. I hear she makes big money."

Grandma Mazur was standing in the hall. She lived with my parents now that Grandpa Mazur was scarfing down his normal two-eggs-and-a-half-pound-of-bacon breakfast in the hereafter.

"We better get a move on with this dinner if we're gonna make the viewing," Grandma Mazur said. "You know how I like to get there early, so I can get a good seat. And the Knights of Columbus will be there tonight. There'll be a big crowd." She smoothed the front of her dress. "What do you think of this dress?" she asked me. "You think it's too flashy?"

Grandma Mazur was seventy-two and didn't look a day over ninety. I loved her dearly, but when you got her down to her skivvies, she resembled a soup chicken. Tonight's dress was a fire-engine-red shirtwaist with shiny gold buttons. "It's perfect," I told her. Especially for the funeral home, which would be cataract central.

My mother brought the mashed potatoes to the table. "Come and eat," she said, "before the mashed potatoes get cold."

"So what did you do today?" Grandma Mazur asked. "You have to rough anyone up?"

"I spent the day looking for Kenny Mancuso, but I didn't have much luck."

"Kenny Mancuso is a bum," my mother said. "All those Morelli and Mancuso men are trash. You can't trust a one of them."

I looked over at my mother. "Have you heard any news about Kenny? Anything going through the gossip mill?"

"Just that he's a bum," my mother said. "Isn't that enough?"

In the burg it is possible to be born into bumhood. The Morelli and Mancuso women are above reproach, but the men are jerks. They drink, they cuss, they slap their kids around and cheat on their wives and girlfriends.

"Sergie Morelli will be at the viewing," Grandma Mazur said. "He'll be there with the K of C. I could grill him for you. I'd be real sneaky about it too. He's always been kind of sweet on me, you know."

Sergie Morelli was eighty-one years old and had a lot of bristly gray hair coming out of ears that were half the size of his withered head. I didn't expect Sergie knew where Kenny was hiding, but sometimes bits and pieces of seemingly benign information turned out to be useful. "How about if I come to the viewing with you," I said, "and we can grill Sergie together?"

"I guess that would be okay. Just don't cramp my style."

My father rolled his eyes and forked into his chicken.

"Do you think I should carry?" Grandma Mazur asked. "Just in case?"

"Jesus," my father said.

We had warm homemade apple pie for dessert. The apples were tart and cinnamony. The crust was flaky and crisp with a sprinkling of sugar. I ate two pieces and almost had an orgasm. "You should open a bakery," I said to my mother. "You could make a fortune selling pies."

She was busy stacking pie plates and gathering up silverware. "I have enough to do to take care of the house and your father. Besides, if I was to go to work, I'd want to be a nurse. I've always thought I'd make a good nurse."

Everyone stared at her openmouthed. No one had ever heard her voice this aspiration. In fact, no one had ever heard her voice *any* aspiration that didn't pertain to new slipcovers or draperies.

"Maybe you should think about going back to school," I told my mother. "You could enroll in the community college. They have a nursing program."

"I wouldn't want to be a nurse," Grandma Mazur said. "They gotta wear them ugly white shoes with the rubber soles, and they empty bedpans all day. If I was going to get a job, I'd want to be a movie star."

There are five funeral homes in the burg. Betty Szajack's brother-in-law, Danny Gunzer, was laid out at Stiva's Mortuary.

"When I die you make sure I'm taken to Stiva," Grandma Mazur said on the way over. "I don't want that no-talent Mosel laying me out. He don't know nothing about makeup. He uses too much rouge. Nobody looks natural. And I don't want Sokolowsky seeing me naked. I heard some funny things about Sokolowsky. Stiva is the best. If you're anybody at all, you go to Stiva."

Stiva's was on Hamilton, not far from St. Francis Hospital, in a large converted Victorian sporting a wraparound porch. The house was painted white with black shutters, and in deference to the wobbly old folks, Stiva had installed green indoor-outdoor carpeting from the front door, down the stairs to the sidewalk. A driveway ran to the back, where a four-car garage housed the essential vehicles. A brick addition had been added to the side opposite the driveway. There were two viewing rooms in the addition. I had never been given the full tour, but I assumed the embalming equipment was there as well.

I parked on the street and ran around the Jeep to help Grandma Mazur get out. She'd decided she couldn't do a good job of worming information out of Sergie Morelli in her standard-fare tennis shoes and was now precariously teetering on black patent leather heels, which she said all babes wore.

I took a firm grip on her elbow and ushered her up the stairs to the lobby, where the K of C were massing in their fancy hats and sashes. Voices were hushed, and footsteps muffled by new carpet. The aroma of cut flowers was overbearing, mingling with the pervasive odor of breath mints that didn't do much in the way of hiding the fact that the K of C had shored themselves up with large quantities of Seagram's.

Constantine Stiva had set up business thirty years ago and had presided over mourners every day since. Stiva was the consummate undertaker, his mouth forever fixed in Muzak mode, his high forehead pale and soothing as cold custard, his movements always unobtrusive and silent. Constantine Stiva . . . the stealth embalmer.

Lately Constantine's stepson, Spiro, had begun making undertaker noises, hovering at Constantine's side during evening viewings and assisting in morning burials. Death was clearly Constantine Stiva's life. It seemed more a spectator sport to Spiro. His smiles of condolence were all lips and teeth and no eyes. If I had to venture a guess as to his industry pleasures, I'd go with the chemistry—the tilt-top tables and the pancreatic harpoons. Mary Lou Molnar's little sister went to grade school with Spiro and reported to Mary Lou that Spiro had saved his fingernail clippings in a glass jar.

Spiro was small and dark with hairy knuckles and a face that was dominated by nose and sloping forehead. The uncharitable truth was that he looked like a rat on steroids, and this rumor about the fingernail-saving did nothing to enhance his image in my eyes.

He'd been friends with Moogey Bues, but he hadn't seemed especially disturbed by the shooting. I'd spoken to him briefly while working my way through Kenny's little black book. Spiro's response had been politely guarded. Yes, he'd hung with Moogey and Kenny in high school. And yes, they'd stayed friends. No, he couldn't think of a motive for either shooting. No, he hadn't seen Kenny since his arrest and hadn't a clue as to his whereabouts.

Constantine was nowhere to be seen in the lobby, but Spiro stood directing traffic in a conservative dark suit and crisp white shirt.

Grandma looked him over as one would a cheap imitation of good jewelry. "Where's Con?" she asked.

"In the hospital. Herniated disk. Happened last week."

"No!" Grandma said on a sharp intake of air. "Who's taking care of the business?"

"Me. I pretty much run the place, anyway. And then Louie's here, of course."

"Who's Louie?"

"Louie Moon," Spiro told her. "You probably don't know him because he mostly works mornings, and sometimes he drives. He's been with us for about six months."

A young woman pushed through the front door and stood halfway into the foyer. She searched the room while she unbuttoned her coat. She caught Spiro's eye, and Spiro did his official undertaker nod of greeting. The young woman nodded back.

"Looks like she's interested in you," Grandma said to Spiro.

Spiro smiled, showing prominent incisors and lowers crooked enough to give an orthodontist wet dreams. "A lot of women are interested in me. I'm a pretty good catch." He spread his arms wide. "This will all be mine someday."

"I guess I never looked at you in that light," Grandma said. "I suppose you could support a woman in fine style."

"I'm thinking of expanding," he said. "Maybe franchising the name."

"Did you hear that?" Grandma said to me. "Isn't it nice to find a young man with ambition."

If this went on much longer, I was going to ralph on Spiro's suit. "We're here to see Danny Gunzer," I told Spiro. "Nice talking to you, but we should be running along before the K of C takes up all the good seats."

"I understand perfectly. Mr. Gunzer is in the green room."

The green room used to be the parlor. It should have been one of the better rooms, but Stiva had painted it a bilious green and had installed overhead lighting bright enough to illuminate a football field.

"I hate that green room," Grandma Mazur said, hustling after me. "Every wrinkle shows in that room what with all those overhead lights. This is what it comes to when you let Walter Dumbowski do the electric. Them Dumbowski brothers don't know nothing. I tell you, if Stiva tries to lay me out in the green room, you just take me home. I'd just as leave be put out on the curb for Thursday trash pickup. If you're anybody at all, you get one of the new rooms in the back with the wood paneling. Everybody knows that."

Betty Szajack and her sister were standing at the open casket. Mrs. Goodman, Mrs. Gennaro, old Mrs. Ciak, and her daughter were already seated. Grandma Mazur rushed forward and put her purse on a folding chair in the second row. Her place secured, she wobbled up to Betty Szajack and made her condolences while I worked the back of the room. I learned that Gail Lazar was pregnant, that Barkolowski's deli was cited by the health department, and that Biggy Zaremba was arrested for indecent exposure. But I didn't learn anything about Kenny Mancuso.

I meandered through the crowd, sweating under my flannel shirt and turtleneck, with visions of my damp hair steaming as it frizzed out to maximum volume. By the time I got to Grandma Mazur I was panting like a dog.

"Just look at this tie," she said, standing over the casket, eyes glued to Gunzer. "It's got little horse heads on it. If this don't beat all. Almost makes me wish I was a man so I could be laid out with a tie like this."

Bodies shuffled at the back of the room and conversation ceased as the K of C made its appearance. The men moved forward two by two, and Grandma Mazur went up on tiptoe, pivoting on her patent-leather spikes to get a good look. Her heel caught in the carpet and Grandma Mazur pitched back, her body board stiff.

She smacked into the casket before I could get to her, flailing with her arms for support, finally finding purchase on a wire stand supporting a large milk-glass vase of gladioli. The stand held, but the vase tipped out, crashing down onto Danny Gunzer, clonking him square in the forehead. Water sloshed into Gunzer's ears and dripped off his chin, and gladioli settled onto Gunzer's charcoal gray suit in colorful confusion. Everyone stared in speechless horror, half expecting Gunzer to jump up and shriek, but Gunzer didn't do anything.

Grandma Mazur was the only one not frozen to the floor. She righted herself and adjusted her dress. "Well, I guess it's a good thing he's dead," she said. "This way no harm's done."

"No harm? *No harm?*" Gunzer's widow yelled,

wild-eyed. "Look at his tie. His tie is ruined. I paid extra for that tie."

I mumbled apologies to Mrs. Gunzer and offered to make good on the tie, but Mrs. Gunzer was in the middle of a fit and wasn't hearing any of it.

She shook her fist at Grandma Mazur. "You ought to be locked up. You and your crazy granddaughter. A bounty hunter! Who ever heard of such a thing?"

"Excuse me?" I said, slitty-eyed with fists on hips.

Mrs. Gunzer took a step back (probably afraid I was going to shoot her), and I used the space to retreat. I snagged Grandma Mazur by the elbow, gathered her belongings together, and steered her toward the door, almost knocking Spiro over in my haste.

"It was an accident," Grandma said to Spiro. "I caught my heel on the carpet. Could have happened to anybody."

"Of course," Spiro said. "I'm sure Mrs. Gunzer realizes this."

"I don't realize nothing," Mrs. Gunzer bellowed. "She's a threat to normal people."

Spiro guided us into the foyer. "Hope this incident won't keep you from returning to Stiva's," he said. "We always like to see pretty women come to visit." He leaned closer, his lips hovering at my ear in a conspiratorial whisper. "I'd like to speak to you in private about some business I need conducted."

"What sort of business?"

"I need something found, and I hear you're very good at finding. I asked around after you inquired about Kenny."

"Actually I'm pretty busy right now. And I'm not a private investigator. I'm not licensed."

"A thousand dollars," Spiro said. "Flat finder's fee."

Time stood still for several heartbeats while I went on a mental spending binge. "Of course if we kept it quiet, I don't see any harm in helping a friend." I lowered my voice. "What are we looking for?"

"Caskets," Spiro whispered. "Twenty-four caskets."

Morelli was waiting for me when I got home. He was slouched against the wall, hands stuffed into pockets, ankles crossed. He looked up expectantly when I stepped out of the elevator and smiled at the brown grocery bag I carried.

"Let me guess," he said. "Leftovers."

"Gee, now I know why you made detective."

"I can do better." He sniffed the air. "Chicken."

"Keep it up and you might make the K-9 Corps."

He held the bag while I opened the door. "Have a tough day?"

"My day passed tough at five o'clock. If I don't get these clothes off soon, I'm going to mildew."

He sidestepped into the kitchen and pulled a foil-wrapped packet of chicken out of the bag, along with a container of stuffing, a container of gravy, and a container of mashed potatoes. He put the gravy, stuffing, and potatoes in the microwave and set it for three minutes. "How'd the list go? Anything interesting turn up?"

I gave him a plate and silverware and took a beer from the refrigerator. "Big zero. No one's seen him."

"You have any clever ideas about where we go from here?"

"No." Yes! The mail! I'd forgotten about the mail in my pocketbook. I hauled it out and spread it on the kitchen counter—phone bill, Master-Card bill, a bunch of junk mail, and a postcard reminder that Kenny was due for a dental checkup.

Morelli glanced over while he ladled gravy on the dressing, potatoes, and cold chicken. "Is that your mail?"

"Don't look."

"Shit," Morelli said. "Isn't anything sacred to you?"

"Mom's apple pie. So what should I do here? Should I steam the envelopes or something?"

Morelli dropped the envelopes on the floor and smushed them with his shoe. I picked them up and examined them. They were torn and dirty.

"Received in damaged condition," Morelli said. "Do the phone bill first."

I paged through the statement and was surprised to find four overseas calls.

"What do you make of this?" I asked Morelli. "You know any of these codes?"

"The top two are Mexico."

"Can you put names to the numbers?"

Morelli set his plate on the counter, slid the antennae up on my portable phone, and dialed. "Hey, Murphy," he said, "I need you to get me names and addresses for numbers." He read the numbers off and ate while he waited. Minutes later, Murphy came back on the line, and Morelli acknowledged information given. His face was impassive when he hung up. I'd come to know this as his cop face.

"The second two numbers are El Salvador. Murphy couldn't get more specific."

I snitched a piece of chicken from his plate and nibbled on it. "Why is Kenny calling Mexico and El Salvador?"

"Maybe he's planning a vacation."

I didn't trust Morelli when he went bland like this. Morelli's emotions were usually clear on his face.

He opened the MasterCard bill. "Kenny's been busy. He charged almost two thousand dollars' worth of stuff last month."

"Any airline tickets?"

"No airline tickets." He handed the bill over to me. "Look for yourself."

"Mostly clothes. All local stores." I laid the bills out on the kitchen counter. "About those phone numbers . . ."

He had his head back in the grocery bag. "Is that apple pie I see?"

"You touch that pie and you're a dead man."

Morelli chucked me under the chin. "I love it

when you talk tough like that. I'd like to stay and hear more, but I have to get moving."

He let himself out, walked the short distance down the hall, and disappeared into the elevator. When the elevator doors clicked closed I realized he'd walked off with Kenny's phone bill. I smacked the heel of my hand to my forehead. "Unh!"

I retreated back into my apartment, locked my front door, shucked my clothes en route to the bathroom, and plunged into a steaming shower. After the shower I dug out a flannel nightie. I towel-dried my hair and padded barefoot into the kitchen.

I ate two pieces of apple pie, gave a couple chunks of leftover apple and a wedge of crust to Rex, and went to bed, wondering about Spiro's caskets. He hadn't given me any further information. Just that the caskets were missing and had to be found. I wasn't sure how one went about losing twenty-four caskets, but I suppose anything is possible. I'd promised to return without Grandma Mazur so we could discuss case details.

I dragged my body out of bed at seven and peered out the window. The rain had stopped, but the sky was still overcast and dark enough to look like the end of the world. I dressed in shorts and a sweatshirt and laced up my running shoes. I did this with the same amount of enthusiasm I could muster for self-immolation. I tried to run at least three times a week. It never ever occurred to me I might enjoy it. I ran to burn off the occasional bottle of beer, and because it was good to be able to outrun the bad guys.

I ran three miles, staggered into the lobby, and took the elevator back to my apartment. No point to overdoing this exercise junk.

I started coffee brewing and ripped through a fast shower. I dressed in jeans and denim shirt, downed a cup of coffee, and made arrangements with Ranger to meet him for breakfast in half an hour. I had access to the burg underground, but Ranger had access to the underground underground. He knew the dealers and pimps and gun runners. This business with Kenny Mancuso was beginning to feel uncomfortable, and I wanted to know why. Not that it affected my job. My job was very straightforward. Find Kenny, bring him in. The problem was with Morelli. I didn't trust Morelli, and I hated the possibility that he knew more than I did.

Ranger was already seated when I got to the coffee shop. He was wearing black jeans, hand-tooled, high-shine, black snakeskin cowboy boots, and a black T-shirt that spanned tight across his chest and biceps. A black leather jacket was draped across the back of his chair, one side hanging lower than the other, weighted by an ominous pocket bulge.

I ordered hot chocolate and blueberry pancakes with extra syrup.

Ranger ordered coffee and half a grapefruit. "What's up?" he asked.

"You hear about the shooting at Delio's Exxon on Hamilton?"

He nodded. "Somebody buzzed Moogey Bues."

"You know who hit him?"

"Don't have a name."

The hot chocolate and coffee arrived. I waited until the waitress left before asking my next question.

"What do you have?"

"A real bad feeling."

I sipped my hot chocolate. "I got one of those, too. Morelli says he's looking for Kenny Mancuso as a favor to Kenny's mother. I think there's more to it."

"Uh-oh," Ranger said. "You been reading those Nancy Drew books again?"

"So what do you think? You hear anything weird about Kenny Mancuso? You think he did Moogey Bues?"

"I think it don't matter to you. All you've got to do is find Kenny and bring him in."

"Unfortunately, I'm all out of bread crumbs to follow."

The waitress brought my pancakes and Ranger's grapefruit.

"Boy, that looks yummy," I said about Ranger's grapefruit as I poured syrup. "Maybe next time I'll get one of those."

"Better be careful," Ranger said. "Nothing uglier than a fat old white woman."

"You're not being much help here."

"What do you know about Moogey Bues?"

"I know he's dead."

He ate a section of grapefruit. "You might check Moogey out."

"And while I'm checking out Moogey, you could put your ear to the ground."

"Kenny Mancuso and Moogey don't necessarily move in my neighborhood."

"Wouldn't hurt, though."

"True," Ranger said. "Wouldn't hurt."

I finished my hot chocolate and pancakes and wished I'd worn a sweater so I could open the top snap to my jeans. I burped discreetly and paid the bill.

I went back to the scene of the crime and identified myself to Cubby Delio, the station owner.

"Can't understand it," Delio said. "I've owned this station for twenty-two years and never had any trouble."

"How long had Moogey worked for you?"

"Six years. Started working here when he was in high school. I'm going to miss him. He was a likable person, and he was real reliable. He always opened up in the morning for me. I never had to worry about a thing."

"He ever say anything about Kenny Mancuso? Do you know why they were arguing?"

He shook his head, no.

"How about his personal life?"

"I don't know much about his personal life. He wasn't married. So far as I know he was between girlfriends. Lived alone." He sifted through some papers on his desk, coming up with a dog-eared, black-smudged list of employees. "Here's the address," he said. "Mercerville. Over by the high school. Just moved there. Rented himself a house."

I copied the information, thanked him for his time, and got back to my Jeep. I took Hamilton to Klockner, passed Stienert High School, and hung a left into a subdivision of single-family homes. Yards were well tended and fenced for small children and dogs. Houses were mostly white sided with conservative trim colors. There were few cars parked in driveways. This was a neighborhood of double-income families. Everyone was out working, earning enough money to maintain the lawn service, pay off Ms. Maid, and warehouse their offspring at day care centers.

I ticked off numbers until I came to Moogey's house. It was indistinguishable from the others, with no sign that a tragedy had just occurred.

I parked, crossed the lawn to the front door, and knocked. No one answered. I hadn't expected anyone would. I peeked into a narrow window bordering the door but saw very little: a foyer with a wood floor, carpeted stairs leading up, a hall extending from the foyer to the kitchen. Everything seemed to be in order.

I walked down the sidewalk to the driveway and peeked into the garage. There was a car in there, and I assumed it was Moogey's. It was a red BMW. I thought it looked a little pricey for a guy who worked in a gas station, but what did I know. I took down the plate number and returned to my Jeep.

I was sitting there, thinking "Now what?" when my cellular phone rang.

It was Connie, the secretary from the bond office. "I've got an easy recovery for you," she said. "Stop by the office when you get the chance, and I'll give you the paperwork."

"How easy is easy?"

"This one's a bag lady. The old babe at the train station. She lifts undies and then forgets her court date. All you have to do is pick her up and get her to the judge."

"Who posts her bond if she's homeless?"

"Some church group has adopted her."

"I'll be right over."

Vinnie had a storefront office on Hamilton. Vincent Plum Bail Bonding Company. Aside from his penchant for kinky sex, Vinnie was a reputable person. For the most part he kept black-sheep miscreants from hardworking blue-collar Trenton families out of the holding pens at police headquarters. Once in a while he got a genuine slimebag, but that sort of case rarely fell into my hands.

Grandma Mazur had a Wild West image of bounty hunters breaking down doors with six-shooters blazing. The reality of my job was that most of my days were spent coercing dummies into my car and then chauffeuring them to the police station, where they were rescheduled and re-released. I picked up a lot of DWIs and disorderlies and occasionally I got a shoplifter or recreational car thief. Vinnie had given me Kenny Mancuso because in the beginning it had looked very straight-forward. Kenny was a first-time offender from a good burg family. And besides, Vinnie knew I'd do the takedown with Ranger.

I parked the Jeep in front of Fiorello's Deli. I had Fiorello make me a tuna on a kaiser and then went next door to Vinnie.

Connie looked up from her desk that sat like a guardhouse blocking the way to Vinnie's inner office. Her hair had been teased out a good six inches, framing her face in a rat's nest of black curls. She was a couple years older than me, three inches shorter, thirty pounds heavier, and, like me, she'd gone back to using her maiden name after a discouraging divorce. In her case, the name was Rosolli, a name given a wide berth in the burg since her Uncle Jimmy had been made. Jimmy was ninety-two now and couldn't find his dick if it glowed in the dark, but still he was made all the same.

"Hey," Connie said. "How's it going?"

"That's a pretty complicated question right now. Do you have the paperwork ready for the bag lady?"

Connie handed me several forms stapled to-gether. "Eula Rothridge. You can find her at the train station."

I leafed through the file. "No picture?"

"You don't need one. She'll be sitting on the bench closest to the parking lot, soaking up rays."

"Any suggestions?"

"Try not to get downwind."

I grimaced and left.

Trenton's placement on the banks of the Delaware River made it ripe for industry and commerce. Over the years, as the Delaware's navigability and importance dwindled, so did Trenton's, bringing the city to its present-day status of being just one more big pothole in the state highway system. Recently, though, we'd gotten minor league baseball, so could fame and fortune be far behind?

The ghetto had crept in around the train station, making it virtually impossible to get to the station without passing through streets of small, yardless, depressed row houses filled with chronically depressed people. During summer months the neighborhoods steeped in sweat and open aggression. When the temperature dropped, the tone turned bleak, and animosity sat behind insulating walls.

I drove along these streets with my doors locked and my windows shut tight. It was more out of habit than conscious protection, since anyone with a paring knife could slash through my canvas roof.

The Trenton train station is small and not especially memorable. There's a curved drop-off driveway at the front entrance where a few taxis wait and a uniformed cop keeps his eye on things. Several municipal-style benches line the driveway.

Eula was sitting on the farthermost bench, dressed in several winter coats, a purple wool cap, and running shoes. Her face was lined and doughy, her steel gray hair was chopped short and stuck out in ragged clumps from the cap. Her legs were ankleless, feeding into her shoes like giant knockwursts, her knees comfortably spread for the world to see sights better left unseen.

I parked in front of her, in a no-parking zone, and received a warning glare from the cop.

I waved my bond papers at him. "I'll only be a minute," I yelled. "I'm here to take Eula to court."

He gave me an *oh yeah, well, good luck* look and went back to staring off into space.

Eula harrumphed at me. "I ain't goin' to court."

"Why not?"

"The sun's out. I gotta get my vitamin D."

"I'll buy you a carton of milk. It's got vitamin D in it."

"What else you gonna buy me? You gonna buy me a sandwich?"

I took the tuna sandwich out of my pocketbook. "I was going to eat this for lunch, but you can have it."

"What kind is it?"

"Tuna on a kaiser. I got it at Fiorello's."

"Fiorello makes good sandwiches. Did you get extra pickles?"

"Yeah. I got extra pickles."

"I don't know. What about my stuff here?"

She had a supermarket cart behind her, and she'd rammed two big black plastic garbage bags filled with God knows what into the cart.

"We'll put your stuff in lockers in the train station."

"Who's gonna pay for the locker? I'm on a fixed income, you know."

"I'll spring for the locker."

"You're gonna hafta carry my stuff. I got a gimpy leg."

I looked over at the cop, who was staring down at his shoes and smiling.

"You want anything out of those bags before I lock them up?" I asked Eula.

"Nope," she said. "I got all I need."

"And when I lock away all your worldly possessions, and get your milk, and give you the sandwich, you're going to come with me, right?"

"Right."

I hauled the bags up the steps, dragged them down the corridor, and tipped a porter a buck to help me wedge the damn things into the lockers. One bag to one locker. I dropped a fistful of quarters into the lockers, took the keys, and leaned against the wall to catch my breath, thinking I should try to make time for the gym and some upper body work. I trotted back to the front of the building, pushed my way through the doors to the McDonald's franchise, and bought Eula a container of lowfat milk. I swung back out the main entrance and looked for Eula. She was gone. The cop was gone too. And, I had a parking ticket on my windshield.

I walked over to the first cab in line and rapped on his window. "Where'd Eula go?" I asked.

"I dunno," he said. "She took a cab."

"She had money for a cab?"

"Sure. She makes out pretty good here."

"Do you know where she lives?"

"She lives on that bench. The last one on the right."

Wonderful. I got into my car and made a U-turn into the small, metered parking lot. I waited until someone pulled out, then I parked in their slot, ate my sandwich, drank the milk, and waited with my arms crossed over my chest.

Two hours later a cab pulled up and Eula got out. She waddled to her bench and sat down with an obvious sense of possession. I pulled out of my parking spot and eased to the curb in front of her. I smiled.

She smiled back.

I got out of the car and walked over to her. "Remember me?"

"Yeah," she said. "You went off with my stuff."

"I put it in a locker for you."

"Took you long enough."

I was born a month premature, and I never did learn the value of patience. "You see these two keys? Your stuff's locked up in lockers that can only be opened with these two keys. Either you get in my car, or I'm flushing these keys."

"That'd be a mean thing to do to a poor old lady."

It was all I could do to keep from growling.

"Okay," she said, heaving herself up. "I guess I may as well go. It ain't so sunny anymore anyway."

The Trenton Police Department houses itself in

a three-story red-brick block-type building. A sister block, attached at street level, provides space for the courts and related offices. On every side of the municipal complex is the ghetto. This is very convenient, as the police never have to go far to find crime.

I parked in the lot attached to the station and squired Eula through the front hall to the cop at the front desk. If it had been after business hours, or if I'd had an unruly fugitive on my hands, I'd have gotten myself buzzed through the back door directly to the docket lieutenant. None of that was necessary for Eula, so I sat her down while I tried to determine if the judge who'd originally set her bond was working cases. It turned out he wasn't, and I had no recourse but to take her to the docket lieutenant anyway and have them hold her.

I gave her the locker keys, picked up my body receipt, and left through the back door.

Morelli was waiting for me in the parking lot, leaning against my car, hands shoved into his pockets, doing his imitation of a street tough, which probably wasn't an imitation.

"What's new?" Morelli said.

"Not much. What's new with you?"

He shrugged. "Slow day."

"Un-huh."

"Got any leads on Kenny?" he asked.

"Nothing I'd share with you. You swiped the phone bill last night."

"I didn't swipe it. I forgot I had it in my hand."

"Un-huh. So why don't you tell me about the Mexican numbers?"

"Nothing to tell."

"I don't believe that for a second. And I don't believe you're putting all this effort into finding Kenny because you're a good family person."

"You have a reason for your doubts?"

"I have a queasy feeling in the pit of my stomach."

Morelli grinned. "You can take that to the bank."

Okay. Different approach. "I thought we were a team."

"There's all kinds of teams. Some teams work more independent of each other."

I felt my eyes roll back in my head. "Let me get this straight," I said. "What this comes down to is that I share all my information, but you don't. Then when we find Kenny you spirit him off for reasons as yet unknown to me and cut me out of my recovery."

"It's not like that. I wouldn't cut you out of your recovery."

Give me a break. It was exactly like that, and we both knew it.

CHAPTER
3

Morelli and I had done battle before with only short-lived victories on both sides. I suspected this would be another war, of sorts. And I figured I'd have to learn how to live with it. If I went head-on with Morelli, he could make my life as a bounty hunter difficult to impossible.

Not to say that I should be a total doormat. What was important was that I *look* like a doormat at appropriate moments. I decided this wasn't one of those moments and that my demeanor now should be angry and offended. This was an easy act to pull off, since it was true. I peeled out of the police lot, pretending to know where I was going when in fact I didn't. It was close to four, and I had no more stones to turn in the hunt for Mancuso, so I headed home, driving on autopilot, reviewing my progress.

I knew I should go see Spiro, but I couldn't

muster a lot of joy over the project. I didn't share Grandma's enthusiasm for mortuaries. Actually, I thought death was just a bit creepy, and I thought Spiro was downright subterranean. Since I wasn't in all that good of a mood anyway, procrastination seemed like the way to go.

I parked behind my building and skipped the elevator in favor of the stairs since the morning's blueberry pancakes were still oozing over the top of my Levi's. I let myself into my apartment and almost stepped on an envelope that had been shoved under the door. It was a plain white business-sized envelope with my name printed in silver paste-on letters. I opened the envelope, removed the single piece of white paper, and read the two-sentence message, which had also been formed from paste-ons.

"Take a vacation. It will be good for your health."

I didn't see any travel agency brochures stuck in the envelope, so I assumed this wasn't a cruise advertisement.

I considered the other option. Threat. Of course, if the threat was from Kenny, that meant he was still in Trenton. Even better, it meant I'd done something to get him worried. Beyond Kenny I couldn't imagine who would be threatening me. Maybe one of Kenny's friends. Maybe Morelli. Maybe my mother.

I said howdy to Rex, dumped my pocketbook and the envelope on the kitchen counter, and accessed my phone messages.

My cousin Kitty, who worked at the bank, called to say she was keeping her eye on Mancuso's account just like I'd asked, but there was no new activity.

My best friend since the day I was born, Mary Lou Molnar, who was now Mary Lou Stankovic, called to ask if I'd dropped off the face of the earth since she hadn't heard from me since God knows when.

And the last message was from Grandma Mazur.

"I hate these stupid machines," she said. "Always feel like a dang fool talking to nobody. I saw in the paper where there's gonna be a viewing for that gas station fellow tonight, and I could use a ride. Elsie Farnsworth said she'd take me, but I hate to go with her because she's got arthritis in her knees and sometimes her foot gets stuck on the gas pedal."

A viewing for Moogey Bues. That seemed worthwhile. I went across the hall to borrow the paper from Mr. Wolesky. Mr. Wolesky kept his TV going day and night, so it was always necessary to pound real loud on his door. Then he'd open it and tell you not to knock his door down. When he had a heart attack four years ago, he called the ambulance but refused to get wheeled out until after *Jeopardy!* was over.

Mr. Wolesky opened the door and glared out at me. "You don't have to knock the door down," he said. "I'm not deaf, you know."

"I was wondering if I could borrow your paper."

"As long as you bring it right back. I need the TV section."

"I just wanted to check the viewings." I opened the paper to the obits and read down. Moogey Bues was at Stiva. Seven o'clock.

I thanked Mr. Wolesky and returned his paper.

I called Grandma and told her I'd pick her up at seven. I declined my mother's dinner invitation, promised her I wouldn't wear jeans to the viewing, disconnected, and, doing pancake damage control, searched my refrigerator for fat-free food.

I was plowing through a salad when the phone rang.

"Yo," Ranger said. "Bet you're eating salad for supper."

I stuck my tongue out and crossed my eyes at the handset. "You have anything to tell me about Mancuso?"

"Mancuso don't live here. He don't visit here. He don't do business here."

"Just out of morbid curiosity, if you were going to look for twenty-four missing caskets, where would you start?"

"Are these caskets empty or full?"

Oh shit, I'd forgotten to ask. I squeezed my eyes closed. Please God, let them be empty.

I hung up and dialed Eddie Gazarra.

"It's your nickel," Gazarra said.

"I want to know what Joe Morelli's working on."

"Good luck. Half the time Morelli's captain doesn't know what Morelli's working on."

"I know, but you hear things."

Heavy sigh. "I'll see what I can dig up."

Morelli was vice, which meant he was in a different building, in a different part of Trenton than Eddie. Vice did a lot of work with DEA and Customs and kept pretty closemouthed about their projects. Still, there was bar talk and clerical gossip and talk among spouses.

I shucked my Levi's and did the panty hose–business suit bit. I slid my feet into heels, fluffed my hair up with some gel and hairspray, and swiped at my lashes with mascara. I stepped back and took a look. Not bad, but I didn't think Sharon Stone would drive off a bridge in a jealous rage.

"Look at that skirt," my mother said when she opened the door to me. "It's no wonder we have so much crime today what with these short skirts. How can you sit in a skirt like that? Everyone can see everything."

"It's two inches above my knee. It's not *that* short."

"I haven't got all day to stand here talking about skirts," Grandma Mazur said. "I got to get to the funeral parlor. I gotta see how they laid this guy out. I hope they didn't smooth over those bullet holes too good."

"Don't get your hopes up," I told Grandma Mazur. "I think this will be closed coffin." Not only was Moogey shot, but he was also autopsied. I figured it would take all the king's horses and all the king's men to put Moogey Bues back together again.

"Closed coffin! Well, that would be darn disappointing. Word gets out that Stiva is having closed coffins and his attendance'll drop like a rock." She buttoned a cardigan sweater over her dress and tucked her pocketbook under her arm. "Didn't say anything in the paper about closed coffins."

"Come back after," my mother said. "I made chocolate pudding."

"You sure you don't want to go?" Grandma Mazur asked my mother.

"I didn't know Moogey Bues," my mother told her. "I've got better things to do than to go to a viewing of some perfect stranger."

"I wouldn't go either," Grandma Mazur said, "but I'm helping Stephanie with this here manhunt. Maybe Kenny Mancuso will show up, and Stephanie will need some extra muscle. I was watching television, and I saw how you stick your fingers in a person's eyes to slow them down."

"She's your responsibility," my mother said to me. "She sticks her finger in anybody's eye I'm holding you accountable."

The double-wide viewing room door was propped open to better accommodate the crush of people who'd come to see Moogey Bues. Grandma Mazur immediately began elbowing her way to the front with me in tow.

"Well, don't that beat all," she said when she reached the end of the chairs. "You were right. They got the lid down." Her eyes narrowed. "How are we supposed to know if Moogey's really in there?"

"I'm sure someone has checked."

"But we don't know for certain."

I gave her the silent stare.

"Maybe we should peek inside and see for ourselves," she said.

"NO!"

Conversation paused as heads swiveled in our direction. I smiled apologetically and put a restraining arm around Grandma.

I lowered my voice and added some stern to my whisper. "It's not polite to peek into a closed casket. And besides, it's none of our business, and it doesn't really matter to us if Moogey Bues is here or there. If Moogey Bues is missing, it's police business."

"It could be important to the case," she said. "It could have to do with Kenny Mancuso."

"You're just nosy. You want to see the bullet holes."

"There's that," she said.

I noticed Ranger had also come to the viewing. As far as I knew, Ranger wore only two colors: army green and bad-ass black. Tonight he was bad-ass black, the monotony broken only by double-stud earrings, sparkling under the lights. As always, his hair was pulled back into a ponytail. As always, he wore a jacket. This time the jacket was black leather. One could only guess what was hidden under the jacket. Probably enough firepower to wipe out a small European country. He'd positioned himself against a back wall, standing with arms crossed, body relaxed, eyes watchful.

Joe Morelli stood opposite him in a similar pose.

I watched a man slide past a knot of people congregated at the door. The man took a fast survey of the room, then acknowledged Ranger with a nod.

Only if you knew Ranger would you know he replied.

I looked at Ranger, and he mouthed "Sandman" to me. Sandman. The name didn't mean anything.

Sandman approached the casket and studied the polished wood in silence. There was no expression to his face. He looked like he'd seen it all and didn't think much of it. His eyes were dark, deep-set, and lined. I guessed the lines were from dissipation more than sun and laughter. His hair was black, oiled back from his face.

He caught me staring and our eyes locked for a moment before he turned away.

"I need to talk to Ranger," I said to Grandma Mazur. "If I leave you alone, will you promise not to get into trouble?"

Grandma sniffed. "Well, that's plain insulting. I guess after all these years I know how to behave myself."

"No fooling around, trying to see in the casket."

"Hmmph."

"Who was the guy that just paid his respects?" I asked Ranger. "Sandman?"

"His name is Perry Sandeman. Got the name of Sandman on account of if you irritate him he'll put you to sleep for a real long time."

"How do you know him?"

"He gets around. Buys a little dope from the brothers."

"What's he doing here?"

"Works at the garage."

"Moogey's garage?"

"Yeah. I hear he was there when Moogey got shot in the knee."

Someone screamed in the front of the room, and there was the sound of a heavy object being slammed shut. A heavy object like a coffin lid. I felt my eyes involuntarily roll skyward.

Spiro appeared in the doorway not far from me. Two small frown lines had fixed themselves between his eyebrows. He strode forward, cutting a swath through the crowd. I had a clear view in his wake, and the view was of Grandma Mazur.

"It was my sleeve," Grandma said to Spiro. "It got caught by accident on the lid and the dang thing just opened up. It could of happened to anyone."

Grandma looked back at me and gave a thumbs-up.

"Is that your granny?" Ranger wanted to know.

"Yup. She was checking to make sure Moogey was here."

"You've got a helluva gene pool, babe."

Spiro tested the lid to make sure it was securely closed and replaced the flower spray that had fallen to the floor.

I hustled up, ready to lend support to the lid-caught-on-the-sleeve theory, but support wasn't necessary. Spiro clearly wanted to minimize the incident. He made some sounds of comfort to the closest mourners and was busy wiping Grandma's fingerprints off the glossy wood.

"I couldn't help but notice while the lid was up that you did a nice job," Grandma said, hovering over Spiro. "Couldn't hardly see those holes at all, except for where your mortician's putty'd sunk in a little."

Spiro nodded solemnly, and with the touch of a fingertip to Grandma's back, deftly turned her away from the casket. "We have tea in the lobby," he said. "Perhaps you would like a cup of tea after this unfortunate experience?"

"I guess a cup of tea wouldn't hurt," Grandma said. "I was pretty much done here anyway."

I accompanied Grandma to the lobby and made sure she was actually going to drink tea. When she settled into a chair with her cup and some cookies, I went on my own in search of Spiro. I found him loitering just outside the side door, standing in a halo of artificial light, sneaking a smoke.

The air had grown cool, but Spiro seemed oblivious to the chill. He dragged the smoke deep into his lungs and exhaled slowly. I figured he was trying to absorb as much tar as possible, the sooner to end his wretched life.

I knocked lightly on the glass door to get his attention. "Would you like to discuss the, um, you know . . . now?"

He nodded to me, took one last long drag, and pitched his cigarette onto the driveway. "I would have called you this afternoon, but I figured you'd come to see Bues tonight. I need these things found yesterday." He shifted his eyes over the lot to make sure we were alone.

"Caskets are like anything else. Manufacturers have surplus, they have seconds, they have sales. Sometimes it's possible to buy bulk and get a good price. About six months ago I put in a bulk bid and got twenty-four caskets below cost. We're short on storage space here, so I stowed the caskets in a rental locker."

Spiro took an envelope from his jacket pocket. He removed a key from the envelope and held it up for my inspection. "This is the key to the locker. The address is inside the envelope. The caskets were wrapped in protective plastic for shipment and crated so they could be stacked. I've also included a photograph of one of the caskets. They were all the same. Very plain."

"Have you reported this to the police?"

"I haven't reported the theft to anyone. I want to get the caskets back and generate as little publicity as possible."

"This is out of my league."

"A thousand dollars."

"Jesus, Spiro, these are caskets we're talking about! What kind of a person would steal caskets? And where would I begin to look? You have clues or something?"

"I have a key and an empty locker."

"Maybe you should cut your losses and collect the insurance."

"I can't file for insurance without a police report, and I don't want to bring in the police."

The thousand dollars was tempting, but the job was beyond bizarre. I honestly didn't know where to start looking for twenty-four lost caskets. "Suppose I actually find the caskets . . . what then? How do you expect to get them back? Seems to me if a person's low enough to steal a casket, he's going to be mean enough to fight to keep it."

"Let's just go one step at a time," Spiro said. "Your finder's fee doesn't involve retrieving. Retrieving will be my problem."

"I suppose I could ask around."

"We need to keep this confidential."

No sweat. As if I'd want people to know I was looking for caskets. Get real. "My lips are sealed." I took the envelope and stuffed it into my pocketbook. "One other thing," I said. "These caskets are empty, right?"

"Right."

I went back to look for Grandma, and I was thinking maybe this wouldn't be so bad. Spiro had lost a shitload of caskets. They wouldn't be that easy to hide. It wasn't as if you could pack them into the trunk of your car and drive away. Someone had come in with a flatbed or a semi and taken those caskets. Maybe it was an internal job. Maybe someone from the locker company had ripped Spiro off. Then what? The market for caskets is pretty limited. You could hardly use them as planters or lamp stands. The caskets would have to be sold to other mortuaries. These thieves had to be on the cutting edge of crime. Black-market caskets.

I found Grandma sipping tea with Joe Morelli. I'd never seen Morelli with a teacup in his hand, and the sight was unnerving. As a teenager Morelli had been feral. Two years in the navy and twelve more on the police force had taught him control, but I was convinced nothing short of removing his gonads would ever completely domesticate him. There was always a barbarous part of Morelli that hummed beneath the surface. I found myself helplessly sucked in by it, and at the same time it scared the hell out of me.

"Well, here she is," Grandma said when she saw me. "Speak of the devil."

Morelli grinned. "We've been talking about you."

"Oh, goody."

"I hear you had a secretive meeting with Spiro."

"Business," I said.

"This business have anything to do with the fact that Spiro and Kenny and Moogey were friends in high school?"

I gave him an eyebrow raise to signify surprise. "They were friends in high school?"

He held three fingers up. "Like this."

"Hmmm," I said.

His grin widened. "I guess you're still in war mode."

"Are you laughing at me?"

"Not exactly laughing."

"Well then, what?"

He rocked back on his heels, hands rammed into his pockets. "I think you're cute."

"Jesus."

"Too bad we're not working together," Morelli said. "If we were working together, I could tell you about my cousin's car."

"What about his car?"

"They found it late this afternoon. Abandoned. No bodies in the trunk. No bloodstains. No Kenny."

"Where?"

"The parking lot at the mall."

"Maybe Kenny was shopping."

"Unlikely. Mall security remembers seeing the car parked overnight."

"Were the doors locked?"

"All but the driver's door."

I considered that for a moment. "If I was abandoning my cousin's car, I'd make sure all the doors were locked."

Morelli and I stared into each other's eyes and let the next thought go unsaid. Maybe Kenny was dead. There was no real basis in fact to draw such a conclusion, but the premonition skittered through my mind, and I wondered how this related to the letter I'd just received.

Morelli acknowledged the possibility with a grim set to his mouth. "Yeah," he said.

Stiva had formed a lobby by removing the walls between what had originally been the foyer and the dining room of the large Victorian. Wall-to-wall carpet unified the room and silenced footsteps. Tea was served on a maple library table just outside the kitchen door. Lights were subdued, Queen Anne–period chairs and end tables were grouped for conversation, and small floral arrangements were scattered throughout. It would have been a pleasant room if it wasn't for the certain knowledge that Uncle Harry or Aunt Minnie or Morty the mailman was naked in another part of the house, dead as a doorknob, getting pumped full of formaldehyde.

"You want some tea?" Grandma asked me.

I shook my head no. Tea held no appeal. I wanted fresh air and chocolate pudding. And I wanted to get out of my panty hose. "I'm ready to leave," I said to Grandma. "How about you?"

Grandma looked around. "It's still kind of early, but I guess I haven't got anybody left to see." She set her teacup on the table and settled her pocketbook into the crook of her arm. "I could use some chocolate pudding anyway."

She turned to Morelli. "We had chocolate pudding for dessert tonight, and there's still some left. We always make a double batch."

"Been a long time since I've had homemade chocolate pudding," Morelli said.

Grandma snapped to attention. "Is that so? Well, you're welcome to join us. We've got plenty."

A small strangled sound escaped from the back of my throat, and I glared *no, no, no* at Morelli.

Morelli gave me one of those ultranaive *what?*

looks. "Chocolate pudding sounds great," he said. "I'd love some chocolate pudding."

"Then it's settled," Grandma announced. "You know where we live?"

Morelli assured us he could find the house with his eyes closed, but just to make sure we'd be safe in the night, he'd follow us home.

"Don't that beat all," Grandma said when we were alone in the car. "Imagine him worrying about our safety. And have you ever met a more polite young man? He's a real looker too. And he's a cop. I bet he has a gun under that jacket."

He was going to need a gun when my mother saw him standing on her doorstep. My mother would look out the storm door, and she wouldn't see Joe Morelli, a man in search of pudding. She wouldn't see Joe Morelli who had graduated from high school and joined the navy. She wouldn't see Morelli the cop. My mother would see Joe Morelli the fast-fingered, horny little eight-year-old who had taken me to his father's garage to play choo-choo when I was six.

"This here's a good opportunity for you," Grandma said as we pulled up to the curb. "You could use a man."

"Not this one."

"What's wrong with this one?"

"He's not my type."

"You've got no taste when it comes to men," Grandma said. "Your ex-husband is a cow's tail. We all knew he was a cow's tail when you married him, but you wouldn't listen."

Morelli pulled up behind me and got out of his truck. My mother opened the storm door and even from a distance I could see the stern set to her mouth and a stiffening of her spine.

"We all came back for pudding," Grandma said to my mother when we reached the porch. "We brought Officer Morelli with us on account of he hasn't had any homemade pudding in an awful long time."

My mother's lips pinched tight.

"I hope I'm not intruding," Morelli said. "I know you weren't expecting company."

This is the opening statement that will get you into any burg house. No housewife worth her salt will ever admit to having her house not up to company twenty-four hours a day. Jack the Ripper would have easy access if he used this line.

My mother gave a curt nod and grudgingly stepped aside while the three of us slid past.

For fear of mayhem, my father had never been informed of the choo-choo incident. This meant he regarded Morelli with no more and no less contempt and apprehension than any of the other potential suitors my mother and grandmother dragged in off the street. He gave Joe a cursory inspection, engaged in the minimum necessary small talk, and returned his attention to the TV, studiously ignoring my grandmother as she passed out pudding.

"They had a closed casket all right for Moogey Bues," my grandmother said to my mother. "I got to see him anyway on account of the accident."

My mother's eyes opened wide in alarm. "Accident?"

I shrugged out of my jacket. "Grandma caught her sleeve on the lid, and the lid accidentally flew open."

My mother raised her arms in appalled supplication. "All day I've had people calling and telling me about the gladioli. Now tomorrow I'll have to hear about the lid."

"He didn't look so hot," Grandma Mazur said. "I told Spiro that he did a good job, but it was pretty much a fib."

Morelli was wearing a blazer over a black knit shirt. He took a seat, and his jacket swung wide, exposing the gun at his hip.

"Nice piece!" Grandma said. "What is it? Is that a forty-five?"

"It's a nine-millimeter."

"Don't suppose you'd let me see it," Grandma said. "I'd sure like to get the feel of a gun like that."

"NO!" everyone shouted in unison.

"I shot a chicken once," Grandma explained to Morelli. "It was an accident."

I could see Morelli searching for a reply. "Where did you shoot it?" he finally asked.

"In the gumpy," Grandma said. "Shot it clear off."

Two puddings and three beers later, Morelli peeled himself away from the TV. We left together and lingered to talk privately at the curb. The sky was starless and moonless and most of the houses were dark. The street was empty of traffic. In other parts of Trenton the night might feel dangerous. In the burg the night felt soft and secure.

Morelli turned my suit collar up against the chill air. His knuckles brushed my neck, and his gaze lingered on my mouth. "You have a nice family," he said.

I narrowed my eyes. "If you kiss me I'll scream, and then my father will come out and punch you in the nose." And before any of those things happened, I'd probably wet my pants.

"I could take your father."

"But you wouldn't."

Morelli still had his hands on my collar. "No, I wouldn't."

"Tell me about the car again. There was no sign of struggle?"

"No sign of struggle. The keys were in the ignition and the driver's door was closed but unlocked."

"Any blood on the pavement?"

"I haven't been out to the scene, but the crime lab checked around and didn't come up with any physical evidence."

"Prints?"

"They're in the system."

"Personal possessions?"

"None found."

"Then he wasn't living out of the car," I reasoned.

"You're getting better at this apprehension agent stuff," Morelli said. "You're asking all the right questions."

"I watch a lot of television."

"Let's talk about Spiro."

"Spiro hired me to look into a mortuarial problem."

Morelli's face creased in laughter. "Mortuarial problem?"

"I don't want to talk about it."

"Doesn't have anything to do with Kenny?"

"Cross my heart and hope to die."

The upstairs window opened and my mother stuck her head out. "Stephanie," she stage-whispered, "what are you doing out there? What will the neighbors think?"

"Nothing to worry about, Mrs. Plum," Morelli called. "I was just leaving."

Rex was running in his wheel when I got home. I switched the light on, and he stopped dead in his tracks, black eyes wide, whiskers twitching in indignation that night had suddenly disappeared.

I kicked my shoes off en route to the kitchen, dropped my pocketbook onto the counter, and punched PLAY on my answering machine.

There was only one message. Gazarra had called at the end of his shift to tell me no one knew much about Morelli. Only that he was working on something big, and that it tied in to the Mancuso-Bues investigation.

I hit the off button and dialed Morelli.

He answered slightly out of breath on the sixth ring. Probably had just gotten into his apartment.

There didn't seem to be much need for small

talk. "Creep," I said, cutting to the heart of the matter.

"Gosh, I wonder who this could be."

"You lied to me. I knew it, too. I knew it right from the beginning, you jerk."

Silence stretched taut between us, and I realized my accusation covered a lot of territory, so I narrowed the field. "I want to know about this big secret case you're working on, and I want to know how it ties in to Kenny Mancuso and Moogey Bues."

"Oh," Morelli said. *"That* lie."

"Well?"

"I can't tell you anything about that lie."

CHAPTER

4

Thoughts of Kenny Mancuso and Joe Morelli had kept me thrashing around most of the night. At seven I rolled myself out of bed, feeling cranky and bedraggled. I showered, dressed in jeans and T-shirt, and made a pot of coffee.

My basic problem was that I had plenty of ideas about Joe Morelli and hardly any about Kenny Mancuso.

I poured out a bowl of cereal, filled my Daffy Duck mug with coffee, and picked through the contents of the envelope Spiro had given me. The storage facility was just off Route 1 in an area of strip-mall-type light-industrial complexes. The photo of the missing casket had been cut from some sort of flyer or brochure and showed a casket that was clearly at the bottom of the funeral food chain. It was little more than a plain pine box, devoid of the carvings and beveled edges usually found on burg caskets. Why Spiro would buy twenty-four of these crates was beyond my comprehension. People spent money on funerals and weddings in the burg. Being buried in one of these caskets would be lower than ring around the collar. Even Mrs. Ciak next door, who was on Social Security and turned her lights off each night at nine to save money, had thousands set aside for her burial.

I finished my cereal, rinsed the bowl and spoon, poured a second cup of coffee, and filled Rex's little ceramic food dish with Cheerios and blueberries. Rex popped out of his soup can with his nose twitching in excitement. He rushed to the dish, crammed everything into his cheeks, and rushed back to his soup can, where he hunkered in butt side out, vibrating with happiness and good fortune. That's the neat part about a hamster. It doesn't take much to make a hamster happy.

I grabbed my jacket and the large black leather pocketbook that held all my bounty-hunter paraphernalia and headed for the stairs. Mr. Wolesky's TV droned through his closed door and the aroma of bacon frying hung in the hallway just in front of Mrs. Karwatt's apartment. I exited the building in solitude and paused for a moment to enjoy the crisp morning air. A few leaves still tenaciously clung to trees, but for the most part limbs were bare and spidery against the bright sky. A dog barked in the neighborhood behind my apartment building and a car door slammed.

Mr. Suburbia was going to work. And Stephanie Plum, bounty hunter extraordinaire, was off to find twenty-four cheap coffins.

Trenton traffic looked insignificant compared to the Holland Tunnel outbound on a Friday afternoon, but it was a pain in the ass all the same. I decided to preserve what little sanity had surfaced this morning and forgo safe, scenic, car-clogged Hamilton. I turned onto Linnert after two blocks of stop-and-go tedium and threaded my way through the blighted neighborhoods that surround center city. I skirted the area around the train station, cut through town, and picked up Route 1 for a quarter mile, getting off at Oatland Avenue.

R and J Storage occupied about a half acre of land on Oatland Avenue. Ten years ago, Oatland Avenue had been a hardscrabble patch of throwaway property. Its spiky grass had been littered with broken bottles and bottle caps, filter tips, condoms, and tumbleweed trash. Industry had recently found Oatland, and now the hardscrabble land supported Gant Printing, Knoblock Plumbing Supply House, and R and J Storage. The spiky grass had given way to blacktop parking lots, but the shards of glass, bottle caps, and assorted urban flotsam had endured, collecting in unattended corners and gutters.

Sturdy chain-link fencing surrounded the self-storage facility, and two drives, designated IN and OUT, led to the honeycomb of garage-sized warehouses. A small sign fixed to the fence stated business hours as 7:00 to 10:00 daily. The gates to the entrance and exit were open, and a small OPEN sign had been hung in the glass-paned office door. The buildings were all painted white with bright blue trim. Very crisp and efficient looking. Just the place to snug away hot caskets.

I pulled into the entrance and crept along, counting off numbers until I reached 16. I parked on the apron in front of the unit, inserted the key in the lock, and pressed the button that triggered the hydraulic door. The door rolled up along the ceiling and, sure enough, the warehouse was empty. Not a coffin or clue in sight.

I stood there for a moment, visualizing the pine boxes stacked chockablock. Here one day, gone the next. I turned to leave and almost crashed into Morelli.

"Jesus," I exclaimed, hand on heart, after squelching a yelp of surprise. "I hate when you creep up behind me like that. What are you doing here, anyway?"

"Following you."

"I don't want to be followed. Isn't that some sort of an infringement of my rights? Police harassment?"

"Most women would be happy to have me follow them."

"I'm not most women."

"Tell me about it." He gestured at the empty bay. "What's the deal?"

"If you must know . . . I'm looking for caskets."

This drew a smile.

"I'm serious! Spiro had twenty-four caskets stored here, and they've disappeared."

"Disappeared? As in stolen? Has he reported the theft to the police?"

I shook my head. "He didn't want to bring the police in. Didn't want word to get out that he'd bulk-bought a bunch of caskets and then lost them."

"I hate to rain on your parade, but I think this smells bad. People who lose things worth lots of money file police reports so they can collect their insurance."

I closed the door and dropped the key into my pocketbook. "I'm getting paid one thousand dollars to find lost caskets. I'm not going to try to identify the odor. I have no reason to believe there's anything bogus going on."

"What about Kenny? I thought you were looking for Kenny."

"Kenny's a dead end right now."

"Giving up?"

"Dropping back."

I opened the door to the Jeep, slid behind the wheel, and shoved the key into the ignition. By the time the engine cranked over, Morelli had seated himself next to me.

"Where are we going?" Morelli asked.

"*I'm* going to the office to talk to the manager."

Morelli was smiling again. "This could be the start of a whole new career. You do good on this one and maybe you can advance to catching grave robbers and headstone vandals."

"Very funny. Get out of my car."

"I thought we were partners."

Yeah, right. I put the Jeep into reverse and K-turned. I parked at the office and swung out of the Jeep, with Morelli following close on my heels.

I stopped and turned, facing him, hand to his chest to keep him at arm's length. "Halt. This is not a group project."

"I could be helpful," Morelli said. "I could lend authority and credibility to your questions."

"Why would you want to do that?"

"I'm a nice guy."

I felt my fingers begin to clutch at his shirt and made an effort to relax. "Try again."

"Kenny, Moogey, and Spiro were practically joined at the hip in high school. Moogey's dead. I've got a feeling Julia, the girlfriend, is out of the picture. Maybe Kenny's turned to Spiro."

"And I'm working for Spiro, and you're not sure you believe the coffin story."

"I don't know what to think of the coffin story. You have any more information on these coffins? Where they were originally purchased? What they look like?"

"They're made of wood. About six foot long . . ."

"If there's one thing I hate, it's a wise-ass bounty hunter."

I showed him the picture.

"You're right," he said. "They're made of wood, and they're about six foot long."

"And they're ugly."

"Yeah."

"And very plain," I added.

"Grandma Mazur wouldn't be caught dead in one of these," Morelli said.

"Not everyone is as discerning as Grandma Mazur. I'm sure Stiva keeps a wide range of caskets on hand."

"You should let me question the manager," Morelli said. "I'm better at this than you are."

"That does it. Go sit in the car."

In spite of all the sparring that went on between us, I sort of liked Morelli. Good judgment told me to stand clear of him, but then I've never been a slave to good judgment. I liked his dedication to the job, and the way he'd risen above his wild teen years. He'd been a street-smart kid, and now he was a street-smart cop. True, he was sort of a chauvinist, but it wasn't entirely his fault. After all, he was from New Jersey, and on top of that he was a Morelli. All things considered, I thought he was coping pretty well.

The office consisted of a small room divided in half by a service counter. A woman wearing a white T-shirt sporting a blue R and J Storage logo stood behind the counter. She was in her late forties–early fifties, with a pleasant face and a body that had comfortably gone to plump. She gave me a perfunctory nod before focusing on Morelli, who had paid no attention to my order and was standing close behind me.

Morelli was wearing washed-out jeans that had suggestively molded to an impressive package in front and the state's best buns in back. His brown leather jacket hid only his gun. The R and J lady swallowed visibly and dragged her eyes upward from Morelli's crotch.

I told her I was checking on some stored items for a friend of mine and that I was concerned with security.

"Who was this friend?" she asked.

"Spiro Stiva."

"No offense," she said, fighting back a grimace, "but he's got that locker filled with coffins. He said they were empty, but I don't care. I wouldn't come within fifty feet of that place. And I don't think you have to worry about security. Who on earth would steal a coffin?"

"How do you know he has coffins in there?"

"Saw them come in. He had so many they had to come in a semi and get off-loaded with a forklift."

"Do you work here full-time?" I asked.

"I work here *all* the time," she said. "My husband and I own it. I'm the R in the R and J. Roberta."

"You have any other big trucks come in here in the last couple of months?"

"A few real big U-Hauls. Is there a problem?"

Spiro had sworn me to secrecy, but I didn't see any way I could get the information I needed without bringing Roberta into the investigation. Besides, she undoubtedly had a master key, and coffins or not, she'd probably check on Spiro's locker when we left and discover it was empty.

"Stiva's coffins are missing," I said. "The locker is empty."

"That's impossible! A person can't just make off with a locker full of caskets. That's a lot of caskets. They filled the locker from one end to the other!

"We have trucks coming and going all the time, but I would have known if they were loading caskets!"

"Locker sixteen is in the back," I said. "You can't see it from here. And maybe they didn't take them all at once."

"How did they get in?" she wanted to know. "Was the lock broken?"

I didn't know how they got in. The lock wasn't broken, and Spiro had been emphatic that the key had never left his possession. Of course, that could be a lie.

"I'd like to see a list of your other renters," I said. "And it would be helpful if you could think back to trucks in the vicinity of Spiro's locker. Trucks big enough to haul those caskets."

"He's insured," she said. "We make everybody take insurance."

"He can't collect on insurance without filing a police report, and at this preliminary stage Mr. Stiva would prefer to keep things quiet."

"Tell you the truth I'm not anxious for this to get around, either. Don't want people thinking our lockers aren't safe." She punched up her computer and produced a printout of renters. "These are renters that are on the books right now. When someone vacates we keep them in file for three months and then the computer drops them."

Morelli and I scanned the list, but we didn't recognize any of the names.

"Do you require identification?" Morelli asked.

"Driver's license," she said. "The insurance company makes us get a photo ID."

I folded the printout, tucked it into my pocketbook, and gave Roberta one of my cards with instructions to call should something turn up. As an afterthought I asked her to use her set of master keys and check each locker on the odd possibility that the caskets weren't taken off the premises.

When we got back to the Jeep, Morelli and I looked the list over one more time and drew a big zero.

Roberta hustled out of her office with keys in hand and the portable phone stuffed into her pocket.

"The great coffin search," Morelli said, watching her disappear around the end of the first row of lockers. He slouched in his seat. "Doesn't compute to me. Why would someone choose to steal caskets? They're big and heavy, and the resale market is limited to nonexistent. People probably have all kinds of things stored here that would be easier to fence. Why steal caskets?"

"Maybe that's what they needed. Maybe some down-on-his-luck undertaker took them. Like Mosel. Ever since Stiva opened up his new addition, Mosel has been on a downslide. Maybe Mosel knew Spiro had caskets stashed here, and he tippytoed in one dark night and swiped them."

Morelli looked at me like I was from Mars.

"Hey, it's possible," I said. "Stranger things have happened. I think we should go around to a bunch of viewings and see if anyone's laid out in one of Spiro's caskets."

"Oh, boy."

I shifted my bag higher onto my shoulder. "There was a guy at the viewing last night named Sandeman. Do you know him?"

"I busted him for possession about two years ago. He got caught in a sweep."

"Ranger tells me Sandeman worked with Moogey at the garage. Said he heard Sandeman was there the day Moogey got shot in the knee. I was wondering if you'd talked to him."

"No. Not yet. Scully was the investigating officer that day. Sandeman gave him a statement, but it didn't say much. The shooting took place in the office, and Sandeman was in the garage working on a car at the time. Had an air wrench going and didn't hear the shot."

"Thought maybe I'd see if he had any ideas on Kenny."

"Don't get too close. Sandeman's a real jerk. Bad temper. Bad attitude." Morelli pulled car keys out of his pocket. "Terrific mechanic."

"I'll be careful."

Morelli gave me a look of total no-confidence.

"You sure you don't want me to go with?" he asked. "I'm good at thumbscrews."

"I'm not really into thumbscrews, but thanks for the offer."

His Fairlane was parked next to my Jeep.

"I like the hula girl in the back window," I said. "Nice touch."

"It was Costanza's idea. It covers an antenna."

I looked at the top of her head and, sure enough, there was the tip of an antenna poking through. I squinted at Morelli. "You're not going to follow me, are you?"

"Only if you say please."

"Not in this lifetime."

Morelli looked like he knew better.

I cut across town and left turned onto Hamilton. Seven blocks later I nosed into a parking slot to the side of the garage. Early morning and evening the pumps were in constant use. At this hour they didn't see much action. The office door was open, but the office was empty. Beyond the office the doors to the bays were up. The third bay had a car on a rack.

Sandeman worked nearby, balancing a tire. He was wearing a faded black Harley tank top that stopped two inches short of low-rider, grease-stained jeans. His arms and shoulders were covered with tattoos of snakes, fangs bared, forked tongues sticking out. Stuck between snakes was a red heart with the inscription I LOVE JEAN. Lucky girl. I decided Sandeman could only be enhanced by a mouthful of rotting teeth and possibly a few festering facial sores.

He straightened when he saw me and wiped his hands on his jeans. "Yeah?"

"You're Perry Sandeman?"

"You got it."

"Stephanie Plum," I said, forgoing the usual formality of an introductory handshake. "I work for Kenny Mancuso's bondsman. I'm trying to locate Kenny."

"Haven't seen him," Sandeman said.

"I understand he and Moogey were friends."

"That's what I hear."

"Did Kenny come around the garage a lot?"

"No."

"Did Moogey ever talk about Kenny?"

"No."

Was I wasting my time? Yes.

"You were here the day Moogey was shot in the knee," I said. "Do you think the shooting was accidental?"

"I was in the garage. I don't know anything about it. End of quiz. I got work to do."

I gave him my card and told him to get in touch if he should think of anything useful.

He tore the card in half and let the pieces float to the cement floor.

Any intelligent woman would have made a dignified retreat, but this was New Jersey, where dignity always runs a poor second to the pleasure of getting in someone's face.

I leaned forward, hands on hips. "You got a problem?"

"I don't like cops. That includes pussy cops."

"I'm not a cop. I'm a bond enforcement agent."

"You're a fucking pussy bounty hunter. I don't talk to fucking pussy bounty hunters."

"You call me pussy one more time, and I'm going to get mad."

"Is that supposed to worry me?"

I had a canister of pepper spray in my pocketbook, and I was itching to give him a blast. I also had a stun gun. The lady who owned the local gun shop had talked me into buying it, and so far it was untested. I wondered if 45,000 volts square in his Harley logo would worry him.

"Just make sure you're not withholding information, Sandeman. Your parole officer might find it annoying."

He gave me a shot to the shoulder that knocked me back a foot. "Somebody yanks my parole officer's chain, and somebody might find out why they call me the Sandman. Maybe you want to think about that."

Not anytime soon.

CHAPTER
5

It was still early afternoon when I left the garage. About the only thing I'd learned from Sandeman was that I thoroughly disliked him. Under ordinary circumstances I couldn't see Sandeman and Kenny being buddies, but these weren't ordinary circumstances, and there was something about Sandeman that had my radar humming.

Poking around in Sandeman's life wasn't high on my list of favored activities, but I thought I should probably spare him some time. At the very least I needed to take a look at his home sweet home and make sure Kenny wasn't sharing the rent.

I drove down Hamilton and found a parking place two doors from Vinnie's office. Connie was stomping around the office, slamming file drawers and cussing when I walked in.

"Your cousin is dog shit," Connie yelled at me. *"Stronzo!"*

"What did he do now?"

"You know that new file clerk we just hired?"

"Sally Something."

"Yeah. Sally Who Knew the Alphabet."

I looked around the office. "She seems to be missing."

"You bet she's missing. Your cousin Vinnie caught her at a forty-five-degree angle in front of the D drawer and tried to play hide the salami."

"I take it Sally wasn't receptive."

"Ran out of here screaming. Said we could give her paycheck to charity. Now there's no one to do the filing, so guess who gets the extra work?" Connie kicked a drawer shut. "This is the third file clerk in two months!"

"Maybe we should chip in and get Vinnie neutered."

Connie opened her middle desk drawer and extracted a stiletto. She pressed the button and the blade flashed out with a lethal click. "Maybe we should do it ourselves."

The phone rang and Connie flipped the knife back into her drawer. While she was talking I thumbed through the file cabinet looking for Sandeman. He wasn't in the file, so either he hadn't bothered making bail on his arrest, or else he'd used another bondsman. I tried the Trenton area phone book. No luck there. I called Loretta Heinz at the DMV. Loretta and I went way back. We'd been Girl Scouts together and had bitched our way through the worst two weeks of my life at Camp Sacajawea. Loretta punched up her handy-dandy computer and, *voilà,* I had Sandeman's address.

I copied the address and mouthed "'bye" to Connie.

Sandeman lived on Morton Street in an area of large stone houses that had gone to trash. Lawns were neglected, torn shades hung limp in dirty windows, cornerstones bore spray-painted gang slogans, and paint blistered from window trim. Most of the houses had been converted to multiple occupancy. A few of the houses had been torched or abandoned and were boarded. A few of the houses had been restored and struggled to recapture some of their original grandeur and dignity.

Sandeman lived in one of the multifamily houses. Not the nicest on the street, but not the worst either. An old man sat on the front stoop. The whites of his eyes had yellowed with age, gray stubble clung to cadaverous cheeks, and his skin was the color of road tar. A cigarette hung from the side of his mouth. He sucked in some smoke and squinted at me.

"Guess I know a cop when I see one," he said.

"I'm not a cop." What was it with this cop stuff? I looked down at my Doc Martens, wondering if it was the shoes. Maybe Morelli was right. Maybe I should get rid of the shoes. "I'm looking for Perry Sandeman," I said, presenting my card. "I'm interested in finding a friend of his."

"Sandeman isn't home. Works at the garage during the day. Not home much at night either. Only comes here when he's drunk or doped up. And then he's mean. You want to stay away from him when he's drunk. Gets extra mean when he's drunk. Good mechanic, though. Everybody says so."

"You know his apartment number?"

"Three C."

"Anybody there now?"

"Haven't seen anybody go in."

I moved past the man, into the foyer, and stood for a moment letting my eyes adjust to the darkness. The air was stagnant, thick with the smell of bad plumbing. Stained wallpaper peeled back at the edges. The wood floor was gritty underfoot.

I transferred the canister of pepper spray from my pocketbook to my jacket pocket and ascended the stairs. There were three doors on the third floor. All were closed and locked. A television droned on behind one of the doors. The other two apartments were silent. I rapped on 3C and waited for a reply. I rapped again. Nothing.

On the one hand, the thought of confronting a felon scared the hell out of me, and I wanted nothing more than to leave pronto. On the other hand, I wanted to catch Kenny and felt obligated to see this through.

There was a window to the back of the hall, and through the window I could see black rusty bars that looked like a fire escape. I moved to the window and looked out. Yep, it was a fire escape all right, and it bordered part of Sandeman's apartment. If I got out onto the fire escape I could probably look in Sandeman's window. No one seemed to be on the ground below. The house to the rear had all the shades drawn.

I closed my eyes and took a deep breath. What was the worst that could happen? I could get arrested, shot, pitched overboard, or beaten to a pulp. Okay, what was the best that could happen? No one would be home, and I'd be off the hook.

I opened the window and crawled out feet first. I was an old hand at fire escapes, since I'd spent many hours on my own. I quickly scuttled to Sandeman's window and looked in. There was an unmade cot that served as his bed, a small Formica kitchen table and chair, a TV on a metal stand, and a dorm-sized refrigerator. Two hooks on the wall held several wire clothes hangers. A hot plate rested on the table, along with crushed beer cans, soiled paper plates, and crumpled food wrappers. There were no doors other than the front door, so I assumed Sandeman had to use the john on the second floor. I bet that was a treat.

Most important, there was no Kenny.

I had one foot through the hall window when I looked down between the bars and saw the old man standing directly below me, looking up, shading his eyes from the sun, my card still pressed between his fingers.

"Anybody home?" he asked.

"Nope."

"That's what I thought," he said. "Won't be home for a while yet."

"Nice fire escape."

"Could use some repair, what with the bolts

being all rusted out. Don't know if I'd trust it. Course if there was a fire a body might not care about rust."

I sent him a tight smile and crawled the rest of the way through the window. I wasted little time getting down the stairs and out of the building. I hopped into my Jeep, locked the doors, and took off.

Half an hour later I was back in my apartment, deciding what to wear for an evening of sleuthing. I settled on boots, a long denim skirt, and a white knit shirt. I spiffed up my makeup and put a few hot rollers in my hair. When the rollers came out I was several inches taller. I still wasn't tall enough to make it in pro ball, but I bet I could intimidate the hell out of the average Pakistani.

I was debating Burger King versus Pizza Hut when the phone rang.

"Stephanie," my mother said, "I have a big potful of stuffed cabbages. And spice cake for dessert."

"Sounds good," I said, "but I've made plans for this evening."

"What plans?"

"Dinner plans."

"Do you have a date?"

"No."

"Then you don't have any plans."

"There's more to life than dates."

"Like what?"

"Like work."

"Stephanie, Stephanie, Stephanie, you work for your no-good cousin Vinnie catching hoodlums. This is no kind of work."

I mentally bashed my head against the wall.

"I've got vanilla ice cream, too, for the spice cake," she said.

"Is it low-fat ice cream?"

"No, it's the expensive kind that comes in the little cardboard tub."

"Okay," I said. "I'll be there."

Rex popped out of his soup can and stretched, front feet out, hindquarters raised. He yawned and I could see down his throat all the way to the insides of his toes. He sniffed at his food cup, found it lacking, and moved on to his wheel.

I gave him a rundown on my night, so he wouldn't worry if I came home late. I left the light burning in the kitchen, turned my answering machine on, grabbed my pocketbook and brown leather bomber jacket, and locked up after myself. I'd be a little early, but that was okay. It'd give me time to read through the obits and decide where to go after supper.

Streetlights were blinking on when I pulled up to the house. A harvest moon hung low and swollen in the dusky evening sky. The temperature had dropped since the afternoon.

Grandma Mazur met me in the foyer. Her steel gray hair was tightly curled in little sausage rolls all over her head. Pink scalp gleamed between the rolls.

"Went to the beauty parlor today," she said. "Thought I might pick up some information for you on the Mancuso case."

"How'd it go?"

"Pretty good. I got a nice set. Norma Szajack, Betty's second cousin, was there getting her hair dyed, and everyone said that's what I should do. I would have tried it out, but I saw on a show that some of them hair dyes give you cancer. I think it might have been Kathy Lee. Had on this woman with a tumor the size of a basketball, and she said it came from hair dye.

"Anyway, Norma and me got to talking. You know Norma's boy Billie went to school with Kenny Mancuso and now Billie works at one of them casinos in Atlantic City. Norma said when Kenny got out of the army he started going down to Atlantic City. She said Billie told her Kenny was one of them high rollers."

"Did she say if Kenny had been to Atlantic City lately?"

"Didn't say. Only other thing was that Kenny called Billie three days ago and asked to borrow some money. Billie said yeah, he could do that, but then Kenny never showed up."

"Billie told all this to his mother?"

"Billie told it to his wife, and she went and told Norma. I guess she wasn't too happy that Billie was gonna loan money to Kenny.

"You know what I think?" Grandma Mazur said. "I think someone whacked Kenny. I bet he's fish food. I saw a show about how real professionals get rid of people. It was on one of them educational channels. What they do is they slit their throats, and then they hang them upside down in the shower to drain all the blood so they don't ruin the carpet what with the bleeding and all. Then the trick is to gut the dead guy and puncture his lungs. If you don't puncture the lungs, they float when you dump them in the river."

My mother made a strangled sound from the kitchen, and I could hear my father choking behind his paper in the living room.

The doorbell rang and Grandma Mazur jumped to attention. "Company!"

"Company," my mother said. "What company? I wasn't expecting company."

"I invited a man for Stephanie," Grandma said. "This one's a real catch. Not much to look at, but he's got a good job with money."

Grandma opened the front door and Spiro Stiva walked in.

My father peered over the top of his paper. "Christ," he said, "it's a fucking undertaker."

"I don't need stuffed cabbage this bad," I said to my mother.

She patted my arm. "It might not be so awful, and it wouldn't hurt to be a little friendly with Stiva. Your grandmother's not getting any younger, you know."

"I invited Spiro over, being his mother's spending all that time with Con in the hospital, and Spiro isn't getting any good home-cooked meals." Grandma winked at me and whispered in my direction. "Got you a live one this time!"

Just barely.

My mother slid an extra plate on the table. "It's certainly nice to have company," she said to

Spiro. "We're always telling Stephanie she should bring her friends home for dinner."

"Yeah, except lately she's gotten so picky with her men friends she don't see much action," Grandma told Spiro. "Just wait until you taste the spice cake for dessert. Stephanie made it."

"No, I didn't."

"She made the cabbages too," Grandma said. "She's gonna make someone a good wife some day."

Spiro glanced at the lace tablecloth and the plates decorated with pink flowers. "I've been shopping around for a wife. A man in my position needs to think about his future."

Shopping around for a wife? Excuse me?

Spiro took the seat next to me at the table, and I discreetly inched my chair away with the hope that distance would get the little hairs on my arm to lie flat.

Grandma passed the cabbages to Spiro. "I hope you don't mind talking about business," she said. "I've got a lot of questions. For instance, I've always wondered about whether you dress the deceased in underwear. It don't seem really necessary, but on the other hand . . ."

My father paused with the tub of margarine in one hand and the butter knife in the other, and for an irrational moment I thought he might stab Grandma Mazur.

"I don't think Spiro wants to talk about underwear," my mother said.

Spiro nodded and smiled at Grandma Mazur. "Trade secret."

At ten minutes to seven Spiro finished off his second piece of cake and announced he would have to leave for the evening viewing.

Grandma Mazur waved to him as he pulled away. "That went pretty good," she said. "I think he likes you."

"Do you want more ice cream?" my mother asked. "Another cup of coffee?"

"No thanks. I'm stuffed. And besides, I have things to do tonight."

"What things?"

"There are some funeral homes I need to visit."

"What funeral homes?" Grandma yelled from the foyer.

"I'm starting with Sokolowsky's."

"Who's at Sokolowsky's?"

"Helen Martin."

"Don't know her, but maybe I should pay my respects all the same if you're such good friends," Grandma said.

"After Sokolowsky's I'm going to Mosel's and then to The House of Eternal Slumber."

"The House of Eternal Slumber? Never been to that one," Grandma said. "Is it new? Is it in the burg?"

"It's over on Stark Street."

My mother crossed herself. "Give me strength," she said.

"Stark Street isn't that bad," I told her.

"It's full of drug dealers and murderers. You don't belong on Stark Street. Frank, are you going to let her go to Stark Street at night?"

My father looked up from his plate at the mention of his name. "What?"

"Stephanie's going to Stark Street."

My father had been engrossed in his cake and was clearly lost. "Does she need a ride?"

My mother rolled her eyes. "You see what I live with."

Grandma was on her feet. "Won't take me a minute. Just let me get my pocketbook, and I'll be ready to go."

Grandma applied fresh lipstick in front of the hall mirror, buttoned herself into her "good wool" coat, and hooked her black patent leather purse over her arm. Her "good wool" coat was a brilliant royal blue with a mink collar. Over the years the coat had seemed to grow in volume in direct proportion to the rate at which Grandma was shrinking, so that the coat was now almost ankle length. I took her elbow and steered her to my Jeep half expecting her knees to buckle under the weight of the wool. I had visions of her lying helpless on the sidewalk in a pool of royal blue, looking like the Wicked Witch of the West with nothing showing but shoes.

We went to Sokolowsky's first as planned. Helen Martin looked fetching in a pale blue lace dress, her hair tinted to match. Grandma studied Helen's makeup with the critical eye of a professional.

"Should have used the green-toned concealer under the eyes," she said. "You got to use a lot of concealer when you got lighting like this. Now

Stiva's got recessed lighting in his new rooms and that makes all the difference."

I left Grandma to her own devices and went in search of Melvin Sokolowsky, locating him in his office just off the front entrance. The door to the office was open, and Sokolowsky was seated behind a handsome mahogany desk, tapping who knows what into a laptop. I rapped lightly to get his attention.

He was a nice-looking man in his mid-forties, dressed in the standard conservative dark suit, white dress shirt, and sober striped tie.

He raised eyebrows at the sight of me standing in his doorway. "Yes?"

"I want to speak to you about funeral arrangements," I said. "My grandmother is getting on in years, and I thought it wouldn't hurt to get some ballpark figures on caskets."

He hauled a large leather-bound catalog up from the bowels of the desk and flipped it open. "We have several plans and a good selection of caskets."

He turned to the casket called the Montgomery.

"This is nice," I said, "but it looks a little pricey."

He thumbed back a couple pages to the pine section. "This is our economy line. As you can see, they're still quite attractive, with a nice mahogany stain and brass handles."

I checked out the economy line but didn't see anything nearly as cheap-looking as Stiva's missing caskets. "Is this as cheap as you get?" I asked. "You have anything without the stain?"

Sokolowsky looked pained. "Who did you say this was for?"

"My grandmother."

"She cut you out of the will?"

Just what the world needs . . . one more sarcastic undertaker. "Do you have any plain boxes or what?"

"Nobody buys plain boxes in the burg. Listen, how about if we put you on a payment plan? Or maybe we could skimp on the makeup . . . you know, only set your grandmother's hair in the front."

I was on my feet and halfway to the door. "I'll think about it."

He was on his feet equally as fast, shoving brochures into my hand. "I'm sure we can work something out. I could get you a real good buy on a plot. . . ."

I ran into Grandma Mazur in the foyer.

"What was he saying about a plot?" she asked. "We already got a plot. It's a good one too. Real close to the water spigot. The whole family's buried there. Of course, when they put your aunt Marion in the ground they had to lower Uncle Fred and put her in on top on account of there wasn't much space left. I'll probably end up on top of your grandfather. Isn't that always the way? Can't even get no privacy when you're dead."

From the corner of my eye I could see Sokolowsky lurking in his doorway, sizing up Grandma Mazur.

Grandma Mazur noticed too.

"Look at that Sokolowsky," she said. "Can't keep his eyes off me. Must be this new dress I'm wearing."

We went to Mosel's next. Then we visited Dorfman's and Majestic Mortuary. By the time we were on the road to The House of Eternal Slumber I was punchy with death. The smell of cut flowers clung to my clothes, and my voice had locked into hushed funereal tones.

Grandma Mazur had enjoyed herself through Mosel but had started to fade toward the end of Dorfman's, and had sat out Majestic Mort, waiting for me in the Jeep while I ran inside and priced burial arrangements.

The House of Eternal Slumber was the only home left on my list. I cut through city center, past the state buildings and turnoffs to Pennsylvania. It was after nine, and the downtown streets were left to the night people—hookers, dealers, buyers, and the kiddie crews.

I turned right onto Stark, instantly plunging us into a despairing neighborhood of dingy brick-fronted row houses and small businesses. Doors to Stark Street bars stood open, spilling rectangles of smoking light onto dark cement sidewalks. Men loitered in front of the bars, passing time, transacting business, looking cool. The colder weather had driven most of the residents inside, leaving the stoops to the even less fortunate.

Grandma Mazur was on the edge of her seat, nose pressed to the window. "So this is Stark Street," she said. "I hear this part of town is filled with hookers and drug dealers. I sure would like to see some of them. I saw a couple hookers on TV once, and they turned out to be men. This one hooker was wearing spandex tights, and he said he had to tape his penis up tight between his legs so it wouldn't show. Can you imagine that?"

I double-parked just short of the mortuary and studied The House of Eternal Slumber. It was one of the few buildings on the street not covered with graffiti. Its white masonry looked freshly scrubbed and an overhead fixture threw a wide arc of light. A small knot of suited men stood talking and smoking in the light. The door opened and two women, dressed in Sunday clothes, exited the building, joined two of the men, and walked to a car. The car left, and the remaining men went into the funeral home, leaving the street deserted.

I zipped into the vacated parking space and did a quick review of my cover story. I was here to see Fred "Ducky" Wilson. Dead at the age of sixty-eight. If anyone asked, I would claim he was my grandfather's friend.

Grandma Mazur and I quietly entered the funeral parlor and scoped the place out. It was small. Three viewing rooms and a chapel. Only one viewing room was being used. The lighting was subdued and the furnishings were inexpensive but tasteful.

Grandma sucked on her dentures and surveyed the crush of people spilling out of Ducky's room. "This isn't gonna float," she said. "We're the wrong color. We're gonna look like hogs in the henhouse."

I'd been thinking the same thing. I'd hoped for a mix of races. This end of Stark Street was pretty much a melting pot, with hard luck being the common denominator more than skin color.

"What's the deal here, anyway?" Grandma asked. "What's with all these funeral homes? I bet you're looking for someone. I bet we're on one of them manhunts."

"Sort of. I can't tell you the details."

"Don't worry about me. My mouth is zipped and locked."

I had a fleeting view of Ducky's casket and even from this distance I knew his family had spared no expense. I knew I should look into it further, but I was tired of doing the bogus pricing out a funeral routine. "I've seen enough," I told Grandma. "I think it's time to go home."

"Fine by me. I could use to get these shoes off. This manhunting stuff takes it out of a body."

We swung through the front door and stood squinting under the overhead light.

"That's funny," Grandma said. "I could have swore we parked the car here."

I heaved a sigh. "We did park the car here."

"It isn't here anymore."

It sure as hell wasn't. The car was gone, gone, gone. I pulled my phone out of my pocketbook and called Morelli. There was no answer at his home number, so I tried his car phone.

There was a short crackle of static and Morelli came on.

"It's Stephanie," I said. "I'm at The House of

Eternal Slumber on Stark Street and my car's been stolen."

There was no immediate response, but I thought I heard some muffled laughter. "Have you called it in?" he finally asked.

"I'm calling it in to you."

"I'm honored."

"Grandma Mazur is with me, and her feet hurt."

"Ten-four, Keemo Sabe."

I dropped my phone back into my pocketbook. "Morelli's on his way."

"Nice of him to come get us."

At the risk of sounding cynical, I suspected Morelli had been camped out in my parking lot, waiting for me to come home so he could get briefed on Perry Sandeman.

Grandma Mazur and I huddled close to the door, ever on the alert should my car cruise by. It was an uneventful, tedious wait, and Grandma seemed disappointed not to have been approached by drug dealers or pimps looking for fresh blood.

"Don't know what all the to-do is about," she said. "Here it is a perfectly good night, and we haven't seen any crime. Stark Street isn't what it's cracked up to be."

"Some slimeball stole my car!"

"That's true. I guess this evening wasn't a complete bust. Still, I didn't see it happen. It just isn't the same if you don't see it happen."

Morelli's truck turned at the corner and made its way up Stark Street. He double-parked, set his flasher, and sauntered around to us. "What happened?"

"The Jeep was parked and locked in this empty space here. We were in the funeral home for less than ten minutes. When we came out, the Jeep was gone."

"Any witnesses?"

"None that I know of. I didn't canvass the neighborhood." If there was one thing I'd learned in my short career as a bounty hunter, it was that no one saw anything on Stark Street. Asking questions was an exercise in futility.

"I had the dispatcher notify all cars as soon as I got your call," Morelli said. "You should come down to the station tomorrow and fill out a report."

"Any chance I'll get my car back?"

"There's always a chance."

"I saw a TV show about stolen cars," Grandma Mazur said. "It was on these chop shops that take cars apart. Probably by now there's nothing left of that Jeep but a grease spot on some garage floor."

Morelli opened the passenger-side door to his pickup and hoisted Grandma onto the seat. I scooched up beside her and told myself to think positive. Not all stolen cars ended up as spare parts, right? My car was so cute that probably someone couldn't resist taking it for a short joyride. Think positive, Stephanie. Think positive.

Morelli made a U-turn and retraced back to the burg. We made a perfunctory stop at my parents' house, only staying long enough to deposit

Grandma Mazur in the La-Z-Boy rocker and re-assure my mother that nothing terrible had happened to us on Stark Street . . . aside from having my car grand-thefted.

On the way out my mother handed me the traditional bag of food. "A little something for a snack," she said. "Some spice cake."

"I love spice cake," Morelli told me when we were back in his truck, heading for my apartment.

"Forget it. You're not getting any."

"Of course I am," Morelli said. "I went out of my way to help you tonight. The least you can do is give me some spice cake."

"You don't really want spice cake, anyway. You just want to come up to my apartment so you can find out about Perry Sandeman."

"That's not the only reason."

"Sandeman wasn't in a talky mood."

Morelli stopped for a light. "Learn anything at all?"

"He hates cops. He hates me. I hate him. He lives in a walkup on Morton Street, and he's a mean drunk."

"How do you know about him being a mean drunk?"

"Went to his home address and talked to one of his neighbors."

Morelli slid a glance at me. "That was pretty ballsy."

"It was nothing," I said, making the most of the lie. "All in a day's work."

"I hope you had the sense not to give out your

name. Sandeman won't be happy to find you snooping around his crib."

"I think I might have left my card." No need to tell him about getting caught on the fire escape. Wouldn't want to weigh him down with unnecessary details.

Morelli gave me a *boy, are you stupid or what* look. "I understand they have positions available for makeover ladies at Macy's."

"Don't start with that makeover stuff again. So I made a mistake."

"Cookie, you're making a career out of making mistakes."

"It's my style. And don't call me Cookie."

Some people learn from books, some listen to the advice of others, some learn from mistakes. I fit into the last category. So sue me. At least I rarely made the same mistake twice . . . with the possible exception of Morelli. Morelli had this habit of periodically screwing up my life. And I had a habit of letting him do it.

"Have any luck on the funeral circuit?"

"None."

He cut the engine and leaned close to me. "You smell like carnations."

"Watch it. You'll crush the cake."

He looked down at the bag. "That's a lot of cake."

"Un-huh."

"You eat all that cake, and it'll go straight to your hips."

I heaved a sigh. "Okay, you can have some of the cake. Just don't try anything funny."

"What's that supposed to mean?"

"You know what that means!"

Morelli grinned.

I thought about looking haughty, but decided it was too late, and I probably couldn't pull it off anyway, so I settled for a grunt of exasperation and levered myself out of the pickup. I stalked off with Morelli following close on my heels. We rode the elevator in silence, exited at the second floor, and stopped short at the sight of my door slightly ajar. There were gouge marks where a tool had been inserted between jamb and door and used to pry the door open.

I heard Morelli unholster his gun, and I slid a glance in his direction. He motioned for me to step aside, his eyes locked on the door.

I pulled the .38 out of my pocketbook and muscled my way in front of him. "My apartment, my problem," I said, not actually anxious to be a hero, but not wanting to relinquish control.

Morelli grabbed me by the back of my jacket and yanked. "Don't be an idiot."

Mr. Wolesky opened his door with a bag of garbage in his arms and caught us scuffling. "What's going on?" he asked. "You want me to call the cops?"

"I am the cops," Morelli said.

Mr. Wolesky gave him a long, considering look, and then turned to me. "He give you any trouble, you let me know. I'm just going down the hall with my garbage."

Morelli stared after him. "I don't think he trusts me."

Smart man.

We both peeked cautiously inside my apartment, entering the foyer glued at the hip like Siamese twins. The kitchen and the living room area were empty of intruders. We immediately went to the bedroom and bath, checking out closets, looking under the bed, peering out at the fire escape beyond the window.

"It's clear," Morelli said. "You assess the damage and see if anything's been stolen. I'll try to secure the front door."

At first glance damage seemed to consist exclusively of spray-painted slogans having to do with female organs and anatomically impossible suggestions. Nothing seemed to be missing from my jewelry box. Sort of insulting since I had a very nice pair of cubic zirconias that I thought looked every bit as good as diamonds. Well, what did this guy know? This was a person who'd misspelled *vagina*.

"The door won't lock, but I was able to attach the security chain," Morelli called from the foyer. I heard him walk to the living room and stop. Silence followed.

"Joe?"

"Un-huh."

"What are you doing?"

"Watching your cat."

"I don't have a cat."

"What do you have?"

"A hamster."

"Are you sure?"

A little ripple of alarm raced through my chest. *Rex!* I rushed from the bedroom into the living room, where Rexy's glass aquarium rested on an end table beside the couch. I halted dead center in the room and clapped a hand to my mouth at the sight of a huge black cat stuffed into the hamster cage, the mesh lid held tight with duct tape.

My heart beat with sickening clarity and my throat closed over. It was Mrs. Delgado's cat, and the cat sat hunkered down, slitty-eyed and as pissed off as any cat could get. It didn't look especially hungry, and Rex was nowhere in sight.

"Shit," Morelli said.

I made a sound that was half gurgle, half sob and bit into my hand to keep from wailing.

Morelli had his arm around me. "I'll buy you a new hamster. I know this guy who owns a pet store. He's probably still up. I'll get him to open the store—"

"I don't want a new h-h-hamster," I cried. "I want Rex. I loved him."

Morelli held me tighter. "It's okay, honey. He had a good life. I bet he was pretty old too. How old was he?"

"Two years."

"Hmmm."

The cat squirmed in the cage and growled low in its throat.

"It's Mrs. Delgado's cat," I said. "She lives directly above me, and the cat lives on the fire escape."

Morelli went into the kitchen and returned

with scissors. He cut the duct tape, lifted the mesh lid, and the cat jumped out and bolted for the bedroom. Morelli followed after the cat, opened the window, and the cat scurried on home.

I looked into the cage, but I didn't see any hamster remains. No fur. No little bones. No yellow fangs. Nothing.

Morelli looked too. "Pretty thorough job," he said.

This drew another sob.

We stayed like that for a minute, squatting in front of the cage, numbly staring at pine shavings and the back of Rex's soup can.

"What's the soup can for?" Morelli wanted to know.

"He slept in the soup can."

Morelli tapped on the can, and Rex rushed out.

I almost fainted with relief, caught midway between laughing and crying, too choked to speak.

Rex was clearly in the same state of emotional overload. He rushed from one end of his cage to the other, nose twitching, beady black eyes bugging out of his head.

"Poor guy," I said, reaching into the aquarium, taking Rex in my hand, raising him up to my face for a closer look.

"Maybe you should let him relax awhile," Morelli said. "He seems pretty agitated."

I stroked his back. "Hear that, Rex . . . are you agitated?"

Rex responded by sinking his fangs into the tip of my thumb. I let out a shriek and jerked my hand away, flipping Rex off into space like a Frisbee. He sailed halfway across the room, landed with a soft thunk, lay stunned for five seconds, and then scrambled behind a bookcase.

Morelli looked at the two puncture wounds in my thumb, then he looked at the bookcase. "You want me to shoot him?"

"No, I don't want you to shoot him. I want you to go into the kitchen, get the big strainer, and trap Rex in it while I wash my hands and get a Band-Aid."

When I came out of the bathroom five minutes later, Rex was crouched still as stone under the strainer, and Morelli was at the dining room table eating the spice cake. He'd set out a wedge for me and poured glasses of milk.

"I think we can hazard a pretty good guess at the identity of the villain here," Morelli said, glancing at my business card impaled on my carving knife, which was sunk into the middle of my square wood table. "Nice centerpiece," he offered. "Did you say you left your calling card with one of Sandeman's neighbors?"

"Seemed like a good idea at the time."

Morelli finished his milk and cake and rocked back in his chair. "How spooked are you about all of this?"

"On a scale of one to ten, I guess I'm at six."

"Do you want me to stay until you can get your door fixed?"

I took a minute to consider. I'd been in worrisome situations before, and I knew it was no fun being alone and scared. Problem was, I didn't want to admit any of this to Morelli. "You think he'll be back?"

"Not tonight. Probably not ever unless you push him again."

I nodded. "I'll be okay. But thanks for the offer."

He stood. "You've got my number if you need me."

I wasn't about to touch that one.

He looked at Rex. "You need any help getting Dracula settled in?"

I knelt down, lifted the strainer, scooped Rex up, and gently set him back in his cage. "He doesn't usually bite," I said. "He was just excited."

Morelli gave me a chuck under the chin. "Happens to me sometimes, too."

I slid the chain home after Morelli left and jury-rigged an alarm system for myself by stacking glasses in front of the door. If the door opened, it'd knock the pyramid over, and the glasses smashing on the linoleum floor would wake me up. There was the added advantage that if the intruder was barefoot, he'd cut himself on the broken glass. Of course, this was unlikely since it was November and forty degrees.

I brushed my teeth, got into my jammies, put my gun on the table beside my bed, and crawled into bed, trying not to be disturbed by the writing on my wall. First thing in the morning I'd call the super to get my door fixed, and while I was at it, I'd mooch some paint.

I lay awake for a long time, unable to sleep. My

muscles were twitchy with nerves and my brain was uneasy. I hadn't shared my opinion with Morelli, but I was pretty sure Sandeman hadn't vandalized my apartment. One of the messages on my wall had mentioned conspiracy, and a silver letter *K* had been pasted below the message. Probably I should have shown Morelli the *K*, and probably I should have shown him the silver-lettered note suggesting I take a vacation. I wasn't sure why I'd held back. I suspected the reason was childish. Sort of like . . . you won't tell me your secret, then I won't tell you mine. Nah, nah, nah, nah, nah.

My mind wandered in the dark. I wondered why Moogey was killed, and why I couldn't find Kenny, and if I had any cavities.

I awoke with a start, finding myself sitting bolt upright in bed. The sun was streaming in through the crack in my bedroom curtains, and my heart was pounding. There was a scraping sound from far away. My mind cleared, and I realized it had been the glasses crashing to the floor that had jolted me awake.

CHAPTER
6

I was on my feet with my gun in my hand, but I couldn't make a decision on direction. I could call the cops, jump out my window, or rush out and attempt to shoot the son of a bitch at my door. Fortunately, I didn't have to choose because I recognized the voice cussing in the hall. Morelli's.

I looked at the bedside clock. Eight. I'd overslept. Happens when you don't close your eyes until daybreak. I slipped my feet into my Doc Martens and shuffled to the foyer, where glass shards were scattered over a four-foot area. Morelli had managed to work the chain off the latch and was standing in the open doorway, surveying the mess.

He raised his eyes and gave me the once-over. "You sleep in those shoes?"

I sent him a nasty look and went to the kitchen

for a broom and dustpan. I handed him the broom, dropped the dustpan on the floor, and crunched my way over glass, back to the bedroom. I exchanged my flannel nightgown for sweatpants and sweatshirt and almost screamed out loud when I caught sight of myself in the oval mirror above my dresser. No makeup, bags under my eyes, hair out to here. I wasn't sure brushing would make much of a difference, so I slapped on my Rangers hat.

When I got back to the foyer the glass was gone, and Morelli was in the kitchen making coffee.

"You ever think of knocking?" I asked him.

"I did knock. You didn't answer."

"You should have knocked louder."

"And disturb Mr. Wolesky?"

I stuck my head in the refrigerator and pulled out the remains of the leftover cake, then divided it up. Half for me. Half for Morelli. We stood at the kitchen counter and ate our cake while we waited on the coffee.

"You're not doing too good here, babe," Morelli said. "You've had your car stolen, your apartment vandalized, and someone tried to snuff your hamster. Maybe you should drop back and punt."

"You're worried about me."

"Yeah."

We both shuffled our feet some at this.

"Awkward," I said.

"Tell me about it."

"Hear anything about my Jeep?"

"No." He pulled some folded papers from his inside jacket pocket. "This is the report of theft. Look it over and sign it."

I did a fast read-through, added my name to the bottom, and returned it to Morelli. "Thanks. I appreciate the help."

Morelli stuffed the papers in his pocket. "I need to get back downtown. Do you have a plan for the day?"

"Fix my door."

"Are you going to report the break-in and vandalism?

"I'm going to make repairs and pretend it didn't happen."

Morelli acknowledged this and stared down at his shoes, making no move to leave.

"Something wrong?" I asked.

"Lots of things." He blew out a long breath. "About this case I'm working on . . ."

"The big top-secret one?"

"Yeah."

"If you tell me about it, I won't tell a soul. I swear!"

"Right," Morelli said. "Only Mary Lou."

"Why would I tell Mary Lou?"

"Mary Lou is your best friend. Women always blab everything to their best friend."

I slapped my forehead. "Unh. That is stupid and sexist."

"So sue me," Morelli said.

"Are you going to tell me, or what?"

"This is to be kept quiet."

"Sure."

Morelli hesitated. Clearly a cop between a rock and a hard place. Another exhale. "If this gets around . . ."

"It won't!"

"Three months ago a cop was killed in Philadelphia. He was wearing a Kevlar vest but he caught a couple high-penetration rounds square in the chest. One tore into his left lung; the other hit the heart."

"Cop killers."

"Exactly. Illegal armor-piercing bullets. Two months ago Newark had a real effective drive-by where the weapon of choice was a LAW—Light Anti-Tank Weapon. Army issue. Significantly decreased the population of the Sherman Street Big Dogs and turned Big Dog Lionel Simms's new Ford Bronco into pixie dust. The casing from the rocket was recovered and traced to Fort Braddock. Braddock ran an inventory and discovered some munitions missing.

"When we got Kenny into custody we put his gun through NCRC, and what do you think?"

"It came from Braddock."

"Yeah."

This was an excellent secret. This made life much more interesting. "What'd Kenny say about the hot gun?"

"Said he bought it on the street. Said he didn't know the vendor by name, but he'd work with us to try to make an ID."

"And then he disappeared."

"This is an interagency operation," Morelli said. "CID wants it kept confidential."

"Why did you decide to tell me?"

"You're in the middle of it. You need to know."

"You could have told me sooner."

"In the beginning it looked like we had good leads. I was hoping we'd have Kenny in custody by now and wouldn't have to involve you."

My mind was moving at warp speed, generating all sorts of wonderful possibilities.

"You could have bagged him in the parking lot when he was doing his thing with Julia," I said to Morelli.

He agreed. "I could have."

"That might not have told you what you really wanted to know."

"Which is?"

"I think you wanted to follow him to see where he was hiding out. I think you aren't just looking for Kenny. I think you're looking for more guns."

"Keep going."

I was feeling really pleased with myself, now, trying hard not to smile too wide. "Kenny was stationed at Braddock. He got out four months ago and started spending money. He bought a car. Paid cash. Then he rented a relatively expensive apartment and furnished it. He filled the closets with new clothes."

"And?"

"And Moogey was doing pretty good, too, considering he was living on a gas station attendant's wages. He had a megabucks car in his garage."

"Your conclusion?"

"Kenny didn't buy that gun on the street. He and Moogey were involved in the Braddock ammo rip-off. What was Kenny doing at Braddock? Where did he work?"

"He was a shipping clerk. He worked in the warehouse."

"And the missing munitions were stored in the warehouse?"

"Actually they were stored in a compound adjacent to the warehouse, but Kenny had access to it."

"Ah-ha!"

Morelli grinned. "Don't get all wired over this. Kenny's working in the warehouse is hardly conclusive proof of guilt. Hundreds of soldiers have access to that warehouse. And as far as Kenny's affluence goes . . . he could be dealing drugs, betting on horses, or blackmailing Uncle Mario."

"I think he was running guns."

"I think so, too," Morelli said.

"Do you know how he got the stuff out?"

"No. CID doesn't know either. It could all have gone out at once, or it could have trickled out over a period of time. No one checks inventory unless something is needed or, in this case, unless something turns up stolen. CID is conducting a background search on Kenny's army friends and coworkers in the warehouse. So far none of those people have been labeled suspects."

"So where do we go from here?"

"Thought it might be helpful to talk to Ranger."

I grabbed the phone off the kitchen counter and tapped out Ranger's number.

"Yo," Ranger answered. "This better be good."

"It has potential," I said. "You free for lunch?"

"Big Jim's at twelve."

"Going to be a threesome," I told him. "You and me and Morelli."

"He there now?" Ranger wanted to know.

"Yeah."

"You naked?"

"No."

"Still early," Ranger said.

I heard the disconnect, and I hung up.

When Morelli left I called Dillon Ruddick, the building superintendent, who was also an all-around good guy and friend. I explained my problem and about half an hour later, Dillon showed up with his trusty box of tools, a half gallon of paint, and assorted paint paraphernalia.

He went to work on the door, and I tackled the walls. It took three coats to cover the spray paint, but by eleven my apartment was threat free and had all new locks installed.

I took a shower, scrubbed my teeth, dried my hair, and got dressed in jeans and black turtleneck.

I placed a call to my insurance company and reported the theft of my car. I was told my policy did not cover car rental and that payment would be made in thirty days if my car didn't turn up by then. I was doing some heavy sighing when my phone rang. Even before I touched the receiver the urge to scream told me it was my mother.

"Have you gotten your car back?" she asked.

"No."

"Not to worry. We have it all figured out. You can use your uncle Sandor's car."

Uncle Sandor had gone into a nursing home last month, at the age of eighty-four, and had given his car to his only living sister, Grandma Mazur. Grandma Mazur had never learned to drive. My parents and the rest of the free world weren't anxious for her to start now.

While I hated to look a gift horse in the mouth, I really didn't want Uncle Sandor's car. It was a 1953 powder blue Buick with a shiny white top, whitewall tires big enough to fit a backhoe, and gleaming chrome portholes. It was the same size and shape as a beluga whale and probably got six miles to the gallon on a good day.

"Wouldn't think of it," I said to my mother. "Nice of you to offer, but that's Grandma Mazur's car."

"Grandma Mazur wants you to have it. Your father's on his way over. Drive it in health."

Damn. I declined her offer of dinner and disconnected. I peeked in at Rex to make sure he wasn't suffering any delayed reactions to last night's ordeal. He seemed in good spirits, so I gave him a broccoli floret and a walnut, grabbed my jacket and pocketbook, and locked the apartment behind me. I slogged down the stairs and stood outside, waiting for my father to appear.

The far-off sound of a mammoth engine arrogantly sucking gas carried to the parking lot, and I shrank back against the building, hoping for a reprieve, praying this wasn't the Buick approaching.

A bulbous-nosed behemoth of a car turned the corner, and I felt my heart beat in time to the pounding of pistons. It was the Buick, all right, in all its glory, not a speck of rust anywhere. Uncle Sandor had bought the car new in 1953 and had kept it in showroom condition.

"I don't think this is a good idea," I said to my father. "What if I scratch it?"

"It won't get scratched," my father said, putting the car in park, sliding over on the big bench seat. "It's a Buick."

"But I like little cars," I explained.

"That's what's wrong with this country," my father said, "little cars. Soon as they started bringing those little cars over from Japan everything went to pot." He thumped on the dash. "Now, this is a car. This baby is made to last. This is the kind of car a man can be proud to drive. This is a car with *cojones*."

I got in next to my father and peered over the wheel, staring openmouthed at the amount of hood. Okay, so it was big and ugly, but hell, it had *cojones*.

I took a firm grip on the wheel and thumped my left foot to the floor before my brain registered "no clutch."

"Automatic," my father said. "That's what America is all about."

I dropped my father at the house and forced a smile. "Thanks."

My mother was at the front stoop. "Be careful," she yelled. "Keep your doors locked."

Morelli and I walked into Big Jim's together. Ranger was already there, sitting with his back to the wall at a table that afforded a good view of the room. Always the bounty hunter, and most likely feeling naked since he'd probably left most of his personal arsenal in the car in honor of Morelli.

There was no need to look at a menu. If you knew anything at all, you ate ribs and greens at Jim's. We ordered and sat in silence until drinks were served. Ranger kicked back in his chair, arms crossed over his chest. Morelli in a less aggressive, more indolent slouch. Me on the edge of my seat, elbows on the table, ready to jump and run should they decide to have a shootout just for the hell of it.

"So," Ranger finally said, "what's going on here?"

Morelli leaned forward slightly. The pitch of his voice was casual and low. "The army's lost some toys. So far they've turned up in Newark and Philadelphia and Trenton. You hear anything about this stuff being out on the street?"

"There's always stuff out on the street."

"This is different stuff," Morelli said. "Cop killers, LAWs, M-16s, new 9mm Berettas stamped 'Property of U.S. Government.'"

Ranger nodded. "I know about the car in Newark and the cop in Philly. What have we got in Trenton?"

"We've got the gun Kenny used to shoot Moogey in the knee."

"No shit?" Ranger tipped his head back and laughed. "This gets better all the time. Kenny Mancuso accidentally shoots his best friend in the knee, is apprehended by a cop who by chance stops in to get gas even as the gun is smoking, and it turns out he's got a funny gun."

"What's the word?" Morelli asked. "You know anything?"

"Nada," Ranger said. "What's Kenny give you?"

"Nada," Morelli said.

Conversation stopped while we shuffled silver and glasses to make room for the plates of ribs and bowls of greens.

Ranger continued to stare at Morelli. "I get the feeling there's more."

Morelli selected a rib and did his lion-on-the-Serengeti imitation. "The stuff was stolen from Braddock."

"While Kenny was stationed there?"

"Possibly."

"I bet the little devil had access too."

"So far all we have is coincidence," Morelli said. "It'd be nice if we could get a line on the distribution."

Ranger did a scan on the room and focused his attention back to Morelli. "Been quiet here. I can ask in Philly."

My pager beeped deep in my pocketbook. I stuck my head in and rummaged around, finally resorting to extracting the contents one by one—cuffs, flashlight, Mace, stun gun, hairspray, hairbrush, wallet, sports Walkman, Swiss army knife, pager.

Ranger and Morelli watched in grim fascination.

I glanced at the digital readout. "Roberta."

Morelli brought his head up from his ribs. "Are you a betting person?"

"Not with you."

Jim had a public phone in the narrow hallway leading to the restrooms. I dialed Roberta's number and leaned a hip against the wall while I waited. Roberta picked up after several rings. I was hoping she'd found the caskets, but no such luck. She'd checked every locker and found nothing unusual, but she'd remembered a truck that had made several trips to a locker in the vicinity of number 16.

"At the end of the month," she said. "I remember because I was doing the monthly billing, and this truck went in and out a couple times."

"Can you describe it?"

"It was fairly large. Like a small moving van. Not an eighteen-wheeler or anything. More that it could hold a couple rooms of furniture. And it wasn't a rental. It was white with black lettering on the door, but it was too far to read from the office."

"Did you see the driver?"

"Sorry, I didn't pay that close attention. I was doing the billing."

I thanked her and hung up. Hard to say if the truck information was worth anything. There had to be a hundred trucks in the Trenton area to fit that description.

Morelli looked at me expectantly when I got back to the table. "Well?"

"She didn't find anything, but she remembered seeing a white truck with black lettering on the door make several passes at the end of the month."

"That narrows it down."

Ranger'd picked his ribs clean. He looked at his watch and pushed back. "Gotta see a man."

He and Morelli did some ritualistic hand thing, and Ranger left.

Morelli and I ate in silence for a while. Eating was one of the few body functions we felt comfortable sharing. When the last of the greens had been consumed we gave a collective sigh of satisfaction and signaled for the check.

Big Jim's didn't have five-star prices, but there wasn't much left in my wallet after I anted up my share. Probably it would be wise to visit Connie and see if she had any more easy pickups for me.

Morelli had parked on the street, and I'd opted to leave the blimp in a public lot two blocks down on Maple. I left Morelli at the door and marched off, telling myself a car was a car. And what did it matter if people saw me driving a 1953 Buick? It was transportation, right? Sure. That's why I'd parked a quarter mile away in an underground garage.

I retrieved the car and motored down Hamilton, past Delio's Exxon and Perry Sandeman, and found an empty parking space in front of the bond office. I squinted at the slope of the baby blue hood and wondered exactly where the car came to an end. I eased forward, rolled up on the curb, and nudged the parking meter. I decided this was close enough, cut the engine, and locked up behind myself.

Connie was at her desk, looking even meaner than usual, with her thick black eyebrows drawn low and menacing, and her mouth held in a tight slash of bloodred lipstick. Unfiled files were stacked on the tops of the cabinets, and her desk was a jumble of loose papers and empty coffee cups.

"So," I said, "how's it going?"

"Don't ask."

"Hire anyone yet?"

"She starts tomorrow. In the meantime I can't find a goddamn thing because nothing's in order."

"You should make Vinnie help."

"Vinnie isn't here. Vinnie went to North Carolina with Mo Barnes to pick up a Failure to Appear."

I took a wad of folders and started alphabetizing. "I'm at a temporary impasse with Kenny Mancuso. Anything new come in that looks like a fast bust?"

She handed me several forms stapled together. "Eugene Petras missed his court appearance yesterday. Probably at home, drunk as a skunk, and doesn't know what day it is."

I glanced at the bond agreement. Eugene Petras showed a burg address. The charge was spousal batterment. "Should I know this guy?"

"You might know his wife, Kitty. Maiden name was Lukach. I think she was a couple years behind you in school."

"Is this his first arrest?"

Connie shook her head. "Got a long history. A real asshole. Everytime he gets a couple beers in him he knocks Kitty around. Sometimes he goes too far and puts her in the hospital. Sometimes she files charges, but eventually she always backs off. Scared, I guess."

"Lovely. What's his bond worth?"

"He's out on two thousand dollars. Domestic violence doesn't count for much of a threat."

I tucked the paperwork under my arm. "I'll be back."

Kitty and Eugene lived in a narrow row house at the corner of Baker and Rose, across from the old Milped Button Factory. The front door sat flush to the sidewalk without benefit of yard or porch. The exterior was maroon asphalt shingle with weathered white trim. Curtains were drawn in the front room. Upstairs windows were dark.

I had the pepper spray easily accessible in my jacket pocket, and my cuffs and stun gun stuck into my Levi's. I knocked on the door and heard scrambling going on inside. I knocked again, and a man's voice shouted something incoherent. Again, more shuffling sounds, and then the door opened.

A young woman peered out at me from behind a security chain. "Yes?"

"Are you Kitty Petras?"

"What do you want?"

"I'm looking for your husband, Eugene. Is he at home?"

"No."

"I heard a man's voice in there. I thought it sounded like Eugene."

Kitty Petras was rail thin with a pinched face and large brown eyes. She wore no makeup. Her brown hair was pulled back in a ponytail at the nape of her neck. She wasn't pretty, but she wasn't unattractive, either. Mostly, she was nothing. She had the forgettable features that abused women get after years of trying to make themselves invisible.

She gave me a wary look. "You know Eugene?"

"I work for his bonding agent. Eugene missed his court date yesterday, and we'd like him to reschedule." Not so much a lie as a half-truth. First we'd reschedule him, and then we'd lock him up in a dingy, smelly cell until his new date came around.

"I don't know . . ."

Eugene reeled into my line of sight through the crack in the door. "What's going on?"

Kitty stepped away. "This woman would like you to reschedule your court date."

Eugene shoved his face up close. All nose and chin and squinty red eyes and 100-proof breath. "What?"

I repeated the baloney about rescheduling and moved to the side so he would be forced to open the door if he wanted to see me.

The chain slid free and clanked against the jamb. "You're shitting me, right?" Eugene said.

I positioned myself halfway into the door, adjusted my pocketbook on my shoulder, and lied my little heart out. "This will only take a few minutes. We need you to stop in at the courthouse and register for a new date."

"Yeah, well, you know what I have to say to that?" He turned his back to me, dropped his pants, and bent over. "Kiss my hairy white ass."

He was facing in the wrong direction to give him a snootful of pepper spray, so I reached into my Levi's and pulled out the stun gun. I'd never used it, but it didn't seem complicated. I leaned forward, firmly pressed the gadget against Eugene's butt, and hit the go button. Eugene gave a short squeak and crumpled to the floor like a sack of flour.

"My God," Kitty cried, "what have you done?"

I looked down at Eugene, who was lying motionless, eyes glazed, drawers at his knees. He was breathing a little shallowly, but I thought that was to be expected from a man who'd just taken enough juice to light up a small room. His color was pasty white, so nothing had changed there. "Stun gun," I said. "According to the brochure it leaves no lasting damage."

"Too bad. I was hoping you'd killed him."

"Maybe you should fix his pants," I said to Kitty. There was already too much ugliness in this world without my having to look at Eugene's Mr. Droopy.

When she had him zipped up I prodded him

with the toe of my shoe and got minimal response. "Probably it'd be best if we get him out to my car before he comes around."

"How're we gonna do that?" she asked.

"Guess we'll have to drag him."

"No way. I don't want no part of this. Lordy, this is terrible. He'll beat the daylights out of me for this."

"He can't beat you if he's in jail."

"He'll beat me when he gets out."

"If you're still here."

Eugene made a feeble attempt to move his mouth, and Kitty yelped. "He's gonna get up! Do something!"

I didn't really want to give him any more volts. Didn't think it would look good if I hauled him into court with his hair curled. So I grabbed him by the ankles and tugged toward the door.

Kitty raced upstairs and I assumed, from the sounds of drawers being wrenched open, she was packing.

I managed to get Eugene out of the house and onto the sidewalk next to the Buick, but there was no way I was going to get Eugene into the car without some help.

I could see Kitty assembling suitcases and tote bags in the front room. "Hey, Kitty," I yelled, "I need a hand here."

She peeked out the open door. "What's the problem?"

"Can't get him into the car."

She chewed on her lower lip. "Is he awake?"

"There are all kinds of awake. This kind of awake isn't nearly so awake as some other kinds."

She inched forward. "His eyes are open."

"True, but the pupils are mostly rolled up behind his lids. I don't imagine he can see much like that."

In response to our conversation, Eugene had begun ineffectually flailing his legs.

Kitty and I each took an arm and hoisted him to shoulder level.

"This would be easier if you'd parked closer," Kitty said, breathing heavily. "You practically parked in the middle of the street."

I steadied myself under the burden. "I can only park on the curb when there's a parking meter to aim for."

We gave a joint heave and slammed up against the rear quarter panel with rubber-limbed Eugene. We shoved him into the backseat and cuffed him to the sissy bar, where he hung like a sandbag.

"What will you do?" I asked Kitty. "Do you have someplace to go?"

"I have a girlfriend in New Brunswick. I can stay with her for a while."

"Make sure you keep the court informed of your address."

She nodded her head and scuttled back into her house. I hopped behind the wheel and threaded my way through the burg to Hamilton. Eugene's head snapped around some on the curves, but aside from that the trip to the police station was uneventful.

I drove to the rear of the building, climbed out of the Buick, hit the attention button on the locked door, which led to the docket desk, and stepped away to wave at the security camera.

Almost instantly the door opened and Crazy Carl Costanza poked his head out at me. "Yeah?"

"Pizza delivery."

"It's against the law to lie to a cop."

"Help me get this guy out of my car."

Carl rocked back on his heels and smiled. "This is your car?"

I narrowed my eyes. "You want to make something of it?"

"Hell no. I'm fucking politically correct. I don't make cracks about women's big cars."

"She electrocuted me," Eugene said. "I want to talk to a lawyer."

Carl and I exchanged looks.

"It's terrible what drink can do to a man," I said, unlocking the cuffs. "The craziest things come out of their mouths."

"You didn't really electrocute him, did you?"

"Of course not!"

"Scrambled his neurons?"

"Buzzed him on the ass."

By the time I got my body receipt it was after six. Too late to stop by the office and get paid. I idled in the parking lot for a few moments, staring beyond the wire fence at the odd assortment of businesses across the street. The Tabernacle Church, Lydia's Hat Designs, a used-furniture store, and a corner grocery. I'd never seen any customers in any of the stores, and I wondered how the owners survived. I imagined it was marginal, although the businesses seemed stable, their facades never changing. Of course, petrified wood looks the same year after year, too.

I was worried my cholesterol level had dropped during the day, so I opted for Popeye's spicy fried chicken and biscuits for dinner. I got it to go, and I drove me and my food to Paterson Street and parked across from Julia Cenetta's house. I figured it was as good a place as any to eat, and who knows, maybe I'd get lucky and Kenny would show up.

I finished my chicken and biscuits with a side of slaw, slurped down a Dr Pepper, and told myself it didn't get much better than this. No Spiro, no dishes, no aggravation.

Lights were on in Julia's house but curtains were drawn, so I couldn't snoop. There were two cars in the driveway. I knew one was Julia's, and I assumed the other belonged to her mother.

A late-model car pulled up to the curb and parked. A hulking blond guy got out of the car and went to the door. Julia answered, wearing jeans and a jacket. She called something over her shoulder to someone in the house and left. The blond guy and Julia sat kissing in the car for a few minutes. The blond guy cranked the engine over and the two of them drove away. So much for Kenny.

I rumbled off to Vic's Video and rented *Ghostbusters*, my all-time favorite inspirational movie. I picked up some microwave popcorn, a KitKat, a bag of bite-sized Reese's peanut butter cups, and a box of instant hot chocolate with marshmallows. Do I know how to have a good time, or what?

The red light was blinking on my answering machine when I got home.

Spiro wondered if I'd made any progress finding his caskets, and did I want to go to dinner with him tomorrow after the Kingsmith viewing? The answer to both questions was an emphatic *NO!* I procrastinated relaying this to him, as even the sound of his voice on my machine gave me bowel problems.

The other message was from Ranger. "Call me."

I tried his home phone. No answer. I tried his car phone.

"Yo," Ranger said.

"It's Stephanie. What's happening?"

"Gonna be a party. Think you should get dressed for it."

"You mean like heels and stockings?"

"I mean like a thirty-eight S and W."

"I suppose you want me to meet you somewhere."

"I'm in an alley at the corner of West Lincoln and Jackson."

Jackson ran for about two miles, skirting junkyards, the old abandoned Jackson Pipe factory, and a ragged assortment of bars and rooming houses. It was an area of town so intensely depressed, it was deemed unworthy even of gang graffiti. Few cars traveled the second mile, beyond the pipe factory. Streetlights had been shot out and never replaced, fires were a common occurrence, leaving more and more buildings blackened and boarded, and discarded drug paraphernalia clogged garbage-filled gutters.

I gingerly took my gun out of the brown bear cookie jar and checked to make sure it was loaded. I slid it into my pocketbook, along with the KitKat, tucked my hair under my Rangers hat so I'd look androgynous, and crammed myself back into my jacket.

At least I was giving up a date with Bill Murray for a good cause. Most likely Ranger had a line on either Kenny or the caskets. If Ranger needed help with the takedown on someone he was personally tracking he wouldn't call me. If you gave Ranger fifteen minutes, he could assemble a team that would make the invasion of Kuwait look like a kindergarten exercise. Needless to say, I wasn't at the head of his commando-for-hire list. I wasn't even on the bottom of it.

I felt fairly safe driving down Jackson in the Buick. Anyone desperate enough to carjack Big Blue would probably be too stupid to pull it off. I figured I didn't even have to worry about a drive-by shooting. It's hard for a person to aim a gun when he's laughing.

Ranger drove a black Mercedes sports car when he wasn't expecting to transport felons. When it was hunting season, he came loaded for bear in a black Ford Bronco. I spotted the Bronco in the alley, and I feared the contents of my intestines would liquefy at the possibility of snagging someone on Jackson Street. I parked directly in front of Ranger and cut my lights, watching him come forward from the shadows.

"Something happen to the Jeep?" he asked.

"Stolen."

"Word is there's going to be a gun deal going down tonight. Military weapons with hard-to-get ammo. The guy with the goods is supposed to be white."

"Kenny!"

"Maybe. Thought we should take a look. My source tells me there's gonna be a yard sale at two-seventy Jackson. That's the house facing us with the broken front window."

I squinted at the street. A rusted Bonneville sat up on blocks two houses down from 270. The rest of the world was empty of life. All houses were dark.

"We're not interested in busting up this business deal," Ranger said. "We're going to stay here and be nice and quiet and try to get a look at the white guy. If it's Kenny, we'll follow him."

"It's pretty dark to make an identification."

Ranger handed me a pair of binoculars. "Night scope."

Of course.

We were heading into the second hour of waiting when a panel van cruised down Jackson. Seconds later the van reappeared and parked.

I trained the scope on the driver. "He seems to be white," I told Ranger, "but he's wearing a ski mask. I can't see him."

A BMW sedan slid into place behind the van. Four brothers got out of the BMW and walked to the van. Ranger had his window down, and the sound of the side door to the van swinging open carried across the street to the alley. Voices were muffled. Someone laughed. Minutes passed. One of the brothers shuffled between the van and the Beemer carrying a large wooden box. He popped the trunk, stored the box, returned to the van, and repeated the procedure with a second wooden box.

Suddenly the door to the house with the car on blocks crashed open and cops bolted out, yelling instructions, guns drawn, running for the Beemer. A police car barreled down the street and swerved to a stop. The four brothers scattered. Shots were fired. The van revved up and jumped away from the curb.

"Don't lose sight of the van," Ranger shouted, sprinting back to the Bronco. "I'll be right behind you."

I slammed the Buick into drive and pressed my foot to the floor. I shot out of the alley as the van roared past, and realized too late that the van was being pursued by another car. There was a lot of screeching tires and cussing on my part, and the car in pursuit bounced off the Buick with a good solid *whump*. A little red flasher popped off the roof of the car and sailed away into the night like a shooting star. I'd hardly felt the impact, but the other car, which I assumed was a cop car, had been propelled a good fifteen feet.

I saw the van's taillights disappearing down the

street and debated following. Probably not a good idea, I decided. Might not look good to leave the scene after trashing one of Trenton's finest unmarked.

I was fishing in my pocketbook, looking for my driver's license, when the door was opened and I was yanked out and onto my feet by none other than Joe Morelli. We stared at each other in openmouthed astonishment for a beat, barely able to believe our eyes.

"I don't believe this," Morelli yelled. "I don't fucking believe this. What do you do, sit in bed at night and think about ways to fuck up my life?"

"Don't flatter yourself."

"You almost killed me!"

"You're overreacting. And it wasn't personal. I didn't even know that was your car." If I'd known, I wouldn't have hung around. "Besides, you don't hear me whining and complaining because *you* got in my way. I would have caught him if it hadn't been for you."

Morelli passed a hand over his eyes. "I should have moved out of state when I had the chance. I should have stayed in the navy."

I looked over at his car. Part of the rear quarter panel had been ripped away, and the back bumper lay on the ground. "It's not so bad," I said. "Probably you can still drive it."

We both turned our attention to Big Blue. There wasn't so much as a scratch on it.

"It's a Buick," I said, by way of apology. "It's a loaner."

Morelli looked off into space. "Shit."

A patrol car pulled up behind Morelli. "You okay?"

"Yeah. Wonderful," Morelli said. "I'm fucking fine."

The patrol car left.

"A Buick," Morelli said. "Just like old times."

When I was eighteen I'd sort of run over Morelli with a similar car.

Morelli looked beyond me. "I suppose that's Ranger in the black Bronco."

I cut my eyes to the alley. Ranger was still there, doubled over the steering wheel, shaking with laughter.

"You want me to file an accident report?" I asked Morelli.

"I wouldn't dignify this with an accident report."

"Did you get a look at the guy in the van? Do you think it was Kenny?"

"Same height as Kenny, but he seemed slimmer."

"Kenny could have lost weight."

"I don't know," Morelli said. "It didn't feel like Kenny to me."

Ranger's lights flashed on, and the Bronco eased around the back of the Buick.

"Guess I'll be leaving now," Ranger said. "I know how three's a crowd."

I helped Morelli load his bumper into his backseat and kick the rest of the debris to the side of the road. Around the corner, I could hear the police packing up.

"I have to go back to the station," Morelli said. "I want to be there when they talk to these guys."

"And you're going to run the plates on the van."

"The van was probably stolen."

I returned to the Buick and backed down the alley to avoid the broken glass in the road. I took the first driveway to Jackson and headed for home. After several blocks I swung around and drove to the police station. I parked deep in shadow, a car length back from the corner, across from the bar with the RC Cola sign. I'd been there for less than five minutes when two blue-and-whites rolled into the station parking lot, followed by Morelli in his bumperless Fairlane, followed by one of the big blue-and-white Suburbans. The Fairlane fit right in with the blue-and-whites. Trenton doesn't waste money on cosmetic surgery. If a cop car gets a dent, it's there for life. There wasn't a car in the lot that didn't look like it'd been used for demolition derby.

At this time of night the side lot was relatively empty. Morelli parked the Fairlane next to his truck and walked into the building. The blue-and-whites lined up at the cage to unload prisoners. I put the Buick into drive, slid into the lot, and parked next to Morelli's truck.

After an hour the chill had begun to creep into the Buick, so I ran the heater until everything was toasty. I ate half the KitKat and stretched out on the bench seat. A second hour passed, and I repeated the procedure. I'd just finished the last morsel of chocolate when the side door to the station opened and the silhouette of a man appeared backlit through the door frame. Even in silhouette I knew it was Morelli. The door closed behind him, and Morelli headed for his truck. Halfway across the lot he spotted me in the Buick. I saw his lips move, and it didn't take a genius to figure out the single word.

I got out of the car so it'd be more difficult to ignore me. "Well," I said, all little Miss Cheerful. "How'd it go?"

"The stuff was from Braddock. That's about it." He took a step closer and sniffed. "I smell chocolate."

"I had half a KitKat."

"I don't suppose you still have the other half?"

"I ate it earlier."

"Too bad. I might have been able to remember some crucial piece of information if I had a KitKat."

"Are you telling me I'm going to have to feed you?"

"You have anything else in your pocketbook?"

"No."

"Any more apple pie at home?"

"I have popcorn and candy. I was going to watch a movie tonight."

"Is it buttered popcorn?"

"Yeah."

"Okay," Morelli said. "I guess I could settle for buttered popcorn."

"You're going to have to give me something

pretty damn good if you expect to get half of my popcorn."

Morelli did the slow smile.

"I was talking about information!"

"Sure," Morelli said.

CHAPTER

7

Morelli followed me from the station, hanging back in his new 4x4, no doubt worried about turbulence caused by the Buick as it plowed through the night.

We pulled into the lot behind my apartment building and parked side by side. Mickey Boyd was lighting up under the back door overhang. Mickey's wife, Francine, got a nicotine patch the week before, and now Mickey wasn't allowed to consume tar in their apartment.

"Whoa," Mickey said, cigarette magically stuck to his lower lip, eye squinting against the smoke, "check out the Buick. Sweet car. I tell you, they don't make cars like that anymore."

I looked sideways at Morelli. "I guess this big car with portholes stuff is another one of those man things."

"It's the size," Morelli said. "A man has to be able to haul."

We took the stairs, and halfway up I felt my heart contract. Eventually the fright of having my apartment violated would dissipate, and the old casual security would return. Eventually. Not today. Today I struggled to hide my anxiety. Didn't want Morelli to think I was a wimp. Fortunately, my door was locked and intact, and when we entered the apartment, I could hear the hamster wheel spinning in the dark.

I flipped the light switch and dropped my jacket and pocketbook onto the little hall table.

Morelli followed me into the kitchen and watched while I slid the popcorn into the microwave. "I bet you rented a movie to go with this popcorn."

I opened the bag of peanut butter cups, and held the bag out to Morelli. *"Ghostbusters."*

Morelli took a peanut butter cup, unwrapped it, and lobbed it into his mouth. "You don't know much about movies either."

"It's my favorite!"

"It's a sissy movie. Hasn't even got DeNiro in it."

"Tell me about the bust."

"We got all four of the guys in the BMW," Morelli said, "but no one knows anything. The deal was set up by phone."

"What about the van?"

"Stolen. Just like I said. Local."

The timer pinged, and I removed the popcorn. "Hard to believe anyone would bop out to Jackson Street in the middle of the night to buy hot GI guns from someone they'd only dealt with on the phone."

"The seller knew names. Guess that was enough for these guys. They're not big players."

"Nothing to implicate Kenny?"

"Nothing."

I dumped the popcorn into a bowl and handed the bowl to Morelli. "So what names did the seller use? Anyone I know?"

Morelli stuck his head into the refrigerator and came out with beer. "You want one?"

I took a can and snapped it open. "About those names . . ."

"Forget about the names. They aren't going to help you find Kenny."

"What about a description? What'd the seller's voice sound like? What color were his eyes?"

"He was an average white guy with an average voice and no outstanding characteristics. No one noticed eye color. The interrogation went in the general direction that the brothers were looking for guns, not a fuckin' date."

"We wouldn't have lost him if we'd been working together. You should have called me," I said. "As an apprehension agent I have the right to be in on combined operations."

"Wrong. Being invited to participate in combined operations is a professional courtesy we can extend to you."

"Fine. Why wasn't it extended?"

Morelli took a handful of popcorn. "There was

no real indicator that Kenny would be driving the van."

"But there was a possibility."

"Yeah. There was a possibility."

"And you chose not to include me. I knew it right from the beginning. I knew you'd cut me out."

Morelli moved to the living room. "So what are you trying to tell me, that we're back to war?"

"I'm trying to tell you that you're slime. And what's more, I want my popcorn back and I want you out of my apartment."

"No."

"What do you mean, no?"

"We made a deal. Information for popcorn. You got your information, and now I'm entitled to my popcorn."

My first thought was of my pocketbook, lying on the hall table. I could give Morelli the Eugene Petras treatment.

"Don't even think about it," Morelli said. "You get anywhere near the hall table, and I'll write you up for carrying concealed."

"That's disgusting. That's an abuse of your power as a police officer."

Morelli took the *Ghostbusters* cartridge from the top of the TV and slid it into the VCR. "Are you going to watch this movie with me, or what?"

I woke up feeling grumpy and not sure why. I suspected it had something to do with Morelli and the fact that I hadn't gotten to gas him or zap him or shoot him. He'd left when the movie had run its course and the popcorn bowl was empty. His parting words were that I should have faith in him.

"Sure," I'd said. When pigs fly.

I got the coffee going, dialed Eddie Gazarra, and left a message for a callback. I painted my toenails while I waited, drank some coffee, and made a pan of Rice Krispies marshmallow treats. I sliced the pan into bars, ate two, and the phone rang.

"Now what?" Gazarra asked.

"I need the names of the four brothers that got busted on Jackson Street last night. And I want the names the van driver gave as reference."

"Shit. I don't have access to that stuff."

"You still need a baby-sitter?"

"I always need a baby-sitter. I'll see what I can do."

I took a fast shower, ran my fingers through my hair, and dressed in Levi's and a flannel shirt. I removed the gun from my pocketbook and cautiously returned it to the cookie jar. I turned on the answering machine and locked up after myself.

The air was crisp and the sky was almost blue. Frost sparkled on the Buick's windows like pixie dust. I slid behind the wheel, powered up, and turned the defroster on full blast.

Going with the philosophy that doing *anything* (no matter how tedious and insignificant) is better than doing nothing, I dedicated the morning to drive-bys on Kenny's friends and relatives. While I drove I kept an eye out for my Jeep and for white trucks with black lettering. I wasn't finding anything, but the list of items to look for was getting longer, so maybe I was making progress. If the list got long enough, sooner or later I was bound to find something.

After the third pass I gave up and headed for the office. I needed to pick up my check for bringing Petras in, and I wanted to access my answering machine. I found a space available two doors down from Vinnie, and I took a stab at parallel-parking Big Blue. In slightly less than ten minutes, I got the car pretty well angled in, with only one rear tire on the sidewalk.

"Nice parking job," Connie said. "I was afraid you were going to run out of gas before you berthed the *QE Two*."

I dumped my pocketbook onto the Naugahyde couch. "I'm getting better. I only hit the car behind me twice, and I missed the parking meter totally."

A familiar face popped up from behind Connie. "Sheee-it, that better not a been my car you hit."

"Lula!"

Lula posed her 230 pounds with hand on outthrust hip. She was wearing white sweats and white sneakers. Her hair had been dyed orange and looked like it had been cut by a bush hog and straightened with wallpaper paste.

"Hey, girl," Lula said. "What you doing dragging your sad ass in here?"

"Came to pick up a paycheck. What are you doing here? Trying to make bail?"

"Hell no. I just been hired to whip this office into shape. I'm gonna file my ass off."

"What about your previous profession?"

"I'm retired. I gave the corner over to Jackie. I couldn't go back to bein' a ho after I was cut so bad last summer."

Connie was smiling ear to ear. "I figure she can handle Vinnie."

"Yeah," Lula said. "He try anything with me, and I'll stomp on the little motherfucker. He mess with a big woman like me, and he be nothin' more than a smelly spot on the carpet."

I liked Lula a lot. We'd met a few months ago, when I was just starting out on my bounty hunter career, and I'd found myself looking for answers on her corner on Stark Street.

"So, do you still get around? You still hear things on the street?" I asked Lula.

"What kinda things?"

"Four brothers tried to buy some guns last night and got busted."

"Hah. Everybody knows about that. That's the two Long boys, and Booger Brown and his dumber'n-cat-shit cousin, Freddie Johnson."

"You know who they were buying the guns from?"

"Some white dude. Don't know more'n that."

"I'm trying to get a line on the white dude."

"Sure does feel funny being on this side of the law," Lula said. "Think this is gonna take some getting used to."

I dialed my number and accessed my messages.

There was another invitation from Spiro and a list of names from Eddie Gazarra. The first four were the same names Lula had given me. The last three were the gangster references given by the gun seller. I wrote them down and turned to Lula.

"Tell me about Lionel Boone, Stinky Sanders, and Jamal Alou."

"Boone and Sanders deal. They go in and out of lockup like it was a vacation condo. Life expectancy don't look good, if you know what I mean. Don't know Alou."

"How about you?" I asked Connie. "You know any of these losers?"

"Not offhand, but you can check the files."

"Whoa," Lula said. "That's my job. You just stand back and watch me do this."

While she was checking the files I called Ranger.

"Talked to Morelli last night," I said to Ranger. "They didn't get a lot out of the brothers in the BMW. Mostly all they got was that the driver of the van used Lionel Boone, Stinky Sanders, and Jamal Alou as references."

"Bunch of bad people," Ranger said. "Alou is a craftsman. Can customize anything that goes bang."

"Maybe we should talk to them."

"Don't think you'd want to hear what they'd have to say to you, babe. Be better if I look the boys up by myself."

"Okay by me. I have other things to do anyway."

"Ain't got none of those assholes on file," Lula called. "Guess we too high-class."

I got my check from Connie and moseyed out to Big Blue. Sal Fiorello had come out of the deli and was peering into Blue's side window. "Will you look at the condition of this honey," he said to no one in particular.

I rolled my eyes and stuck the key in the door lock. "Morning Mr. Fiorello."

"That's some car you got here," he said.

"Yep," I replied. "Not everyone can drive a car like this."

"My uncle Manni had a fifty-three Buick. They found him dead in it. Found him at the landfill."

"Gee, I'm really sorry."

"Ruined the upholstery," Sal said. "Was a damn shame."

I drove to Stiva's and parked across the street from the mortuary. A florist's truck pulled into the service driveway and disappeared around the side of the building. There was no other activity. The building seemed eerily still. I wondered about Constantine Stiva in traction in St. Francis. I'd never known Constantine to take a vacation, and now here he was flat on his back with his business turned over to his ratty stepson. It had to be killing him. I wondered if he knew about the caskets. My guess was no. My guess was that Spiro had screwed up and was trying to keep it from Con.

I needed to give Spiro a no-progress report and decline his dinner invitation, but I was having a hard time motivating myself to cross the street. I could manage a mortuary at seven at night when it was filled with the K of C. I wasn't crazy about tippytoeing around at eleven in the morning, just me and Spiro and the dead people.

I sat there awhile longer, and I got to thinking how Spiro, Kenny, and Moogey had been best friends all through school. Kenny, the wise guy. Spiro, the not-too-bright kid with bad teeth and an undertaker for a stepfather. And Moogey, who as far as I could tell was a good guy. It's funny how people form alliances around the common denominator of simply needing a friend.

Now Moogey was dead. Kenny was missing in action. And Spiro was out twenty-four cheap caskets. Life can get pretty strange. One minute you're in high school, shooting baskets and stealing little kids' lunch money, and then next thing you know you're using mortician's putty to fill in the holes in your best friend's head.

A weird thought steamed from my brain like the Phoenix rising. What if this was all tied together? What if Kenny stole the guns and hid them in Spiro's caskets? Then what? I didn't know then what.

Feathery clouds had stolen into the sky, and the wind had picked up since I left my apartment this morning. Leaves rattled across the street and whipped against the windshield. I thought if I sat there long enough I'd probably see Piglet soar by.

By twelve it was clear that my feet weren't going to bypass my chicken heart. No problem. I'd go with plan number two. I'd go home to my parents, mooch lunch, and drag Grandma Mazur back with me.

• • •

It was almost two o'clock when I pulled into Stiva's small side lot with Grandma perched beside me on the big bench seat, straining to see over the dashboard.

"Ordinarily I don't go to afternoon viewings," Grandma said, gathering her purse and gloves together. "Sometimes in the summer when I feel like taking a walk I might stop in, but usually I like the crowd that comes in the evening. Of course things are all different when you're bounty hunters . . . like us."

I helped Grandma out of the car. "I'm not here as a bounty hunter. I'm here to talk to Spiro. I'm helping him with a small problem."

"I bet. What's he lost? I bet he lost a body."

"He didn't lose a body."

"Too bad. I wouldn't mind looking for a body."

We made our way up the stairs and through the door. We stopped for a moment to study the viewing schedule.

"Who're we supposed to be here to see?" Grandma wanted to know. "We gonna see Feinstein or Mayer?"

"Do you have a preference?"

"I guess I could go see Mayer. Haven't seen him in years. Not since he quit working at the A and P."

I left Grandma to herself and went looking for Spiro. I found him in Con's office, sitting behind the big walnut desk, phone in hand. He broke the connection and motioned me into a chair.

"That was Con," he said. "He calls all the time.

I can't get off the phone with him. He's getting to be a real pain in the ass."

I thought it would be nice if Spiro made a move on me, so I could give him some volts. Maybe I could give the little jerk some anyway. If I could get him to turn around I could give it to him in the back of the neck and claim it was someone else. I could say some crazed mourner ran into the office and stuck it to Spiro and then ran off.

"So, what's the word?" Spiro asked.

"You're right about the caskets. They're gone." I put the locker key on his desk. "Let's think about the key again. You only got one, right?"

"Right."

"Did you ever make a duplicate?"

"No."

"Did you ever pass it on to someone else?"

"No."

"How about valet parking? Was it on your key chain?"

"No one had access to the key. I kept the key at home, in the top drawer of my dresser."

"What about Con?"

"What about him."

"Did he ever have access to the key?"

"Con doesn't know about the caskets. I did this on my own."

I wasn't surprised. "Just out of morbid curiosity, what did you expect to do with these caskets? You're not going to sell them to anyone in the burg."

"I was sort of a middleman. I had a buyer."

A buyer. Unh! Mental head slap. "Does this buyer know his coffins are history?"

"Not yet."

"And you'd prefer not to ruin your credibility."

"Something like that."

I didn't think I wanted to know any more. I wasn't even sure I wanted to continue to look for the caskets.

"Okay," I said. "New subject. Kenny Mancuso."

Spiro sunk deeper into Con's chair. "We used to be friends," Spiro said. "Me and Kenny and Moogey."

"I'm surprised Kenny didn't ask you for help. Maybe ask you to hide him out."

"I should be so lucky."

"You want to enlarge on that?"

"He's out to get me."

"Kenny?"

"He was here."

This brought me out of my chair. "When? Did you see him?"

Spiro slid the middle drawer open and extracted a sheet of paper. He flipped the paper over to me. "I found this on my desk when I came in this morning."

The message was cryptic. "You have something that's mine, now I have something that's yours." The message was formed from silver paste-on letters. It was signed with a silver *K*. I stared at the paste on the letters and swallowed audibly. Spiro and I had a common pen pal.

"What does this mean?" I asked Spiro.

Spiro was still sunk into the chair. "I don't know what it means. It means he's crazy. You're going to keep looking for the caskets, aren't you?" Spiro asked. "We made a deal."

Here Spiro is, totally stressed over this bizarre note from Kenny, and in the next breath he's quizzing me about the caskets. Very suspicious, Dr. Watson.

"I suppose I'll keep looking," I told him, "but in all honesty, I'm stumped."

I found Grandma still in the Mayer room, manning the command post at the head of the casket with Marjorie Boyer and Mrs. Mayer. Mrs. Mayer was nicely snockered on 100-proof tea, entertaining Grandma and Marjorie with a slightly slurred version of the story of her life, concentrating on the seamier moments. She was swaying and gesturing, and every now and then a splot of whatever would slurp out of her teacup and splatter onto her shoe.

"You have to see this," Grandma said to me. "They gave George a dark blue satin liner on account of his lodge colors are blue and gold. Isn't that something?"

"All the lodge brothers'll be here tonight," Mrs. Mayer said. "They're gonna have a ceremony. And they sent a spray . . . THIS BIG!"

"That's a pip of a ring George is wearing," Grandma said to Mrs. Mayer.

Mrs. Mayer chugged the rest of her tea. "It's his lodge ring, the Lord rest his soul, George wanted to be buried with his lodge ring."

Grandma bent down for a better look. She leaned into the casket and touched the ring. "Uh-oh."

We were all afraid to ask.

Grandma straightened and turned to face us. "Well, will you look at this," she said, holding an object the size of a Tootsie Roll in her hand. "His finger came off."

Mrs. Mayer fainted crash onto the floor, and Marjorie Boyer ran screaming out of the room.

I inched forward for a better look. "Are you sure?" I asked Grandma Mazur. "How could that happen?"

"I was just admiring his ring, feeling the smooth glass stone, and next thing I knew his finger came off in my hand," she said.

Spiro charged into the room with Marjorie Boyer close on his heels. "What's this about a finger?"

Grandma held it out for him to see. "I was just taking a close look, and next thing I knew here was the finger."

Spiro snatched at the finger. "This isn't a real finger. This is wax."

"It came off his hand," Grandma said. "See for yourself."

We all peered into the casket, staring at the little stump where George's middle finger used to be.

"There was a man on TV the other night said aliens were snatching up people and doing scientific experiments on them," Grandma said. "Maybe that's what happened here. Maybe aliens got George's finger. Maybe they got some other parts too. You want me to check out the rest of George's parts?"

Spiro flipped the lid closed. "Sometimes accidents happen during the preparation process," he said. "Sometimes it's necessary to do a little artificial enhancement."

A creepy thought skittered into my mind regarding George's finger loss. Nah, I told myself. Kenny Mancuso wouldn't do something like that. That would be too gross even for Mancuso.

Spiro stepped over Mrs. Mayer and moved to the intercom just outside the door. I followed after him and waited while he instructed Louie Moon to call the ERT and then to bring some putty to room number four.

"About that finger," I said to Spiro.

"If you were doing your job, he'd be locked up by now," Spiro said. "I don't know why I ever hired you to find the caskets when you can't find Mancuso. How hard can it be? The guy's freaking nuts, leaving me notes, hacking up stiffs."

"Hacking up stiffs as in cutting off fingers?"

"Only one finger," Spiro said.

"Have you called the police?"

"What, are you serious? I can't call the police. They'll go right to Con. Con finds out about any of this he'll go ape-shit."

"I'm still sort of shaky on the finer points of the law, but it seems to me you have an obligation to report this stuff."

"I'm reporting it to you."

"Oh no, I'm not taking responsibility for this."

"It's my business if I want to report a crime," Spiro said. "There's no law says you have to tell the cops everything."

Spiro's gaze settled on a spot over my left shoulder. I turned to see what had caught his attention and was unnerved to see Louie Moon standing just inches from me. He was easy to identify because his name was written in red thread just over the breast pocket of his white cotton jumpsuit. He was average height and average weight and probably in his thirties. His skin was very pale, and his eyes were flat and faded blue. His blond hair had started to recede. He gave me a fast glance, just enough to acknowledge my presence, and handed Spiro the putty.

"We have a fainter in here," Spiro told him. "How about if you direct the ERT to the back door and then send them up here?"

Moon left without saying a word. Very mellow. Maybe working with dead people does that for you. I suppose it could be peaceful once you get over the body fluids stuff. Not much conversation going on, but probably good for the blood pressure.

"How about Moon?" I said to Spiro. "Did he ever have access to the locker key? Does he know about the caskets?"

"Moon doesn't know about anything. Moon has the IQ of a lizard."

I didn't exactly know how to reply to this, since Spiro was so lizardlike himself.

"Let's go through this from the beginning," I said. "When did you get the note?"

"I came in to make some phone calls and found the note on my desk. It must have been a few minutes before twelve."

"How about the finger? When did you find out about the finger?"

"I always do a walk-through before viewings. I noticed old George was short a finger and gave him a patch-up job."

"You should have told me."

"It wasn't something I wanted to share. I didn't think anybody'd find out. I didn't count on Granny Disaster showing up."

"You have any idea how Kenny got in?"

"Must have just walked in. When I leave at night I set the alarm. I shut it off when I open up in the morning. During the day the back door is always open for deliveries. Usually the front door's open too."

I'd watched the front door for a good part of the morning and no one had used it. A florist had pulled around back. That was about it. Of course, Kenny could have waltzed in before I got there.

"You didn't hear anything?"

"Louie and I were working in the addition most of the morning. People know to use the intercom if they need us."

"So who was in and out?"

"Clara does hair for us. She got here around nine-thirty to work on Mrs. Grasso. She left about an hour later. I guess you could talk to her. Just don't tell her anything. Sal Munoz delivered some flowers. I was up here when he came and left, so I know he won't be any help."

"Maybe you should check around. Make sure you're not missing anything else."

"I don't want to know what else I'm missing."

"So what is it that you have and Kenny wants?"

Spiro grabbed his crotch and gave a hoist. "He was small. You know what I mean?"

I felt my upper lip curl back. "You're kidding, right?"

"You never know what motivates people. Sometimes these things eat at them."

"Yeah, well, if you come up with anything else let me know."

I went back to the room and collected Grandma Mazur. Mrs. Mayer was on her feet, looking okay. Marjorie Boyer seemed a little green, but maybe it was just the lighting.

When we got to the lot I noticed an odd tilt to the Buick. Louie Moon was standing beside it, his expression serene, his eyes locked onto a large screwdriver sticking out of the whitewall. He could just as well have been watching grass grow.

Grandma squatted down to get a better look. "Don't seem right that someone should do this to a Buick," she said.

I hated to give in to paranoia, but I didn't for a minute think this was an act of random vandalism.

"Did you see who did this?" I asked Louie.

He shook his head no. When he spoke his voice

was soft and as flat as his eyes. "I just came out here to wait for the ERT."

"And no one was in the lot? You didn't see any cars driving away?"

"No."

I allowed myself the luxury of a sigh and went back inside to call for road service. I used the pay phone in the hall, unhappy to find that my hand was shaking as I fumbled to find a quarter in the bottom of my pocketbook. It's just a punctured tire, I told myself. It's no big deal. It's a car, for chrissake . . . an old car.

I had my father come to rescue Grandma Mazur, and while I waited for the tire to be replaced, I tried to imagine Kenny sneaking into the funeral home and leaving the note. It would have been fairly easy for Kenny to come in the back door and not be seen. Slicing off a finger would have been more difficult. It would have taken time.

CHAPTER

8

The back door to the funeral home opened to a short hall, which led to the lobby. The door to the basement, the side door to the kitchen, and Con's office all opened from the hall. A small vestibule and double glass door, located between Con's office and the basement door, gave access to the macadam driveway running back to the garages. It was through this door that the deceased rolled on his last journey.

Two years ago Con had hired a decorator to spiff the place up. The decorator's colors of choice, mauve and lime, dotted the walls with pastoral landscapes. The floors were heavily padded and carpeted. Nothing squeaked. The entire house was designed to keep noise to a minimum, and now Kenny was sneaking about and not being heard.

I ran into Spiro in the hall. "I want to know

more about Kenny," I said to him. "Where would Kenny go to hide out? Someone must be helping him. Who would he turn to?"

"Morellis and Mancusos always go back to the family. Someone dies, it's like they all died. They come in here in their ugly black dresses and coats and cry buckets for each other. My guess is he's living in a Mancuso attic."

I wasn't so sure. Seemed to me Joe would know by now if Kenny was hiding in a Mancuso attic. The Mancusos and Morellis weren't known for their ability to keep secrets from each other.

"If he wasn't in a Mancuso attic?"

Spiro shrugged. "He went to Atlantic City a lot."

"He seeing any girls besides Julia Cenetta?"

"You want to go through the phone book?"

"That many, huh?"

I left through the side door and waited impatiently while Al from Al's Auto Body unjacked my car. Al stood and wiped his hands on his coveralls before handing me the bill.

"Weren't you driving a Jeep last time I gave you a new tire?"

"The Jeep got stolen."

"You ever think about using public transportation?"

"What happened to the screwdriver?"

"I put it in your trunk. Never know when you need a screwdriver."

Clara's Beauty Parlor was three blocks down Hamilton, next to Buckets of Donuts. I found a parking space, gritted my teeth, held my breath, and backed the Buick in at warp speed. Better to get it over with. I knew I was close when I heard glass breaking.

I slunk out of the Buick and assessed the damage. None to the Buick. Broken headlight on the other guy's car. I left a note with insurance information and made for Clara's.

Bars, funeral homes, bakeries, and beauty parlors form the hub of the wheel that spins the burg. Beauty parlors are especially important because the burg is an equal-opportunity neighborhood caught in a 1950s time warp. The translation of this is that girls in the burg become obsessed with hair at a very early age. The hell with coed peewee football. If you're a little girl in the burg, you spend your time combing out Barbie's hair. Barbie sets the standard. Big gunky black eyelashes, electric-blue eye shadow, pointy outthrust breasts, and a lot of platinum-blond phony-looking hair. This is what we all aspire to. Barbie even teaches us how to dress. Tight glittery dresses, skimpy shorts, an occasional feather boa, and, of course, spike heels with everything. Not that Barbie doesn't have more to offer, but little girls in the burg know better than to get sucked in by yuppie Barbie. They don't buy into any of that tasteful sportswear, professional business suit stuff. Little girls in the burg go for the glamour.

The way I see it is, we're so far behind we're actually ahead of the rest of the country. We never had to go through any of that messy readjustment with roles stuff. You are who you want to be in the burg. It's never been men against women. In the burg it's always been weak against strong.

When I was a little girl I got my bangs cut at Clara's. She set my hair for my first communion and for my high school graduation. Now I go to the mall to get my hair trimmed by Mr. Alexander, but I still go to Clara sometimes to get my nails done.

The beauty parlor is in a converted house that was gutted to form one large room with a bathroom at the rear. There are a few chrome-and-upholstered chairs in the front where you can wait your turn and read dog-eared magazines or flip through hairdressing books showing styles no one can duplicate. Beyond the waiting area the washing bowls face off with the comb-out chairs. Just in front of the bathroom is a small manicure station. Posters showing more exotic, unobtainable hairstyles line the walls and reflect in the bank of mirrors.

Heads swiveled under dryers when I walked in.

Under the third dryer from the rear was my archenemy, Joyce Barnhardt. When I was in the second grade Joyce Barnhardt spilled a paper cup filled with water onto the back of my chair and told everyone I'd wet my pants. Twenty years later I'd caught her flagrante delicto on my dining room table, riding my husband like he was Dickie the Wonder Horse.

"Hello, Joyce," I said. "Long time no see."

"Stephanie. How's it going?"

"Pretty good."

"I understand you lost your job selling undies."

"I didn't sell undies." Bitch. "I was the lingerie buyer for E.E. Martin, and I lost my job when they consolidated with Baldicott."

"You always did have a problem with undies. Remember when you wet your pants in the second grade?"

If I'd been wearing a blood pressure cuff, it would have popped off my arm. I punched the hood back on the dryer and got so far in her face our noses were touching. "You know what I do for a living now, Joyce? I'm a bounty hunter, and I carry a gun, so don't piss me off."

"Everybody in New Jersey carries a gun," Joyce said. She reached into her pocketbook and pulled out a 9mm Beretta.

This was embarrassing because not only didn't I have my gun with me, but my gun was smaller.

Bertie Greenstein was under the dryer next to Joyce. "I like a forty-five," Bertie Greenstein said, hauling a Colt government model out of her tote bag.

"Too much kick," Betty Kuchta told Bertie from across the room. "And it takes up too much room in your pocketbook. You're better off with a thirty-eight. That's what I carry now. A thirty-eight."

"I carry a thirty-eight," Clara said. "I used to carry a forty-five but I got bursitis from the weight, so my doctor said to switch to a lighter gun. I carry pepper spray, too."

Everyone but old Mrs. Rizzoli, who was getting a perm, had pepper spray.

Betty Kuchta waved a stun gun in the air. "I've got one of these, too."

"Kiddie toy," Joyce said, brandishing a taser.

Nobody could one-up the taser.

"So, what'll it be?" Clara asked me. "Manicure? I just got in some new polish. Luscious Mango."

I looked at the bottle of Luscious Mango. I hadn't actually intended to get my nails done, but the Luscious Mango was pretty awesome. "Luscious Mango will be good," I said. I dropped my jacket and pocketbook over the back of the chair, sat down at the little manicure stand, and plunged my fingers into the soaking bowl.

"Who are you after now?" old Mrs. Rizzoli wanted to know. "I heard it was Kenny Mancuso."

"Have you seen him?"

"Not me," Mrs. Rizzoli said. "But I heard Kathryn Freeman saw him coming out of that Zaremba girl's house at two in the morning."

"That wasn't Kenny Mancuso," Clara said. "That was Mooch Morelli. I heard it right from Kathryn herself. She lives across the street, and she was up letting her dog out. He had diarrhea from eating chicken bones. I told her not to give that dog chicken bones, but she never listens."

"Mooch Morelli!" Mrs. Rizzoli said. "Can you imagine? Does his wife know?"

Joyce pulled the dryer back over her head. "I hear she's filing for divorce."

They all went back under the dryers and buried their faces in magazines since this was getting kind of close to home for Joyce and me. It was common knowledge who'd been caught with whom on my dining room table, and no one wanted to risk being present at a shootout with her hair in curlers.

"How about you?" I asked Clara while she filed a nail into a perfect oval. "Have you seen Kenny?"

She shook her head. "Not in a long time."

"I heard someone saw him sneaking into Stiva's this morning."

Clara stopped filing, and her head came up. "Holy mother. I was at Stiva's this morning."

"You see or hear anything?"

"No. It must have been after I left. I guess it doesn't surprise me. Kenny and Spiro were real good friends."

Betty Kuchta leaned forward from the dryer hood. "He was never all there, you know," she said, pointing a finger to her head. "He was in my Gail's class in the second grade. The teachers all knew never to turn their back."

Mrs. Rizzoli nodded in agreement. "A bad seed. Too much violence in the blood. Like his uncle Guido. *Pazzo*."

"You want to be careful of that one," Mrs. Kuchta said to me. "You ever notice his pinky finger? When Kenny was ten he chopped off the end of his pinky finger with his father's ax. Wanted to see if it would hurt."

"Adele Baggionne told me all about it," Mrs.

Rizzoli said. "Told me about the finger and lots of other things, too. Adele said she was watching out her back window, wondering what Kenny was going to do with the ax. Said she saw him put his hand on the wood stump next to the garage and chop his finger off. Said he never cried. Said he just stood there looking at it, smiling. Adele said he would have bled to death if she hadn't called the rescue squad."

It was close to five when I left Clara's. The more I heard about Kenny and Spiro the creepier I felt. I'd started the search thinking Kenny was a wise-ass, and now I was worried he was crazy. And Spiro didn't sound any better.

I drove straight home with my mood darkening by the minute. I was so spooked by the time I reached my apartment I had my pepper spray in my hand when I unlocked my front door. I flashed the lights on and relaxed a little when everything seemed in order. The red light was blinking on my answering machine.

It was Mary Lou. "So what's the deal here? You shacked up with Kevin Costner or something and don't have time to call?"

I shrugged out of my jacket and dialed her number. "I've been busy," I told her. "Not with Kevin Costner."

"Then with who?" she asked.

"With Joe Morelli, for one."

"Even better."

"Not that way. I've been looking for Kenny Mancuso and not having any luck."

"You sound depressed. You should get a mani-cure."

"I got a manicure, and it didn't help."

"Then there's only one thing left."

"Shopping."

"Fuckin' A," Mary Lou said. "I'll meet you at Quaker Bridge at seven. Macy's shoes."

Mary Lou was already deep into shoes when I showed up.

"What do you think of these shoes?" she asked, pirouetting in black ankle-high boots with stiletto heels.

Mary Lou is five foot three and built like a brick shithouse. She had a lot of hair, which happened to be red this week, and she favored huge hoop earrings and the wet look in lipstick. She'd been happily married for six years and had two kids. I liked her kids, but for right now I was content with a hamster. A person doesn't need a diaper pail with a hamster.

"They look familiar," I said about the shoes. "I think Witch Hazel was wearing shoes like that when she found Little Lulu picking beebleberries in her front yard."

"You don't like them?"

"Are these special occasion shoes?"

"New Year's Eve."

"What, no sequins?"

"You should get shoes," she said. "Something sexy."

"I don't need shoes. I need a night scope. You think they sell night scopes someplace here?"

"Omigod," Mary Lou said, holding up a pair

of purple suede platform pumps. "Look at these shoes. These shoes were made for you."

"I don't have the money. I'm between pay-checks."

"We could steal them."

"I don't do that anymore."

"Since when?"

"Since a long time. Anyway, I never stole any-thing big. There was just that once we took some gum from Sal's because we hated Sal."

"What about the jacket from Salvation Army?"

"It was MY jacket!" When I was fourteen my mother gave my favorite denim jacket to Salva-tion Army, and Mary Lou and I retrieved it. I told my mother I'd bought it back, but really we'd shoplifted it.

"You should at least try them on," Mary Lou said. She snagged a salesman. "We want these shoes in a size seven and a half."

"I don't want new shoes," I said. "I need too many other things. I need a new gun. Joyce Barn-hardt has a bigger gun than me."

"Ah-ha! Now we're getting somewhere."

I sat down and unlaced my Doc Martens. "I saw her in Clara's today. It was all I could do to keep from choking her."

"She did you a favor. Your ex-husband was a jerk."

"She's evil."

"She works here, you know. Cosmetics. I saw her doing a makeover when I came in. Had some old lady looking like Lily Munster."

I took the shoes from the salesman and slid them on.

"Are they wonderful, or what?" Mary Lou said.

"They're pretty nice, but I can't shoot anyone with them."

"You never shoot anyone anyway. Well, okay, maybe once."

"You think Joyce Barnhardt has purple shoes?"

"I happen to know Joyce Barnhardt has size ten feet and would look like a cow in these shoes."

I walked over to the mirror at the end of the shoe department and admired the shoes. Eat your heart out, Joyce Barnhardt.

I turned to look at them from the back and slammed into Kenny Mancuso.

He had my arms in an iron grip, and he yanked me flat to his chest. "Surprised to see me?"

I was speechless.

"You're a real pain in the ass," he said. "You think I didn't see you sneaking around in the bushes at Julia's house? You think I don't know about you telling her I fucked Denise Barkolowski?" He gave me a shake that made my teeth clack together. "And now you've got this cozy deal going with Spiro, don't you? The two of you think you're both so smart."

"You should let me take you back to court. If Vinnie assigns another bounty hunter, he might not be gentle about bringing you in."

"Haven't you heard? I'm special. I don't feel pain. Probably I'm freaking immortal."

Oh boy.

He flicked his hand, and a knife appeared. "I keep sending you messages, but you aren't listening," he said. "Maybe I should cut off your ear. Would that get your attention?"

"You don't scare me. You're a coward. You can't even face up to a judge." I'd tried this tack before on belligerent FTAs and found it helpful.

"Of course I scare you," Kenny said. "I'm a scary guy." The knife flashed out and slashed into my sleeve. "Now your ear," Kenny said, hanging tight to my jacket.

My pocketbook, with my bounty hunter paraphernalia, was on the seat beside Mary Lou, so I did what any intelligent, unarmed woman would do. I opened my mouth and screamed at the top of my lungs, startling Kenny enough to screw up his aim, so that I lost some hair but kept my ear.

"Jesus," Kenny said. "You're freaking embarrassing me." He shoved me into a shoe display, gave a backward skip, and took off.

I scrambled to my feet and charged after him, blasting through handbags and junior wear, operating on a surplus of adrenaline and a shortage of common sense. I could hear Mary Lou and the shoe clerk running hard behind me. I was swearing at Kenny and bitching about being in pursuit in goddamn platform heels when I slammed into an old lady at the cosmetics counter and almost knocked her on her ass.

"Jeez," I yelled at her. "I'm sorry!"

"Go!" Mary Lou shouted at me from junior wear. "Catch that sonovabitch!"

I reeled off the old lady and barreled into two other women. One of the women was Joyce Barnhardt in her makeover smock. We all went down in a heap on the floor, grunting and thrashing.

Mary Lou and the shoe clerk waded in to separate us, and somehow in the confusion of the moment, Mary Lou gave Joyce a good hard kick in the back of her knee. Joyce rolled away, howling in pain, and the shoe clerk quickly hoisted me to my feet.

I looked for Kenny, but he was long gone.

"Holy crap," Mary Lou said. "Was that Kenny Mancuso?"

I nodded my head yes while I struggled for air.

"What'd he say to you?"

"Asked me for a date. Said he liked the shoes."

Mary Lou snorted.

The shoe clerk was smiling. "You'd have caught him if you'd been trying on sneakers."

In all honesty I wasn't sure what I would have done if I'd caught him. He had a knife, and all I had were sexy shoes.

"I'm calling my lawyer," Joyce said, pulling herself up. "You attacked me! I'm going to sue the shit out of you."

"It was an accident," I told her. "I was chasing after Kenny, and you got in my way."

"This is the cosmetics department," Joyce shouted. "You can't just go around being a lunatic, chasing people through the cosmetics department."

"I was not being a lunatic. I was doing my job."

"Of course you were being a lunatic," Joyce said. "You're a dented can. You and your grand-mother are screwy tunes."

"Well, at least I'm not a slut."

Joyce's eyes got as big as golf balls. "Who are you calling a slut?"

"You." I leaned forward in my purple pumps. "I'm calling you a slut."

"If I'm a slut, then you're a tramp."

"You're a liar and a sneak."

"Bitch."

"Whore."

"So what do you think?" Mary Lou said to me. "Are you going to get these shoes, or what?"

By the time I got home I wasn't so sure I'd done the right thing with the shoes. I shifted the box under my arm while I unlocked my door. True, they were gorgeous shoes, but they were purple. What was I going to do with purple shoes? I'd have to buy a purple dress. And what about makeup? A person couldn't wear just any old makeup with a purple dress. I'd have to buy new lipstick and eyeliner.

I flipped the light switch and closed the door behind me. I dumped my pocketbook and new shoes on the kitchen counter and jumped back with a yelp when the phone rang. Too much ex-citement for one day, I told myself. I was on over-load.

"How about now?" the caller said. "Are you scared now? Have I got you thinking?"

My heart missed a beat. "Kenny?"

"Did you get my message?"

"What message are you talking about?"

"I left a message for you in your jacket pocket. It's for you and your new buddy, Spiro."

"Where are you?"

The disconnect clicked in my ear.

Shit.

I plunged my hand into my jacket pocket and started pulling stuff out . . . used Kleenex, lipstick, a quarter, a Snickers wrapper, a dead finger. "YOW!"

I dropped everything on the floor and ran out of the room. "Shit, damn, shit!" I stumbled into the bathroom and stuck my head into the toilet to throw up. After a few minutes I decided I wasn't going to throw up (which was kind of too bad since it'd be good to get rid of the hot fudge sundae I'd had with Mary Lou).

I washed my hands with a lot of soap and hot water and crept back to the kitchen. The finger was lying in the middle of the floor. It looked very embalmed. I snatched at the phone, staying as far away from the finger as was humanly possible, and dialed Morelli.

"Get over here," I said.

"Something wrong?"

"JUST GET OVER HERE!"

Ten minutes later the elevator doors opened and Morelli stepped out.

"Uh-oh," he said, "the fact that you're waiting for me in the hall is probably not a good sign." He looked at my apartment door. "You don't have a dead body in there, do you?"

"Not entirely."

"You want to enlarge on that?"

"I have a dead finger on my kitchen floor."

"Is the finger attached to anything? Like a hand or an arm?"

"It's just a finger. I think it belongs to George Mayer."

"You recognized it?"

"No. It's just that I know George is missing one. You see, Mrs. Mayer was going on about George's lodge, and how he wanted to be buried with his ring, and so Grandma had to check the ring out, and in the process broke off one of George's fingers. Turns out the finger was wax. Somehow Kenny got into the mortuary this morning, left Spiro a note, and chopped off George's finger. And then while I was at the mall tonight with Mary Lou, Kenny threatened me in the shoe department. That must have been when he put the finger in my pocket."

"Have you been drinking?"

I gave him a don't-be-stupid look and pointed to my kitchen.

Morelli moved past me and stood hands on hips, staring down at the finger on the floor. "You're right. It's a finger."

"When I came in tonight the phone was ringing. It was Kenny, telling me he left a message in my jacket pocket."

"And the message was the finger."

"Yeah."

"How did it get on the floor?"

"It sort of dropped there when I went to the bathroom to throw up."

Morelli helped himself to a paper towel and used it to pick up the finger. I gave him a plastic bag, he dropped the finger in, sealed the bag, and slipped the bag into his jacket pocket. He leaned against the kitchen counter and crossed his arms over his chest. "Let's start from the beginning."

I gave him all the details except for the part about Joyce Barnhardt. I told him about the silver-lettered note I'd received, and about the silver *K* on my bedroom wall, and about the screwdriver, and about how it would seem they'd come from Kenny.

He was quiet when I finished. After several seconds he asked me if I bought the shoes.

"Yeah," I said.

"Let's see."

I showed him the shoes.

"Very sexy," he said. "I think I'm getting excited."

I quickly put the shoes back in the box. "You have any idea what Kenny meant when he said Spiro had something of his?"

"No. Do you?"

"No."

"Would you tell me if you did?"

"I might."

Morelli opened the refrigerator and stared at the shelves. "You're out of beer."

"I had to choose between food and the shoes."

"You made the right choice."

"I bet this all has to do with the stolen guns. I bet Spiro was in on it. Maybe that's why Moogey got killed. Maybe Moogey found out about Spiro and Kenny stealing guns from the army. Or maybe all three of them did the job, and Moogey got cold feet."

"You should encourage Spiro," Morelli said. "You know, go to the movies with him. Let him hold your hand."

"Oh, ugh! Gross. Yuk!"

"I wouldn't let him see you in the shoes, though. He might go berserk. I think you should save the shoes for me. Wear something slinky with them. And a garter belt. They're definitely garter belt shoes."

Next time I find a finger in my pocket I'll flush it down the toilet. "It bothers me that we haven't been able to spot Kenny, but he doesn't seem to be having any trouble tailing me."

"How did he look? He grow a beard? Dye his hair?"

"He looked just like himself. Didn't look like he was living in dark alleys. He was clean, fresh shaven. Didn't look hungry. Had on clean clothes. Seemed to be alone. Was a little, um, upset. Said I was a pain in the ass."

"No! You? A pain in the ass? I can't imagine why anyone would think that."

"Anyway, he's not living hand to mouth. If he's selling guns, maybe he has money. Maybe he's staying in motels out of the area. Maybe in New Brunswick or down by Burlington or Atlantic City."

"His picture's been circulated in Atlantic City. Nothing's turned up. To tell you the truth, his trail has been dead cold. Having him pissed off at you is the best news I've had all week. All I have to do now is follow you around and wait for him to make another move."

"Oh good. I love being bait for a homicidal mutilator."

"Don't worry. I'll take care of you."

I didn't bother to hold back the grimace.

"Right," Morelli said, cop face in place. "Time out on the flirting and bullshit. We need some serious conversation here. I know what people say about the Morelli and Mancuso men . . . that we're bums and drunks and womanizers. And I'll be the first to admit that it's pretty much true. The problem with this kind of blanket judgment is that it makes it hard for the occasional good guy, like me . . ."

I rolled my eyes.

"And it tags a guy like Kenny a congenital wise-ass when anyplace else on the planet he'd be labeled a sociopath. When Kenny was eight years old he set fire to his dog and never showed a flicker of remorse. He's a manipulative user. He's totally self-centered. He's fearless because he feels no pain. And he's not stupid."

"Is it true he cut off his finger?"

"Yeah. It's true. If I'd known he was threatening you, I'd have done things differently."

"Like what?"

Morelli stared at me for a few moments before answering. "I'd have given you the sociopath lecture sooner, for one thing. And I wouldn't have left you alone in an unlocked apartment protected by juice glasses."

"I wasn't actually sure it was Kenny until I saw him tonight."

"From now on carry your pepper gas on your belt, not in your pocketbook."

"At least we know Kenny's still in the area. My guess is that whatever Spiro has is keeping Kenny here. Kenny isn't going to take off without it."

"Did Spiro seem rattled about the finger?"

"Spiro seemed . . . annoyed. Inconvenienced. He was worried Con would find out things weren't running smoothly. Spiro has plans. He expects to take over and franchise."

Morelli's face creased into a broad smile. "Plans to franchise the funeral parlor?"

"Yeah. Like McDonald's."

"Maybe we should just let Kenny and Spiro go at each other and scrape the remains off the floor when they're done."

"Speaking of remains, what are you going to do with the finger?"

"See if it matches up to what's left of George Mayer's stump. And while I'm doing that I thought I'd subtly ask Spiro what the hell is going on."

"I don't think that's a good idea. He doesn't want the police involved. Wouldn't report the mutilation or the note. If you go barging in there, he's going to kick me out of the loop."

"What do you suggest?"

"Give me the finger. I'll take it back to Spiro tomorrow. See if I can learn anything interesting."

"I can't let you do that."

"The hell you can't! It's my finger, dammit. It was in my coat."

"Give me a break. I'm a cop. I have a job to do."

"I'm a bounty hunter. I have a job to do too."

"Okay, I'll give you the finger, but you have to promise to keep me informed. The first hint I get that you're holding out on me I'll pull the plug."

"Good. Now give me the finger, and go home before you change your mind."

He took the plastic bag out of his jacket pocket and plunked it into my freezer. "Just in case," he said.

When Morelli left I locked the door and checked on the windows. I looked under the bed and in all the closets. When I was confident my apartment was secure I went to bed and slept like a rock, with all the lights blazing.

The phone rang at seven. I squinted at the clock and then at the phone. There is no such thing as a good call at 7 A.M. It's been my experience that all calls between the hours of 11 P.M. and 9 A.M. are disaster calls.

"'Lo," I said into the phone. "What's wrong?"

Morelli's voice came back at me. "Nothing's wrong. Not yet anyway."

"It's seven o'clock. Why are you calling me at seven o'clock?"

"Your curtains are closed. I wanted to make sure you were okay."

"My curtains are closed because I'm still in bed. How do you know my curtains are closed?"

"I'm in your parking lot."

CHAPTER
9

I dragged myself out of bed, pulled the curtain aside, and looked down into the lot. Sure enough, the tan Fairlane was parked next to Uncle Sandor's Buick. I could see the bumper still in Morelli's backseat, and someone had spray-painted PIG on his driver-side door. I opened my bedroom window and stuck my head out. "Go away."

"I have a staff meeting in fifteen minutes," Morelli yelled up. "Shouldn't take more than an hour, and then I'll be free for the rest of the day. I want you to wait for me to get back before you go to Stiva's."

"No problem."

By the time Morelli got back to me it was nine-thirty, and I was feeling restless. I was watching at the window when he pulled into the lot, and I was out of the building like a flash with the finger rolling around in my pocketbook. I was wearing my Doc Martens in case I had to kick someone, and I'd attached the pepper spray to my belt for instant access. I had my stun gun fully charged and stuffed into my jacket pocket.

"In a hurry?" Morelli asked.

"George Mayer's finger is making me nervous. I'll feel a lot better when it's back home with George."

"If you need to talk to me, just give me a call," Morelli said. "You have my car phone number?"

"Committed to memory."

"My pager?"

"Yes."

I powered up the Buick and rumbled out of the lot. I could see Morelli keeping a respectable distance behind me. Half a block from Stiva's I caught sight of the flashing lights of a motorcycle escort. Great. A funeral. I pulled to the side and watched the hearse roll by, followed by the flower car, followed by the limo with the immediate family. I glanced in the limo window and recognized Mrs. Mayer.

I checked my rearview mirror and saw Morelli parked directly behind me, shaking his head as if to say *don't even think about it.*

I punched his number into my phone. "They're burying George without his finger!"

"Trust me. George doesn't care about his finger. You can give it back to me. I'll save it for evidence."

"Evidence of what?"

"Tampering with a dead body."

"I don't believe you. You'll probably toss it into a Dumpster."

"Actually, I was thinking of putting it in Goldstein's locker."

The cemetery was a mile and a half from Stiva's. There were maybe seven or eight cars in front of me, crawling along in the somber procession. Outside, the air was mid-thirties and the sky was a wintery blue, and it felt more like I was in traffic to go to a football game than a funeral. We pulled through the cemetery gates and wound our way to the middle of the cemetery where the grave had been prepared and chairs set up. By the time I parked, Spiro had the widow Mayer already seated.

I sidled up to Spiro and leaned close. "I have George's finger."

No response.

"George's finger," I repeated in my mommy-to-three-year-old voice. "The real one. The one he's missing. I've got it in my pocketbook."

"What the hell is George's finger doing in your pocketbook?"

"It's sort of a long story. What we have to do now is get George put back together again."

"What, are you crazy? I'm not going to open that casket to give George his finger back! No one gives a shit about George's finger."

"I do!"

"Why don't you do something useful like find my damn caskets? Why are you wasting your time finding things I don't want? You don't expect to get paid for finding the finger, do you?"

"Jesus, Spiro, you're such a slime sucker."

"Yeah, so what's your point?"

"My point is that you better figure out how to get old George his finger, or I'm going to make a scene."

Spiro didn't look convinced.

"I'll tell Grandma Mazur," I added.

"Shit, don't do that."

"What about the finger?"

"We don't drop the casket until everyone's in the cars with motors running. We can pitch the finger in then. Will that work for you?"

"Pitch the finger?"

"I'm not opening the casket. You're gonna have to settle for having it buried in the same hole."

"I feel a scream coming on."

"Christ." He pressed his lips together, but his lips weren't ever able to entirely close over his overbite. "All right. I'll open the casket. Anyone ever tell you you're a pain in the ass?"

I moved away from Spiro to the edge of the gathering, where Morelli stood watching. "Everyone tells me I'm a pain in the ass."

"Then it must be true," Morelli said, throwing an arm around my shoulders. "Have any luck getting rid of the finger?"

"Spiro's going to give it back to George after the ceremony, after the cars have cleared out."

"Are you going to stay?"

"Yes. It'll give me a chance to talk to Spiro."

"I'm going to leave with the rest of the warm bodies. I'll be in the area if you need me."

I tilted my face to the sun and let my mind float

through the short prayer. When the temperature dropped below fifty Stiva didn't waste time at graveside. No widow in the burg ever wore sensible shoes to a funeral, and it was the funeral director's responsibility to keep old feet warm. The entire service took less than ten minutes, not even enough time to turn Mrs. Mayer's nose red. I watched the old folks beating their retreat over the blighted grass and hard ground. In a half hour they'd all be at the Mayer house, eating pencil points and drinking highballs. And by one o'clock Mrs. Mayer would be alone, wondering what she was going to do rattling around in the family house all by herself for the rest of her life.

Car doors slammed closed and engines revved. The cars drove away.

Spiro stood hands on hips, a study of the long-suffering undertaker. "Well?" he said to me.

I pulled the bag out of my pocketbook and handed it over.

Two cemetery employees stood on either side of the casket. Spiro gave the baggie to one of them with instructions to open the casket and lay the bag inside.

Neither man blinked an eye. I guess when you make a living dropping lead-lined boxes into the ground you aren't necessarily the inquisitive type.

"So," Spiro said, turning to me. "How'd you get the finger?"

I gave him the rundown on Kenny in the shoe department and how I found the finger when I got home.

"You see," Spiro said, "this is the difference between Kenny and me. Kenny always has to grandstand. Likes to set things up and then see how they play. Everything's a game to Kenny. When we were kids, I'd step on a bug and squash it dead, and Kenny'd stick it with a pin to see how long it'd take the bug to die. Guess Kenny likes to see things squirm, and I like to get the job done. If it was me, I'd have gotten you in a dark, empty parking lot, and I'd have shoved the finger up your butt."

I felt my head go light.

"Just talking theoretically, of course," Spiro said. "I wouldn't ever do that to you on account of you're such a fox. Not unless you wanted me to."

"I have to go now."

"Maybe we could see each other later. Like for dinner or something. Just because you're a pain in the ass, and I'm a slime sucker, doesn't mean we can't get together."

"I'd rather stick a needle in my eye."

"You'll come around," Spiro said. "I got what you want."

I was afraid to ask. "Apparently you've got what Kenny wants, too."

"Kenny's a jerk."

"He used to be your friend."

"Things happen."

"Like what?" I asked.

"Like nothing."

"I got the impression Kenny thought we were partners in some sort of plot against him."

"Kenny's nuts. Next time you see him you should shoot him. You can do that, can't you? You got a gun?"

"I really do have to go."

"Later," Spiro said, making a gun with his hand and pulling the trigger.

I practically ran back to the Buick. I slid behind the wheel, locked the door, and called Morelli.

"Maybe you're right about my going into cosmetology."

"You'd love it," Morelli said. "You'd get to draw eyebrows on a bunch of old babes."

"Spiro wouldn't tell me anything. At least not anything I wanted to hear."

"I picked up something interesting on the radio while I was waiting for you. There was a fire on Low Street last night. It was in one of the buildings belonging to the old pipe factory. Clearly arson. The pipe factory's been boarded up for years, but it seems someone was using the building to store caskets."

"Are you telling me someone torched my caskets?"

"Did Spiro put any contingencies on casket condition, or do you get paid dead or alive?"

"I'll meet you over there."

The pipe factory was on a mean piece of land caught between Low Street and the train tracks. It had been shut down in the seventies and left to decay. On either side were flat fields of no value. Beyond the fields were surviving industries: an auto graveyard, a plumbing supply house, Jackson Moving and Storage.

The gate leading to the pipe factory lot was rusted open, the blacktop cracked and pocked, littered with glass and weathered refuse. A leaden sky reflected in pools of sooty water. A fire truck idled in the lot. An official-type car had been parked next to the truck. A blue-and-white and a fire marshal's car were angled closer to the loading dock, where the fire had obviously taken place.

Morelli and I parked side by side and walked toward a group of men who were talking and writing on clipboards.

They looked up when we approached and nodded acknowledgment to Morelli.

"What's the story?" Morelli said.

I recognized the man who answered. John Petrucci. When my father worked in the post office Petrucci was his supervisor. Now Petrucci was the fire marshal. Go figure.

"Arson," Petrucci said. "Pretty much confined to the one bay. Somebody soaked a bunch of caskets in gasoline and set a fuse. The fire trail is clear."

"Any suspects?" Morelli asked.

They looked at him like he was crazy.

Morelli grinned. "Just thought I'd ask. Mind if we look around?"

"Help yourself. We're done here. The insurance investigator's already gone through. There wasn't much structural damage. Everything's cement. Someone's coming over to board things up."

Morelli and I scrambled up to the loading

dock. I pulled my flashlight out of my pocketbook and flicked it on a heap of charred, waterlogged trash sitting in the middle of the bay. Only at the far perimeter of the sodden mess were remains that could be recognized as a casket. An outer wood box and an inner wood box. Nothing fancy. Both blackened from fire. I reached out to touch a corner, and the casket and packaging collapsed in on itself, settling with a sigh.

"If you wanted to be real diligent about this, you could tell how many caskets were here by collecting the hardware," Morelli said. "Then you could take the hardware back to Spiro and see if he could identify it."

"How many caskets do you think were here?"

"A bunch."

"Good enough for me." I selected a clasp, wrapped it in Kleenex, and slid it into my jacket pocket. "Why would someone steal caskets and then burn them?"

"A lark? A grudge? Maybe ripping off caskets seemed like a good idea at the time, but whoever took them couldn't get rid of them."

"Spiro isn't going to be happy."

"Yeah," Morelli said. "Kind of warms your heart, doesn't it?"

"I needed that money."

"What were you going to do with it?"

"Pay off my Jeep."

"Honey, you don't have a Jeep."

The casket clasp felt heavy in my pocket. Not in terms of ounces and pounds, but in measurements of dread. I didn't want to go knocking on Spiro's door. When in dread, my rule was always to procrastinate.

"I thought maybe I'd go home for lunch," I said to Morelli. "And then I could bring Grandma Mazur back to Stiva's with me. There'll be someone new in George Mayer's room, and Grandma really likes to get out to afternoon viewings."

"Very thoughtful of you," Morelli said. "Am I invited for lunch?"

"No. You already had pudding. If I bring you home for a meal, they'll never let up. Two meals are as good as engaged."

I stopped for gas on the way to my parents' and was relieved not to see Morelli anywhere. Maybe this wouldn't be so bad, I thought. I probably wouldn't get the finder's fee, but at least I'd be done with Spiro. I turned at Hamilton and drove past Delio's Exxon.

My heart dropped when I hit High Street and saw Morelli's Fairlane parked in front of my parents' house. I attempted to park behind him, misjudged, and took out his right taillight.

Morelli got out of his car and examined the damage. "You did that on purpose," he said.

"I didn't! It's this Buick. You can't tell where it ends." I gave him the evil eye. "What are you doing here? I told you no lunch."

"I'm protecting you. I'll wait in the car."

"Fine."

"Fine," Morelli said.

"Stephanie," my mother called from the door.

"What are you doing standing out there with your boyfriend?"

"You see?" I said to Morelli. "What did I tell you? Now you're my boyfriend."

"Lucky you."

My mother was waving us forward. "Come in. What a nice surprise. Good thing I have extra soup. And we have some fresh bread your father just got from the bakery."

"I like soup," Morelli said.

"No. No soup," I told him.

Grandma Mazur appeared at the door. "What are you doing with him?" she asked. "I thought you said he wasn't your type."

"He followed me home."

"If I'd known, I'd have put on some lipstick."

"He's not coming in."

"Of course he's coming in," my mother said. "I have plenty of soup. What would people think if he didn't come in?"

"Yeah," Morelli said to me. "What would people think?"

My father was in the kitchen putting a new washer in the kitchen faucet. He looked relieved to see Morelli standing in the hallway. He'd probably prefer I bring home someone useful, like a butcher or a car mechanic, but I guess cops are a step up from undertakers.

"Sit at the table," my mother said. "Have some bread with cheese. Have some cold cuts. I got the cold cuts at Giovichinni's. He's always got the best cold cuts."

While everyone was ladling out soup and scarfing up cold cuts I pulled the paper with the casket photo out of my pocketbook. The detail in the photo wasn't especially good, but the hardware looked similar to what I'd seen at the fire site.

"What's that?" Grandma Mazur wanted to know. "Looks like a picture of a casket." She took a closer look. "You aren't thinking of buying that for me, are you? I want one with some carving. I don't want one of them military caskets."

Morelli's head came up. "Military?"

"Only place they got caskets this ugly is the military. I saw on TV about how they got all these caskets left over from Desert Storm. Not enough Americans died over there and now they have acres of caskets to get rid of, so the army's been auctioning them off. They're—what do you call it—surplus."

Morelli and I looked at each other. Duh.

Morelli put his napkin on the table and slid his chair back. "I need to make a phone call," he said to my mother. "Is it okay if I use your phone?"

It seemed pretty far-fetched to think Kenny had smuggled the guns and ammo off the base in caskets. Still, crazier things have been known to happen. And it would explain Spiro's casket anxiety.

"How'd it go?" I asked when Morelli returned to the table.

"Marie's checking for me."

Grandma Mazur paused with a spoonful of

soup halfway to her mouth. "Is this police business? Are we working on a case?"

"Trying to get a dental appointment," Morelli said. "I've got a loose filling."

"You need teeth like mine," Grandma told him. "I can mail them to the dentist."

I was having second thoughts about dragging Grandma off to Stiva's. I figured she could hold her own with a disgusting undertaker. I didn't want her involved with a dangerous one.

I finished my soup and bread and helped myself to a handful of cookies from the cookie jar, glancing at Morelli, wondering at his lean body. He'd eaten two bowls of soup, half a loaf of bread slathered in butter, and seven cookies. I'd counted.

He saw me staring and raised his eyebrows in silent question.

"I suppose you work out," I said, more statement than question.

"I run when I can. Do some weights." He grinned. "Morelli men have good metabolism."

Life was a bitch.

Morelli's beeper went off, and he returned the call from the kitchen phone. When he came back to the table he looked like the cat that swallowed the canary. "My dentist," he said. "Good news."

I stacked all the soup bowls and plates and hustled them into the kitchen. "Got to go," I said to my mother. "Got work to do."

"Work," my mother said. "Hah! Some work."

"It was wonderful," Morelli said to my mother. "The soup was terrific."

"You should come again," she told him. "We're having pot roast tomorrow. Stephanie, why don't you bring him back tomorrow?"

"No."

"That's not polite," my mother said. "How is that to treat a boyfriend?"

When my mother was willing to accept a Morelli as a boyfriend, this only went to show how desperate my mother was to get me married, or at least for me to have a social life. "He's not my boyfriend."

My mother gave me a bag of cookies. "I'll make cream puffs tomorrow. I haven't made cream puffs in a long time."

When we got outside I stood straight and tall and looked Morelli square in the eye. "You are *not* coming to dinner."

"Sure," Morelli said.

"What about the phone call?"

"Braddock had a shitload of surplus caskets. The DRMO conducted a sale six months ago. That was two months before Kenny was discharged. Stiva's Mortuary bought twenty-four. The caskets were stored in the same general area as the munitions, but we're talking about a lot of ground. A couple warehouses and an acre or two of open yard, all behind fence."

"Of course the fence was no problem for Kenny, because he worked in the compound."

"Yep. And when bids were accepted the caskets were marked for pickup. So Kenny knew which caskets were assigned to Spiro." Morelli snitched a cookie from my bag. "My uncle Vito would have been proud."

"Vito stole a few caskets in his day?"

"Mostly Vito filled caskets. Hijacking was a sideline."

"So you think it's possible Kenny used the caskets to smuggle the guns off the base?"

"Seems risky and unnecessarily melodramatic, but yeah, I think it's possible."

"Okay, so Spiro, Kenny, and probably Moogey maybe stole all this stuff from Braddock, and stored it at R and J. Then all of a sudden the stuff is missing. Someone pulled a double cross, and we know it wasn't Spiro because Spiro hired me to find the caskets."

"Doesn't seem like it was Kenny either," Morelli said. "When he said Spiro had something that belonged to him, my guess is he was talking about the stolen guns."

"So who does that leave? Moogey?"

"Dead men don't set up late-night sales meetings with the Long brothers."

I didn't want to run over the jagged remnants of Morelli's taillight, so I picked the major pieces out of the gutter, and for lack of something better to do with them, handed the chunks of plastic to Morelli. "Probably you're insured for this," I said.

Morelli looked pained.

"Are you still following me?" I asked.

"Yeah."

"Then watch out for my tires when I go into Stiva's."

Stiva's little side lot was totally filled with the matinee crowd, forcing me to park on the street. I got out of the Buick and tried to be cool about looking for Morelli. I couldn't find him, but I knew he was close because my stomach felt hot and squishy.

Spiro was in the lobby doing his best impersonation of God directing traffic.

"How's it going?" I said.

"Busy. Joe Loosey came in last night. Aneurysm. And Stan Radiewski is here. He was an Elk. The Elks always get a big turnout."

"I have some good news and some bad news," I said. "The good news is . . . I think I found your caskets."

"And the bad news?"

I took the blackened clasp out of my pocket. "The bad news is . . . this is all that's left."

Spiro looked at the clasp. "I don't get it."

"Someone barbecued a bunch of caskets last night. Had them all stacked up in one of the loading bays at the pipe factory, soaked the caskets in gasoline, and lit a fuse. They were pretty badly burned, but there was enough of one to identify as a casket in a crate."

"And you saw this? What else got burned? Was there anything else?"

Like a few LAWs? "From what I could see there were just caskets. You might want to check for yourself."

"Christ," Spiro said. "I can't go now. Who's gonna baby-sit all these fucking Elks?"

"Louie?"

"Jesus. Not Louie. It's going to have to be you."

"Oh no. Not me."

"All you have to do is make sure there's hot tea and say a lot of crapola like . . . the Lord moves in mysterious ways. I'll only be gone a half hour." He dug his keys out of his pocket. "Who was there when you got to the pipe factory?"

"The fire marshal, a uniform, some guy I didn't know, Joe Morelli, a bunch of firemen packing up."

"They say anything worth remembering?"

"Nope."

"You tell them the caskets belonged to me?"

"No. And I'm not staying. I want my finder's fee, and then I'm out of here."

"I'm not handing over any money until I see this for myself. For all I know they could be someone else's caskets. Or maybe you're making all this up."

"Half hour," I yelled to his back. "That's all you get!"

I checked the tea table. Nothing to do there. Lots of hot water and cookies set out. I sat down in a side chair and contemplated some nearby cut flowers. The Elks were all in the new addition with Radiewski, and the lobby was uncomfortably quiet. No magazines to read. No television. Music to die by softly filtered over the sound system.

After what seemed like four days, Eddie Ragucci ambled in. Eddie was a CPA and a big magoo in the Elks.

"Where's the weasel?" Eddie asked.

"Had to go out. He said he wouldn't be long."

"It's too hot in Stan's room. The thermostat must be broken. We can't get it to cut off. Stan's makeup is starting to run. Things like this never happened when Con was here. It's a damn shame Stan had to go when Con was in the hospital. Talk about the lousy breaks."

"The Lord moves in mysterious ways."

"Ain't that the truth."

"I'll see if I can find Spiro's assistant."

I pushed a few buttons on the intercom, yelling Louie's name into the thing, telling him to come to the lobby.

Louie appeared just as I got to the last button. "I was in the workrooms," he said.

"Anybody else in there?"

"Mr. Loosey."

"I mean, are there any other employees? Like Clara from the beauty parlor?"

"No. Just me."

I told him about the thermostat and sent him to take a look.

Five minutes later he trundled back. "The little thing was bent," he said. "It happens all the time. People lean on it, and the little thing gets bent."

"You like working in a funeral home?"

"I used to work in a nursing home. This is a lot easier on account of you can just hose people down here. And once you get them on the table they don't move around."

"Did you know Moogey Bues?"

"Not until after he was shot. Took about a pound of putty to fill in his head."

"How about Kenny Mancuso?"

"Spiro said it was Kenny Mancuso that shot Moogey Bues."

"You know what Kenny looks like? He ever come around here?"

"I know what he looks like, but I haven't seen him in a while. I hear people say how you're a bounty hunter, and that you're looking for Kenny."

"He failed to appear in court."

"If I see him, I'll tell you."

I gave him a card. "Here are some numbers where I can be reached."

The back door banged open and was slammed closed. A moment later Spiro stalked into the room. His black dress shoes and the cuffs of his slacks were powdered with ash. His cheeks were an unhealthy red, and his little rodent eyes were dilated black.

"Well?" I asked.

His eyes fixed over my shoulder. I turned and saw Morelli cross the lobby.

"You looking for someone?" Spiro said to Morelli. "Radiewski's in the addition."

Morelli flashed his badge.

"I know who you are," Spiro said. "There a problem here? I leave for a half hour, and I come back to a problem."

"Not a problem," Morelli told him. "Just trying to find the owner of some caskets that burned."

"You found him. And I didn't set the fire. The caskets were stolen from me."

"Did you report the theft to the police?"

"I didn't want the publicity. I hired Ms. Marvel here to find the damn things."

"The one casket that was left looked a little plain for a burg casket," Morelli said.

"I got them on sale from the army. Surplus. I was thinking maybe I'd franchise out into other neighborhoods. Maybe take them down to Philly. Lot of poor people in Philly."

"I'm curious about this army surplus stuff," Morelli said. "How does this work?"

"You submit a bid to the DRMO. If the bid gets picked up, you've got a week to haul your shit off the base."

"Which base are we talking about?"

"Braddock."

Morelli was a study of calm. "Wasn't Kenny Mancuso stationed at Braddock?"

"Yeah. A lot of people are stationed at Braddock."

"Okay," Morelli said, "so they accept your bid. How do you get the caskets back here?"

"Me and Moogey went down with a U-Haul."

"One last question," Morelli said. "You have any idea why someone would steal your caskets and then set a match to them?"

"Yeah. They were stolen by a nut. I've got things to do," Spiro said. "You're done here, right?"

"For now."

They locked eyes, a muscle worked in Spiro's jaw, and he wheeled off to his office.

"See you back at the ranch," Morelli said to me, and he was off, too.

The door to Spiro's office was closed. I knocked and waited. No answer. I knocked louder. "Spiro," I yelled, "I know you're in there!"

Spiro ripped the door open. "Now what?"

"My money."

"Christ, I have more things to think about than your chickenshit money."

"Like what?"

"Like crazy Kenny Mancuso setting fire to my goddamn caskets."

"How do you know it was Kenny?"

"Who else could it be? He's looney tunes, and he's threatening me."

"You should have told Morelli."

"Yeah, right. That's all I need. Like I haven't got enough problems, I should have the cops looking up my butt."

"I've noticed you're not fond of cops."

"Cops suck."

I felt breath on the back of my neck and turned to find Louie Moon standing almost on top of me.

"Excuse me," he said, "I've got to talk to Spiro."

"Talk," Spiro said.

"It's about Mr. Loosey. There's been an accident."

Spiro didn't say a word, but his eyes bore like drill bits into Louie's forehead.

"I had Mr. Loosey on the table," Louie said, "and I was gonna get him dressed, and then I had to go fix the thermostat, and when I got back to Mr. Loosey I noticed he was missing his . . . um, private part. I don't know how this could happen. One minute it was there, and then the next minute it was gone."

Spiro knocked Louie aside with a sweep of his hand and charged out, yelling, "Jesus H. Christ and motherfucker."

Minutes later, Spiro was back in his office, his face mottled, his hands clenched. "I don't fucking believe this," he roared through clenched teeth. "I leave for half an hour, and someone comes in and hacks off Loosey's dick. You know who that someone was? Kenny, that's who. I leave you in charge, and you let Kenny come in and hack off a dick."

The phone rang and Spiro snatched at it. "Stiva."

His lips narrowed, and I knew it was Kenny.

"You're nuts," Spiro said. "Too much nose candy. Too many of those little tattoos."

Kenny did some talking, and Spiro cut in.

"Shut up," Spiro said. "You don't know what the fuck you're talking about. And you don't know what the fuck you're doing when you mess with me. I see you around here, and I'll kill you. And if I don't kill you, I'll have Cookie here kill you."

Cookie? Was he talking about me? "Excuse me," I said to Spiro, "what was that last part?"

Spiro slammed the phone down. "Fucking jerk."

I put palms flat on his desk and leaned forward. "I am *not* a cookie. And I am *not* a hired gun. And if I was in the protection business, I would *not* protect *your* slimy body. You are a mold spore, a boil, a dog turd. If you ever tell anyone I will kill them on your behalf again, I'll make sure you sing soprano for the rest of your life."

Stephanie Plum, master of the empty threat.

"Let me guess . . . you're on the rag, right?"

Good thing I didn't have my gun with me, because I might have shot him.

"There are a lot of people who wouldn't pay you anything for finding burned-up stuff," Spiro said, "but because I'm such a good guy I'm going to write you a check. We could consider it like a retainer. I could see where it'd be handy to have a chick like you around."

I took the check and left. I didn't see the value in talking any further since there clearly wasn't anyone home. I stopped to get gas and Morelli pulled in behind me.

"This is getting strange," I said to Morelli. "I think Kenny's gone over the edge."

"Now what?"

I told him about Mr. Loosey and his mishap, and about the phone call.

"You should be giving this car high-test," Morelli said. "You're going to get engine knock."

"God forbid I'd get engine knock."

Morelli looked disgusted. "Shit," he said.

I thought this seemed like a strong reaction to my lack of automotive maintenance. "Is engine knock that bad?"

He leaned against the fender. "A cop was killed in New Brunswick last night. Took two hits through his vest."

"Army ammo?"

"Yeah." He raised his eyes to me. "I have to find this stuff. It's right under my nose."

"You think Kenny could be right about Spiro? You think Spiro could have emptied the caskets and hired me to cover his ass?"

"I don't know. Doesn't feel right. My gut instinct is that this started off with Kenny, Moogey, and Spiro, and somehow a fourth player came in and screwed everything up. I think someone snatched the stuff out from under Kenny, Moogey, and Spiro and started them fighting among themselves. And it's probably not someone from Braddock, because it's being sold piecemeal in Jersey and Philly."

"It would have to be someone close to one of those three. A confidant . . . like a girlfriend."

"It could be someone who found out by accident," Morelli said. "Someone who overheard a conversation."

"Like Louie Moon."

"Yeah. Like Louie Moon," Morelli said.

"And it would have to be someone who had access to the locker key. Like Louie Moon."

"There are probably lots of people Spiro could have talked to and who would have had access to his key. Everyone from his cleaning lady to Clara. Same with Moogey. Just because Spiro told you no one but him had a key doesn't mean it's true. Probably all three of them had keys."

"If that's the case, then what about Moogey's key? Has that been accounted for? Was it on his key chain when he was killed?"

"His key chain was never found. It was assumed that he left his keys somewhere in the garage and sooner or later they'd turn up. It didn't seem like an important issue at the time. His parents came with an extra key and drove his car home.

"Now that the caskets have surfaced I have some cause to harass Spiro. I think I'll go back and lean on him. And I want to talk to Louie Moon. Can you keep out of trouble for a while?"

"Don't worry about me. I'm fine. I thought maybe I'd go shopping. See if I could find a dress to go with the purple shoes."

The line of Morelli's mouth tightened. "You're lying. You're going to do something stupid, aren't you?"

"Boy, that really hurts. I thought you'd be excited about a purple dress with the purple shoes. I was going to look for spandex, too. A short spandex dress with bugle beads and sequins."

"I know you, and I know you're not going shopping."

"Cross my heart and hope to die. I'm going shopping. I swear to you."

One corner of Morelli's mouth hitched up a fraction of an inch. "You'd lie to the Pope."

I caught myself halfway through the sign of the cross. "I almost never lie." Only when it's absolutely necessary. And on those occasions when the truth doesn't seem appropriate.

I watched Morelli drive away, and then I headed over to Vinnie's office to get some addresses.

CHAPTER

10

Connie and Lula were yelling at each other when I walked into the office.

"Dominick Russo makes his own sauce," Connie shouted. "With plum tomatoes. Fresh basil. Fresh garlic."

"I don't know about any of that plum tomato shit. All I know is the best pizza in Trenton comes from Tiny's on First Street," Lula shouted back. "Ain't nobody makes pizza like Tiny. That man makes soul pizza."

"Soul pizza? What the hell is soul pizza?" Connie wanted to know.

They both turned and glared at me.

"You settle it," Connie said. "Tell know-it-all here about Dominic's pizza."

"Dom makes good pizza," I said. "But I like the pizza at Pino's."

"Pino's!" Connie curled her upper lip. "They use marinara sauce that comes in five-gallon cans."

"Yeah," I said. "I love that canned marinara sauce." I dropped my pocketbook on Connie's desk. "Glad to see you two getting along so well."

"Hunh," Lula said.

I plopped onto the couch. "I need some addresses. I want to do some snooping."

Connie got a directory from the bookcase behind her. "Who you need?"

"Spiro Stiva and Louie Moon."

"Wouldn't want to look under the cushions in Spiro's house," Connie said. "Wouldn't look in his refrigerator, either."

Lula grimaced. "He the undertaker guy? Shoot, you aren't gonna do breaking and entering on an undertaker, are you?"

Connie wrote an address on a piece of paper and searched for the second name.

I looked at the address she'd gotten for Spiro. "You know where this is?"

"Century Court Apartments. You take Klockner to Demby." Connie gave me the second address. "I haven't a clue on this one. Somewhere in Hamilton Township."

"What are you looking for?" Lula asked.

I stuffed the addresses into my pocket. "I don't know. A key, maybe." Or a couple crates of guns in the living room.

"Maybe I should come with you," Lula said. "Skinny ass like you shouldn't be sneaking around all by yourself."

"I appreciate your offer," I told her, "but riding shotgun isn't part of your job description."

"Don't think I got much of a job description," Lula said. "Seems to me I do whatever got to be done, and right now I've done it all unless I want to sweep the floor and scrub the toilet."

"She's a filing maniac," Connie said. "She was born to file."

"You haven't seen anything yet," Lula said. "Wait'll you see me be an assistant bounty hunter."

"Go for it," Connie said.

Lula packed herself into her jacket and grabbed her pocketbook. "This is gonna be good," she said. "This is gonna be like Cagney and Lacey."

I searched the big wall map for Moon's address. "Okay by me if it's okay with Connie, but I want to be Cagney."

"No way! I want to be Cagney," Lula said.

"I said it first."

Lula stuck her lower lip out and narrowed her eyes. "Was my idea, and I'm not doing it if I can't be Cagney."

I looked at her. "We aren't serious about this, are we?"

"Hunh," Lula said. "Speak for yourself."

I told Connie not to wait up, and held the front door for Lula. "We're going to check out Louie Moon first," I said to her.

Lula stopped in the middle of the sidewalk and looked at Big Blue. "We going in this big motherfucker Buick?"

"Yep."

"I knew a pimp once had a car like this."

"It belonged to my uncle Sandor."

"He a businessman?"

"Not that I know of."

Louie Moon lived on the far perimeter of Hamilton Township. It was almost four when we turned onto Orchid Street. I counted off homes, searching for 216, amused that such an exotically named street had been blessed with a lineup of unimaginative crackerbox houses. It was a neighborhood built in the sixties when land was available, so the plots were large, making the two-bedroom ranches seem even smaller. Over the years homeowners had personalized their carbon-copy houses, adding a garage here, a porch there. The houses had been modernized with vinyl siding of various muted shades. Bay windows had been inserted. Azalea bushes had been planted. And still the sameness prevailed.

Louie Moon's house was set apart by a bright turquoise paint job, a full array of Christmas lights, and a five-foot-tall plastic Santa strapped to a rusted TV antenna.

"Guess he gets into the spirit early," Lula said.

From the droop of the lights haphazardly stapled to his house and the faded look to Santa, I'd guess he was in the spirit all year long.

The house didn't have a garage, and there were no cars in the driveway or parked at the curb. The house looked dark and undisturbed. I left Lula in the car and went to the front door. I knocked twice. No answer. The house was one floor built on a slab. The curtains were all open. Louie had nothing to hide. I circled the house, peeking into windows. The inside was neat and furnished with what I guessed to be an accumulation of discards. There was no sign of recent wealth. No boxes of ammo stacked on the kitchen table. Not a single assault rifle in sight. It looked to me like he lived alone. One cup and one bowl in the dish drain. One side of the double bed had been slept in.

I could easily see Louie Moon living here, content with his life because he had a little blue house. I toyed with the idea of illegal entry, but I couldn't produce enough motivation to warrant the intrusion.

The air was damp and cold and the ground felt hard underfoot. I pulled my jacket collar up and returned to the car.

"That didn't take long," Lula said.

"Not much to see."

"We going to the undertaker next?"

"Yeah."

"Good thing he don't live where he do his thing. I don't want to see what they collect in those buckets at the end of those tables."

It was heavy twilight by the time we got to Century Court. The two-story buildings were red brick with white window trim. Doors were set in four-door clusters. There were five clusters to a building, which meant there were twenty apartments. Ten up and ten down. All of the buildings were set on pipestems coming off Demby. Four buildings per pipestem.

Spiro had an end unit on the ground floor. His windows were dark, and his car wasn't in the lot. With Con in the hospital, Spiro was forced to keep long hours. The Buick was easily recognizable, and I didn't want to get caught if Spiro should decided to bop in for a fast change of socks, so I drove one pipestem over and parked.

"I bet we find some serious shit here," Lula said, getting out of the car. "I got a feeling about this one."

"We're just going to scope things out," I said. "We're not going to do anything illegal . . . like breaking and entering."

"Sure," Lula said. "I know that."

We cut across the grassy area to the side of the buildings, walking casually, as if we were out for a stroll. Curtains were drawn on the windows in the front of Spiro's apartment, so we went to the back. Again, curtains were drawn. Lula tested the sliding patio door and the two windows and found them both to be locked.

"Ain't this a bitch?" she said. "How we supposed to find anything out this way? And just when I had a feeling, too."

"Yeah," I said. "I'd love to get into this apartment."

Lula swung her pocketbook in a wide arc and crashed it into Spiro's window, shattering the glass. "Where there's a will, there's a way," she said.

My mouth dropped open, and when words finally came out they were in a whispered screech.

"I don't believe you did that! You just broke his window!"

"The Lord provides," Lula said.

"I told you we weren't doing anything illegal. People can't just go around breaking windows."

"Cagney would of done it."

"Cagney would *never* have done that."

"Would of."

"Would not!"

She slid the window open and poked her head inside. "Don't look like nobody home. Guess we should go in and make sure this broken glass didn't do any damage." She had the entire upper half of her body shoved into the window. "Could of made this window bigger," she said. "Can't hardly fit a full-bodied woman like me in this sucker."

I gnawed on my lower lip and held my breath, not sure whether I should push her through or pull her out. She looked like Pooh when he was stuck in the rabbit hole.

She gave a grunt and suddenly the back half of her disappeared behind Spiro's curtain. A moment later the patio door clicked open and Lula poked her head out. "You gonna stand out there all day, or what?"

"We could get arrested for this!"

"Hah, like you never did any illegal entry shit?"

"I never broke anything."

"You didn't this time neither. I did the breaking. You just gonna do the entering."

I supposed it was okay since she put it that way.

I slipped behind the patio curtain and let my eyes adjust to the darkness. "Do you know what Spiro looks like?"

"Ratty-faced little guy?"

"Yeah. You do lookout on the front porch. Knock three times if you see Spiro drive up."

Lula opened the front door and peeked out. "Everything clear," she said. Then she let herself out and closed the door.

I locked both doors and flipped the dining room light on, turning the dimmer until the light was low. I started in the kitchen, methodically going through cabinets. I checked the refrigerator for phony jars and did a cursory search of the kitchen trash.

I made my way through the dining room and living room without discovering anything worthwhile. Breakfast dishes were still in the sink, the morning paper was strewn across the table. A pair of black dress shoes had been kicked off and left in front of the TV. Other than that the apartment was clean. No guns, no keys, no threatening notes. No addresses hastily scribbled on a pad beside the kitchen wall phone.

I flicked on the light in the bathroom. Dirty clothes lay in a heap on the bathroom floor. There wasn't enough money in the world to get me to touch Spiro's dirty clothes. If there was a clue in his pocket, it was safe from me. I went through the medicine chest and glanced at the wastebasket. Nothing.

His bedroom door was closed. I held my breath,

opened the door, and almost fainted with the relief of finding the room empty. The furniture was Danish modern, the bedspread was black satin. The ceiling over the bed had been covered with paste-on mirror tiles. Porn magazines were stacked on a chair beside the bed. A used condom was stuck to one of the covers.

Soon as I got home I was going to take a shower in boiling water.

A desk hugged the wall in front of his window. I thought this looked promising. I sat in the black leather chair and carefully riffled through the junk mail, bills, and personal correspondence that lay scattered across the polished desktop. The bills all seemed within reason, and most of the correspondence related to the funeral home. Thank-you notes from the recently bereaved. "Dear Spiro, thank you for overcharging me in my time of sorrow." Phone messages had been recorded on whatever was handy . . . backs of envelopes and letter margins. None of the messages were labeled "death threats from Kenny." I made a list of unexplained phone numbers and stuffed it into my pocketbook for future investigation.

I opened the drawers and poked through paper clips, rubber bands, and other assorted stationery flotsam. There were no messages on his answering machine. Nothing under his bed.

I found it hard to believe there were no guns in the apartment. Spiro seemed like the kind of person to take trophies.

I pawed through his clothes in the dresser and

turned to his closet. The closet was filled with undertaker suits and shirts and shoes. Six pairs of black shoes lined up on the floor, and six shoe boxes. Hmmm. I opened a shoe box. Bingo. A gun. A Colt .45. I opened the other five boxes and ended up with a tally of three handguns and three shoe boxes filled with ammo. I copied the serial numbers off the guns and took down the information on the boxes of ammo.

I pulled the bedroom window aside and peeked out at Lula. She was sitting on the stoop, filing her nails. I rapped on the windowpane, and the file flew from her fingers. Guess she wasn't as calm as she looked. I motioned to her that I was leaving and would meet her out back.

I made sure everything was as I'd found it, shut off all lights, and exited through the patio door. It would be obvious to Spiro that someone had broken into his apartment, but chances were good he'd blame it on Kenny.

"Give me the shit," Lula said. "You found something, didn't you?"

"I found a couple guns."

"That don't float my boat. Everybody got guns."

"Do you have a gun?"

"Yo, momma. Damn right I got a gun." She pulled a big black gun out of her pocketbook. "Blue steel," she said. "Got it off Harry the Horse back when I was a ho. You want to know why we call him Harry the Horse?"

"Don't tell me."

"That mother was fearful. He just wouldn't fit

in anywhere. Hell, I had to use two hands to give him the poor man's special."

I dropped Lula back at the office and went on home. By the time I pulled into my lot, the sky had blackened under the cloud cover and a light rain had begun to fall. I slung my pocketbook over my shoulder and hurried into the building, happy to be home.

Mrs. Bestler was doing hall laps with her walker. Step, step, clomp. Step, step, clomp.

"Another day, another dollar," she said.

"True enough," I replied.

I could hear the rise and fall of audience participation as Mr. Wolesky's TV droned on behind his closed door.

I plugged my key into my lock and did a quick, suspicious look around my apartment. All was secure. There were no messages on the machine, and there'd been no mail downstairs.

I made hot chocolate and a peanut butter and honey sandwich. I stacked the plate on top of the mug, tucked the phone under my arm, grabbed the list of numbers I'd retrieved from Spiro's apartment, and carted everything off to the dining room table.

I dialed the first number and a woman answered.

"I'd like to speak to Kenny," I said.

"You must have the wrong number. There's no Kenny here."

"Is this the Colonial Grill?"

"No, this is a private number."

"Sorry," I said.

I had seven numbers to check out. The first four were exactly alike. All private residences. Probably clients. The fifth was pizza delivery. The sixth was St. Francis Hospital. The seventh was a motel in Bordentown. I thought this last one had some potential.

I gave Rex a corner of my sandwich, heaved a sigh at having to leave the warmth and comfort of my apartment, and shrugged back into my jacket. The motel was on Route 206, not far from the turnpike entrance. It was a cut-rate motel, built before the motel chains moved in. There were forty units, all ground floor, opening to a narrow porch. Lights shone from two. The neon sign at roadside advertised efficiencies available. The exterior was neat, but it was a foregone conclusion that the inside would be dated, the wallpaper faded, the chenille spread threadbare, the bathroom sink rust-stained.

I parked close to the office and hustled inside. An elderly man sat behind the desk, watching a small TV.

"Evening," he said.

"Are you the manager?"

"Yep. The manager, the owner, the handyman."

I took Kenny's picture out of my pocketbook. "I'm looking for this man. Have you seen him?"

"Mind telling me why you're looking for him?"

"He's in violation of a bond agreement."

"What's that mean?"

"It means he's a felon."

"Are you a cop?"

"I'm an apprehension agent. I work for his bonding company."

The man looked at the picture and nodded. "He's in unit seventeen. Been there for a couple days." He thumbed through a ledger on the counter. "Here he is. John Sherman. Checked in on Tuesday."

I could hardly believe it! Damned if I wasn't good. "Is he alone?"

"So far as I know."

"Do you have vehicle information?"

"We don't bother with that. We got lots of parking space here."

I thanked him and told him I'd hang around for a while. I gave him my card and asked that he didn't give me away should he see Sherman.

I drove to a dark corner of the lot, shut the engine off, locked the windows, and hunkered down for the duration. If Kenny showed up, I'd call Ranger. If I couldn't reach Ranger, I'd go to Joe Morelli.

By nine o'clock I was thinking I might have chosen the wrong profession. My toes were frozen, and I had to pee. Kenny hadn't materialized, and there was no activity at the motel to break the monotony of waiting. I ran the engine to warm things up and did some isometrics. I fantasized about going to bed with Batman. He was a little dark, but I liked the look of the codpiece on his rubber suit.

At eleven I begged the manager to let me use

his bathroom. I mooched a cup of coffee from him and returned to Big Blue. I had to admit, while the wait was uncomfortable, it was immeasurably better than it would have been in my little Jeep. There was a feeling of encapsulation in the Buick. Sort of like being in a rolling bomb shelter with windows and overstuffed furniture. I was able to stretch my legs across the front bench seat. Behind me, the backseat had real boudoir potential.

I dozed off somewhere around twelve-thirty and woke up at one-fifteen. Kenny's unit was still dark, and there were no new cars in the lot.

I had several choices available to me. I could try to stick it out myself, I could ask Ranger to rotate shifts with me, or I could pack it in for the night and return before daybreak. If I asked Ranger to rotate shifts, I'd have to give him a bigger piece of the pie than I'd originally intended. On the other hand, if I tried to stick it out by myself, I was afraid I'd nod off and freeze to death like the little match girl. I chose door number three. If Kenny returned tonight, it would be to sleep, and he'd still be here at six in the morning.

I sang "Row, row, row your boat" all the way home to keep awake. I dragged myself into my apartment building, up the stairs, and down the hall. I let myself into my foyer, locked the door behind me, and crawled into bed fully clothed, shoes and all. I slept flat out until six, when an inner alarm clock prodded me awake.

I stumbled out of bed, relieved to find I was already dressed and could forgo that chore. I did the bare minimum in the bathroom, grabbed my jacket and my pocketbook, and trudged out to the parking lot. It was pitch black above the lot lights, still drizzly, and ice had formed on car windows. Lovely. I started the car, turned the heater on full blast, took the scraper out of the map pocket and chipped the windows free. By the time I was done chipping I was pretty much awake. I stopped at a 7-Eleven en route to Bordentown and stocked up on coffee and doughnuts.

It was still dark when I reached the motel. There were no lights on in any of the units, and there were no new cars in the lot. I parked to the dark side of the office and cracked the lid on my coffee. I was feeling less optimistic today and considered the possibility that the old man in the office had been having some fun at my expense. If Kenny didn't show by midafternoon, I'd ask to be let into his room.

If I'd been clever, I'd have changed my socks and brought a blanket. If I'd been *really* clever, I'd have given the guy in the office a twenty and asked him to call me if Kenny showed up.

At ten minutes to seven a woman drove up in a Ford truck and parked in front of the office. She gave me a curious look and went inside. Ten minutes later the old man came out and ambled across the lot to a beat-up Chevy. He waved and smiled and drove off.

There was no way I could be sure the old guy had told the woman about me, and I didn't want her calling the police to report a strange person loitering on the premises, so I hauled myself over to the office and went through the same drill as the night before.

The answers were the same. Yes, she recognized the picture. Yes, he was registered as John Sherman.

"Good-looking guy," she said. "But not real friendly."

"Did you notice the car he was driving?"

"Honey, I noticed everything about him. He was driving a blue van. Wasn't one of those fancy conversion vans. Was more of a work van. The kind without all the windows."

"Did you get a plate number?" I asked.

"Hell no. I wasn't interested in his plates."

I thanked her and retreated to my car to drink cold coffee. Every now and then I got out and stretched and stomped my feet. I took a half-hour break for lunch, and nothing had changed when I got back.

Morelli pulled his cop car beside me at three. He got out and slid onto the seat next to me.

"Christ," he said. "It's freezing in this car."

"Is this a chance meeting?"

"Kelly drives by here on his way to work. He saw the Buick and started a pool on who you were shacked up with."

I gritted my teeth. "Unh."

"So what *are* you doing here?"

"Through some superb detective work, I discovered that Kenny is staying here, registered as John Sherman."

A spark of excitement flickered across Morelli's face. "You have an ID?"

"Both the night clerk and the day clerk recognized Kenny from his picture. He's driving a blue panel van and was last seen yesterday morning. I got here early last night and sat until one. I was back here at six-thirty this morning."

"No sign of Kenny."

"None."

"Have you been through his room?"

"Not yet."

"The maid been through?"

"Nope."

Morelli opened his door. "Let's take a look."

Morelli identified himself to the day clerk and got a key to number 17. He rapped on the unit's door twice. No answer. He unlocked the door, and we both entered.

The bed was unmade. A navy duffel bag sat open on the floor. The bag contained socks and shorts and two black T-shirts. A flannel shirt and a pair of jeans had been tossed across the back of a chair. A shaving kit sat open in the bathroom.

"Looks to me like he's been scared off," Morelli said. "My guess is he spotted you."

"Impossible. I parked in the darkest part of the lot. And how did he know it was me?"

"Sweet thing, everyone knows it's you."

"It's this awful car! It's ruining my life. It's sabotaging my career."

Morelli grinned. "That's a lot to ask of a car."

I tried to look contemptuous, but it was hard

with my teeth chattering from the cold. "Now what?" I asked.

"Now I talk to the clerk and ask her to call me if Kenny returns." He gave me a fast head-to-foot appraisal. "You look like you slept in those clothes."

"How'd it go with Spiro and Louie Moon yesterday?"

"I don't think Louie Moon is involved. He doesn't have what it takes."

"Intelligence?"

"Contacts," Morelli said. "Whoever has the guns is selling them off. I did some checking. Moon doesn't move in the right circles. Moon wouldn't even know how to go about finding the right circles."

"What about Spiro?"

"Wasn't ready to give me a confession." He flipped the light off. "You should go home and take a shower and get dressed for dinner."

"Dinner?"

"Pot roast at six."

"You aren't serious."

The grin was back. "I'll pick you up at quarter to six."

"No! I'll drive myself."

Morelli was wearing a brown leather bomber jacket and a red wool scarf. He took the scarf off and wrapped it around my neck. "You look frozen," he said. "Go home and warm up." Then he sauntered off to the motel office.

It was still drizzling. The sky was gunmetal

gray, and my mood was equally grim. I'd had a good line on Kenny Mancuso, and I'd blown it. I smacked the heel of my hand against my forehead. Stupid, stupid, stupid. I'd sat out there in this big dumb Buick. What was I thinking?

The motel was twelve miles from my apartment building, and I berated myself all the way home. I made a quick stop at the supermarket, fed Big Blue more gas, and by the time I pulled into my lot, I was thoroughly disgusted and demoralized. I'd had three chances to nail Kenny: at Julia's house, at the mall, and now at the motel, and I'd screwed up every time.

Probably at this stage in my career I should stick to the low-level criminals, like shoplifters and drunk drivers. Unfortunately, the payout on those criminals wasn't sufficient to keep me afloat.

I did more self-flagellation while I rode the elevator and made my way down the hall. A sticky note from Dillon was taped to my door. Got a package for you, the note said.

I went back to the elevator and hit the button for basement. The elevator opened to a small vestibule with four closed, locked doors freshly painted battleship gray. One door led to storage cages for the use of the residents, the second door opened into the boiler room with its ominous rumblings and gurglings, the third door gave way to a long corridor and rooms dedicated to building maintenance, and Dillon lived in rent-free contentment behind the fourth door.

I always felt claustrophobic when I came down here, but Dillon said that it suited him fine and that he found the boiler noises soothing. He'd stuck a note to his door, saying that he'd be home at five.

I returned to my apartment, gave Rex some raisins and a corn chip, and took a long, hot shower. I staggered out red as a boiled lobster and foggy-brained from the chlorine gas. I flopped on the bed and contemplated my future. It was a short contemplation. When I woke up it was quarter to six, and someone was pounding on my door.

I wrapped myself in a robe and padded into the foyer. I put my eye to the peephole. It was Joe Morelli. I cracked the door and looked at him over the security chain. "I just got out of the shower."

"I'd appreciate it if you'd let me in before Mr. Wolesky comes out and gives me the third degree."

I slipped the chain and opened the door.

Morelli stepped into the foyer. His mouth curved at the edges. "Scary hair."

"I sort of slept on it."

"No wonder you have no sex life. It'd take a lot out of a man to wake up to hair like that."

"Go sit in a chair in the living room, and don't get up until I tell you. Don't eat my food, and don't scare my hamster, and don't make any long-distance calls."

He was watching television when I came out of my bedroom ten minutes later. I was wearing a granny dress over a white T-shirt, with ankle-high brown lace-up boots, and an oversized, loose-weave cardigan sweater. It was my Annie Hall look, and it made me feel feminine, but it always had the opposite effect on the opposite sex. Annie Hall was guaranteed to wilt the most determined dick. It was better than Mace on a blind date.

I wrapped Morelli's red scarf around my neck and buttoned myself into my jacket. I grabbed my pocketbook and shut the lights off. "There's going to be hell to pay if we're late."

Morelli followed me out the door. "I wouldn't worry about it. Once your mother sees you in that get-up, she'll forget about the time."

"It's my Annie Hall look."

"Looks to me like you've put a jelly doughnut in a bag labeled bran muffin."

I rushed down the hall and took the stairs. I got to the ground floor and remembered the package Dillon was holding. "Wait a minute," I yelled to Morelli. "I'll be right back."

I scrambled down the stairs to the cellar and pounded on Dillon's door.

Dillon peered out.

"I'm late, and I need my package," I said.

He handed me a bulky overnight mail enve-lope, and I ran back up the stairs.

"Three minutes one way or the other can make or break a pot roast," I told Morelli, grabbing him by the hand, dragging him across the lot to his truck. I hadn't intended to go with him, but I figured if we hit traffic he could use his rooftop flasher. "You have a flasher on this truck?" I asked, climbing on board.

Morelli buckled himself in. "Yeah, I have a flasher. You don't expect me to use it for pot roast, do you?"

I swiveled in my seat and stared out the back window.

Morelli cut his eyes to the rearview mirror. "Are you looking for Kenny?"

"I can feel him out there."

"I don't see anyone."

"That doesn't mean he isn't there. He's good at this sneaking around stuff. He walks into Stiva's and chops off body parts, and nobody sees him. He came out of nowhere at the mall. He spotted me at Julia Cenetta's house and in the motel parking lot, and I never had a clue. Now I have this creepy feeling he's watching me, following me around."

"Why would he be doing that?"

"For starters, Spiro told Kenny I'd kill him if he continued to harass him."

"Oh boy."

"Probably I'm just being paranoid."

"Sometimes paranoia is justified."

Morelli stopped for a light. The digital readout on his dashboard clock blinked to 5:58. I cracked my knuckles, and Morelli glanced over at me, eyebrows raised.

"Okay," I said, "so my mother makes me nervous."

"It's part of her job," Morelli said. "You shouldn't take it personally."

We turned off Hamilton, into the burg, and traffic disappeared. There were no car lights behind us, but I couldn't shake the feeling that Kenny had me in his sights.

My mother and Grandma Mazur were at the door when we parked. Usually it was the differences between my mother and grandmother that caught my attention. Today it was the similarities that seemed obvious. They stood tall, with their shoulders back. It was a defiant posture, and I knew it was my posture, too. Their hands were clasped in front of them, their gaze was unwavering, fixed on Morelli and me. Their faces were round; their eyes were hooded. Mongol eyes. My Hungarian relatives had come from the steppes. Not a city dweller among them. My mother and grandma were small women and had grown even smaller with age. They were dainty-boned and petite, with baby-fine hair. Probably they were descended from pampered, caravan-cosseted Gypsy women.

I, on the other hand, was a throwback to some plow-pulling, rawboned wife of a barbarian farmer.

I hiked up my skirt to jump from the truck, and saw my mother and grandmother flinch at the sight.

"What's this outfit?" my mother demanded. "Can't you afford clothes? Are you wearing other people's? Frank, give Stephanie some money. She needs to buy clothes."

"I don't need to buy clothes," I said. "This is new. I just bought it. It's the style."

"How will you ever get a man when you're dressed like this?" My mother turned to Morelli. "Am I right?"

Morelli grinned. "I think she's kind of cute. It's the Monty Hall look."

I still had the package in my hand. I set it on the foyer table and took my jacket off. "Annie Hall!"

Grandma Mazur picked the envelope up and studied it. "Overnight mail. Must be something important. Feels like there's a box in here. Return address says R. Klein from Fifth Avenue in New York. Too bad it isn't for me. I wouldn't mind getting some overnight mail."

I hadn't thought much about the package until now. I didn't know anyone named R. Klein, and I hadn't ordered anything from New York. I took the envelope from Grandma and peeled the flap back. There was a little cardboard box inside. It was taped closed. I took the box out, and held it in my hand. It wasn't especially heavy.

"Smells funny," Grandma said. "Like insecticide. Or maybe it's one of them new perfumes."

I ripped the tape away, opened the box, and sucked in my breath. There was a penis inside the box. The penis was neatly sliced off at the root, perfectly embalmed, and secured to a square of Styrofoam with a hat pin.

Everyone stared at the penis in dumbfounded horror.

Grandma Mazur spoke first, and when she did it was with a touch of wistfulness. "Been a long time since I've seen one of those," she said.

My mother started screaming, hands in air, eyes bugging out of her head. "Get it out of my house! What's the world coming to? What will people think?"

My father left his chair in the living room and padded out to the hall to see what the fuss was all about. "What's going on?" he asked, sticking his head into the huddle.

"It's a penis," Grandma said. "Stephanie got it in the mail. It's a pretty good one too."

My father recoiled. "Jesus and Joseph!"

"Who would do such a thing?" my mother shouted. "What is it? Is it rubber? Is it one of those rubber penises?"

"Don't look rubber to me," Grandma Mazur said. "Looks to me like a real penis, except it's kind of discolored. I don't remember them being this color."

"That's crazy!" my mother said. "What person would mail his penis?"

Grandma Mazur looked at the envelope. "Says Klein on the return address. I always thought that was a Jewish name, but this doesn't look to me like a Jewish penis."

Everyone turned their attention to Grandma Mazur.

"Not that I'd know much about it," Grandma said. "It's just that I might have seen one of them Jewish ones in *National Geographic*."

Morelli took the box from me and replaced the lid. We both knew the name to attach to the penis. Joseph Loosey.

"I'm going to take a raincheck on dinner," Morelli said. "I'm afraid this is a police matter." He snagged my pocketbook off the hall table and draped it over my shoulder. "Stephanie needs to come too, so she can make a statement."

"It's that bounty hunter job," my mother said to me. "You meet all the wrong kinds of people. Why can't you get a good job like your cousin Christine? No one ever sends Christine these things in the mail."

"Christine works in a vitamin factory. She spends her whole day watching the cotton stuffer to make sure it doesn't malfunction."

"She makes good money."

I zipped my jacket. "I make good money . . . sometimes."

CHAPTER 11

Morelli yanked the door to the truck open, tossed the overnight envelope onto the seat, and made an impatient gesture for me to follow. His face was composed, but I could feel the vibrations of anger radiating in waves from his body.

"Goddamn him," Morelli said, slamming the truck into gear. "He thinks this is fucking funny. Him and his damn games. When he was a kid he used to tell me stories about the things he'd done. I never knew what was real and what was made up. I'm not sure Kenny knew. Maybe it was all real."

"Were you serious about this being a police matter?"

"The post office frowns on the mailing of human body parts for sport purposes."

"That was why you rushed us out of my parents' house?"

"I rushed us out of your parents' house because I didn't think I could manage two hours at the dinner table with everyone focused on Joe Loosey's joystick sitting in the refrigerator next to the applesauce."

"I'd appreciate it if you could keep this quiet. I wouldn't want people to get the wrong idea about me and Mr. Loosey."

"Your secret is safe."

"Do you think we should tell Spiro?"

"I think *you* should tell Spiro. Let him think the two of you are in this together. Maybe you can learn something."

Morelli eased the truck into the Burger King drive-through and got a couple bags of food. He rolled the window up, pulled out into traffic, and the truck immediately filled with the smell of America.

"It's not pot roast," Morelli said.

That was true, but with the exception of dessert, food is food. I stuck the straw into my milk shake and dug around in the bag for the french fries. "These stories Kenny used to tell you . . . what were they about?"

"Nothing you want to hear. Nothing I even want to remember. Very sick shit."

He took a handful of fries. "You never told me how you happened to locate Kenny in the motel."

"Probably I shouldn't divulge my professional secrets."

"Probably you should."

Okay, public relations time. Time to appease

Morelli by giving him some worthless information. With the added advantage of implicating him in an illegal activity. "I broke into Spiro's apartment and went through his trash. I found some phone numbers, ran them down, and came up with the motel."

Morelli stopped for a light and turned his face to me. His expression was unreadable in the dark. "You broke into Spiro's apartment? Was this by way of an accidentally unlocked door?"

"It was by way of a window that managed to get broken by a pocketbook."

"Shit, Stephanie, that's breaking and entering. People get arrested for that kind of stuff. They go to jail."

"I was careful."

"That makes me feel a lot better."

"I figure Spiro will think it was Kenny and not report it."

"So Spiro knew where Kenny was staying. I'm surprised Kenny wasn't more cautious."

"Spiro has a caller ID device on his phone at the funeral parlor. Maybe Kenny didn't realize he could be picked up like that."

The light changed, Morelli moved forward, and we rode in silence for the rest of the trip. He swung into the lot, parked, and cut his lights.

"Do you want to come in, or would you prefer to be left out of the loop?" he wanted to know.

"I'd rather be left out of the loop. I'll wait here."

He took the envelope with the penis, and he took a bag of food. "I'll do this as fast as I can."

I gave him the paper with the guns and ammo information from Spiro's apartment. "I found some hardware in Spiro's bedroom. You might want to check to see if it came from Braddock." I wasn't enamored with the idea of helping Morelli when he was still holding back on me, but I had no way of tracing the guns on my own, and besides, if the stuff was stolen, Morelli'd owe me.

I watched him jog to the side door. The door opened, showing a fleeting rectangle of light in the otherwise dark brick facade. The door closed, and I unwrapped my cheeseburger, wondering if Morelli would have to bring someone in to identify the evidence. Louie Moon or Mrs. Loosey. I hoped he had the sense to remove the hat pin before lifting the lid for Mrs. Loosey.

I scarfed down my cheeseburger and fries and worked at the milk shake. There was no activity in the lot or on the street, and the silence in the truck was deafening. I listened to myself breathe for a while. I snooped in the glove compartment and map pockets. I found nothing interesting. According to Morelli's dashboard clock he'd been gone for ten minutes. I finished the milk shake and crammed all the wrappers back in the bag. Now what?

It was almost seven. Visiting hours for Spiro. The perfect time to tell him about Loosey's dick. Unfortunately, I was stuck twiddling my thumbs in Morelli's truck. The glint of keys dangling from the ignition caught my eye. Maybe I should borrow the truck and slip over to the funeral parlor. Take care of business. After all, who knows how long it would take Morelli to do the paperwork? I could be stuck here for hours! Morelli would probably be grateful to me for getting the job done. On the other hand, if he came out and found his truck missing it could get ugly.

I dug around in my pocketbook and came up with a black Magic Marker. I couldn't find paper, so I wrote a note on the side of the food bag. I backed the truck up a few feet, deposited the bag in the empty space, jumped back in the truck, and took off.

Lights were blazing from Stiva's, and a crowd of people milled about on the front porch. Stiva always got a big draw on Saturdays. The lot was full and there were no parking places for two blocks down on the street, so I zoomed into the driveway reserved for "funeral cars only." I would only be a few minutes, and besides, nobody was going to tow away a truck with a PBA shield in the back window.

Spiro did a double take when he saw me. The first reaction was relief; the second was reserved for my dress.

"Nice outfit," he said. "You look like you just got off the bus from Appalachia."

"I've got news for you."

"Yeah, well, I've got news for you, too." He jerked his head in the direction of the office. "In here."

He hotfooted it across the lobby, wrenched the door to the office open, and closed it behind us with a slam.

"You're not going to believe this," he said. "That asshole Kenny is such a prick. You know what he did now? He broke into my apartment."

My eyes rounded in surprise. "No!"

"Yeah. Can you believe it? Broke a goddamn window."

"Why would he break into your apartment?"

"Because he's fucking crazy."

"Are you sure it was Kenny? Was anything missing?"

"Of course it was Kenny. Who the hell else could it be? Nothing was stolen. The VCR is still there. My camera, my money, my jewelry weren't touched. It was Kenny, all right. The dumb crazy fucker."

"Did you report this to the police?"

"What's between me and Kenny is private. No police."

"You might have to change that game plan."

Spiro's eyes contracted and dulled and focused on mine. "Oh?"

"You remember the little incident yesterday concerning Mr. Loosey's penis?"

"Yeah?"

"Kenny mailed it to me."

"No shit?"

"It came Express Mail."

"Where is it now?"

"The police have it. Morelli was there when I opened the package."

"*Fuck!*" He kicked his wastebasket across the room. "Fuck, fuck, fuck, fuck, fuck."

"I don't know why you're so upset about all this," I cooed. "Seems to me this is crazy Kenny's problem. I mean, after all, you didn't do anything wrong." Humor the jerk, I thought. See where he runs with it.

Spiro stopped raving and looked at me, and I imagined I heard the sound of little bitty gears meshing in his head. "That's true," he said. "I didn't do anything wrong. I'm the victim here. Does Morelli know the package came from Kenny? Was there a note? A return address?"

"No note. No return address. Hard to say what Morelli knows."

"You didn't tell him it came from Kenny?"

"I have no real proof that it came from Kenny, but the thing clearly had been embalmed, so the police will be checking funeral parlors. I imagine they'll want to know why you didn't report the . . . um, theft."

"Maybe I should just come clean. Tell the cops about how crazy Kenny is. Tell them about the finger and about my apartment."

"What about Con? You coming clean to him too? Is he still in the hospital?"

"Came home today. Got a week of rehab, and then he'll be back at work part-time."

"He's not going to be happy when he finds out his clients have been getting parts whacked off."

"Tell me about it. I've heard enough of his 'the body is holy' crap to last me three lifetimes. I mean, what's the big deal? It isn't like Loosey was gonna use his dick."

Spiro dropped into the padded executive chair behind the desk and slid into a slouch. The mask of civility dropped from his face, and his sallow skin tightened over slanted cheekbones and pinched across spiky teeth as he morphed into Rodent Man. Furtive, foul-breathed, evil-spirited. Impossible to tell if he'd been born the rodent, or if years of schoolyard taunts had shaped his soul to suit his face.

Spiro leaned forward. "You know how old Con is? Sixty-two. Anyone else would be thinking retirement, but not Constantine Stiva. I'll be dead from natural causes, and Stiva'll still be kissing ass. He's like a snake with a heart rate of twelve. Pacing himself. Sucking formaldehyde like the elixir of life. Hanging on just to piss me off.

"Should have been cancer instead of a back injury. What the hell good is a back injury? You don't die from a damn back injury."

"I thought you and Con got along."

"He drives me nuts. Him and his rules and goody-goody attitude. You should see him in the embalming room. Everything just so. You'd think it was a fucking shrine down there. Constantine Stiva at the altar of the fucking dead. You know what I think of the dead? I think they stink."

"Why do you work here?"

"There's money to be made, chicky. And I like money."

I held myself tight in check to keep from physically recoiling. Here was the muck and slime of Spiro's brain, spilling out of every orifice, dribbling down his corded neck onto his pristine white undertaker's shirt. Butthead, all dressed up with no place to go. "Have you heard from Kenny since he broke into your apartment?"

"No." Spiro turned broody. "Used to be we were friends. Him and Moogey and me used to do everything together. Then Kenny went into the army, and he got different. Thought he was smarter than the rest of us. Had all these big ideas."

"Like what?"

"I can't tell you, but they were big. Not that I couldn't come up with ideas like that, but I'm busy with other stuff."

"He include you in these big ideas? You make any money from them?"

"Sometimes he included me. You never knew with Kenny. He was slick. He'd hold out, and you never knew. He was like that with women. They all thought he was this cool guy." Spiro's lips pulled back in a smile. "Used to crack us up how he'd play the faithful-till-death-do-us-part-boyfriend role and all the while he'd be porking everyone in sight. He could really sucker women in. Even when he smacked them around they kept coming back for more. You had to admire the guy, you know. He had something. I've seen him burn women with cigarettes and stick them with pins, and they'd still suck up to him."

The cheeseburger slid in my stomach. I didn't know who was more disgusting . . . Kenny for sticking pins in women, or Spiro for admiring him. "I should be moving along," I said. "Got things to do." Like maybe fumigating my mind after talking to Spiro.

"Wait a minute. I wanted to talk to you about security. You're an expert in this kind of stuff, right?"

I wasn't an expert at anything. "Right."

"So, what should I do about Kenny? I was thinking about a bodyguard again. Just for at night. Someone to close up with me here, and make sure I got into my apartment okay. I figure I was lucky Kenny wasn't waiting for me in my apartment."

"You're afraid of Kenny?"

"He's like smoke. You can't put your finger on him. He's always in a shadow somewhere. He watches people. He plans things." Our eyes locked. "You don't know Kenny," Spiro said. "Sometimes he's a real fun guy, and sometimes the things he thinks are pure evil. Believe me, I've seen him in action, you don't want to be on the receiving side of the evil."

"I told you before . . . I'm not interested in guarding your body."

He took a pack of twenties from his top desk drawer and counted them out. "Hundred dollars a night. All you have to do is get me into my apartment safe and sound. I'll take it from there."

Suddenly I saw the value of guarding Spiro. I'd be right there on the spot if Kenny actually did show up. I'd be in a position to wheedle information. And I could legally search through Spiro's house every night. Okay, so along with all that I was selling out for the money, but hell, it could be worse. I could have sold out for fifty. "When do I start?"

"Tonight. I close up at ten. Get here five or ten minutes ahead."

"Why me? Why don't you get some big tough guy?"

Spiro put the money back in the drawer. "I'd look like a fag. This way people think you're after my ass. Better for my image. Unless you keep wearing dresses like that. Then I might reconsider."

Wonderful.

I left his office and caught sight of Morelli slouched against the wall next to the front door, hands shoved in pants pockets, clearly pissed off. He spotted me, and his expression didn't change, but the rise and fall of his chest picked up. I plastered a phony smile on my face and breezed across the lobby to him, whisking out the door before Spiro had a chance to see us together.

"I see you got my message," I said when we reached the truck, turning up the wattage on the smile.

"Not only did you steal my truck, but you parked it illegally."

"You park illegally all the time."

"Only when it's official police business, and I have no other choice . . . or when it's raining."

"I don't know why you're upset. You wanted me to talk to Spiro. So that's what I did. I came here and talked to Spiro."

"For starters, I had to flag down a blue-and-white to get a ride over here. And more important, I don't like you running around on your own. I want you in eyesight until we nail Mancuso."

"I'm touched you're worried about my safety."

"Safety hasn't got much to do with it, Skippy. You have an uncanny knack for running into people you're looking for, and you're completely inept at taking them down. I don't want you screwing up another encounter with Kenny. I want to make sure I'm around next time you stumble across him."

I settled onto the seat with a sigh. When you're right, you're right. And Morelli was right. I wasn't totally up to speed as a bounty hunter.

We were silent for the ride back to my apartment. I knew these streets like I knew my own hand. Half the time, I drove them unconsciously, suddenly realizing I was in my parking lot, wondering how the devil I'd gotten there. Tonight I paid closer attention. If Kenny was out there, I didn't want to miss him. Spiro had said Kenny was like smoke, that he lived in the shadows. I told myself this was a romanticized vision. Kenny was your everyday sociopath who went sneaking around thinking he was God's second cousin.

The wind had picked up, and clouds scudded overhead, periodically obliterating the sliver of moon. Morelli parked next to the Buick and cut the engine. He reached over and toyed with the collar on my jacket. "Do you have any plans for tonight?"

I told him about the bodyguard deal.

Morelli just stared at me. "How do you do it?" he asked. "How do you walk into this stuff? If you knew what you were doing, you'd be a real threat."

"Guess I lead a charmed life." I looked at my watch. It was 7:30, and Morelli was still working. "You put in long hours," I said. "I thought cops clocked on in eight-hour shifts."

"Vice is flexible. I work when I need to."

"You have no life."

He shrugged. "I like my job. When I need a break I take off for a weekend at the shore or a week in the Islands."

This was pretty interesting. I'd never thought of Morelli as being an "Islands" person. "What do you do when you go to the Islands? What's the appeal?"

"I like to dive."

"And what about the shore? What do you do at the Jersey shore?"

Morelli grinned. "I hide under the boardwalk and abuse myself. Old habits die hard."

I had a tough time visualizing Morelli diving off the coast of Martinique, but the thought of him abusing himself under the boardwalk was crystal clear. I could see him as a horny little eleven-year-old, hanging outside the Seaside bars, listening to the bands, eyeballing the women in their elastic tank tops and skimpy shorts. And later, crawling under the boardwalk with his cousin Mooch, the two of them whacking off together before they had to meet up with Uncle Manny and Aunt Florence for the ride back to the bungalow in Seaside Heights. Two years later he would have substituted his cousin Sue Ann Beale for his cousin Mooch, but the basic routine would be the same.

I pushed the truck door open and lurched out into the parking lot. The wind whistled around Morelli's antennae and whipped at my skirt. My hair flew about my face in a frenzied explosion of tangled frizz.

I made an attempt to tame it in the elevator while Morelli looked on, calmly curious about my efforts to shove the mess into an elastic band I'd found in my jacket pocket. He stepped into the hall when the doors opened. Waited while I fumbled for the key.

"How scared is Spiro?" Morelli wanted to know.

"Scared enough to hire me to protect him."

"Maybe it's just a ploy to get you into his apartment."

I stepped into the entrance hall, flipped the light switch, and shrugged out of my jacket. "It's an expensive ploy."

Morelli went straight to the TV and buzzed in ESPN. The Rangers' blue jerseys blinked onto the screen. The Caps were at home in white. I watched a face-off before bobbing into the kitchen to check my answering machine.

There were two messages. The first from my mother, calling to say she heard First National had openings for tellers and that I should be sure to wash my hands if I touched Mr. Loosey. The second call was from Connie. Vinnie had gotten back from North Carolina and wanted me to stop in the office tomorrow. Pass on that one. Vinnie was worried about the Mancuso money. If I stopped in to see him, he'd yank Mancuso out from under me, and give it to someone with more experience.

I pushed the off button, grabbed a bag of blue corn chips from the cupboard, and snagged a couple beers from the refrigerator. I slouched next to Morelli on the couch, setting the corn chips between us. Ma and Pa on a Saturday night.

Halfway through the first period the phone rang.

"How's it going?" the caller asked. "You and Joe doing it doggy style? I hear he likes that. You really are something. Doing both Spiro and Joe-boy."

"Mancuso?"

"Just thought I'd call to see if you enjoyed your surprise package."

"It was a real kick. What's the point?"

"No point. Just having fun. I was watching when you opened it in the hall. Nice touch bringing the old lady into it. I like old ladies. You might say they're my specialty. You'll have to ask Joe about the things I do to old ladies. No wait, better yet, why don't I show you firsthand?"

"You're sick, Mancuso. You need help."

"It's your granny who's gonna need help. Maybe

you, too. Wouldn't want you to feel left out. In the beginning I was pissed off. You kept bungling around in my business. Now I'm seeing this from a new angle. Now I think I could have a good time with you and Granny Halfwit. It's always best when you have someone watching, waiting their turn.

"Maybe I could even get you to tell me about Spiro, and how he steals from his friends."

"How do you know it wasn't Moogey who stole from his friends?"

"Moogey didn't know enough to steal from his friends."

The disconnect clicked in my ear.

Morelli was standing beside me in the kitchen, beer bottle dangling from one hand, looking casual, but his eyes were still and hard.

"That was your cousin," I said. "He was calling to see if I enjoyed my surprise package, and then he suggested he might have some fun with me and Grandma Mazur."

I thought I was doing a pretty good imitation of the tough-as-nails bounty hunter, but the truth is I was shaking inside. I wasn't going to ask Morelli what Kenny Mancuso did to old women. I didn't want to know. And whatever it was, I didn't want it done to Grandma Mazur.

I called my parents' house to make sure Grandma Mazur was safe at home. Yes, she was watching television, my mother said. I assured her I'd washed my hands, and begged off on coming back for dessert.

I changed out of the dress into jeans and sneakers and a flannel shirt. I retrieved my .38 from the cookie jar, made sure it was loaded, and slipped it into my pocketbook.

When I came back to the living room Morelli was hand-feeding a corn chip to Rex.

"Looks to me like you're dressed for action," Morelli said. "I heard you lifting the lid on the cookie jar."

"Mancuso made threatening sounds about my grandmother."

Morelli pulled the power on the Rangers. "He's getting restless and frustrated, and he's getting stupid. It was stupid to come after you in the mall. It was stupid of him to sneak into Stiva's. And it was stupid to call you. Every time he does something like that he risks exposure. Kenny can be cunning when he's on top of himself. When he loses it, he's all ego and impulse.

"He's feeling desperate because his gun deal got screwed up. He's looking for a scapegoat, looking for someone to punish. Either he had a buyer who paid him some front money, or else he sold off a batch of shit before the bulk of it was stolen. My money's on the buyer theory. I think he's in a sweat because he can't meet his contract and the front money's been spent."

"He thinks Spiro has the stuff."

"These two would eat their young if you gave them the chance."

I had my jacket in my hand when the phone rang again. It was Louie Moon.

"He was here," Moon said. "Kenny Mancuso. He came back, and he cut Spiro."

"Where's Spiro now?"

"He's at St. Francis. I took him there, and then I came back to see to things. You know, close up and all."

Fifteen minutes later we were at St. Francis. Two uniforms, Vince Roman and a new guy I didn't know, stood flatfooted, weighted to the earth by their gun belts, at the emergency room desk.

"What's the deal?" Morelli asked.

"Took a statement from Stiva's kid. Got slashed by your cousin." Vince cut his eyes to the door behind the desk. "Got Spiro back there, stitching him up."

"How bad?"

"Could have been worse. Guess Kenny tried to cut Spiro's hand off, but the blade glanced off the rodent's big gold ID bracelet. Wait'll you see the bracelet. Right out of the Liberace collection."

This got a chuckle out of Vince and his partner.

"Don't suppose anyone tagged Kenny?"

"Kenny's the wind."

Spiro was sitting up on a hospital bed in the ER when we found him. There were two other people in the ER, and Spiro was separated from them by a privacy curtain partially pulled closed. His right arm was heavily bandaged from hand to forearm. His white shirt was blood-splattered, open at the neck. A blood-soaked necktie and kitchen towel had been tossed onto the floor beside the bed.

Spiro came out of his stupor when he saw me. "You were supposed to protect me!" he yelled. "Where the hell were you when I needed you?"

"I don't go on duty until ten of ten, remember?"

His eyes swiveled to Morelli. "He's nuts. Your cousin is fucking nuts. He tried to chop my goddamn hand off. He should be locked up. He should be in a looney bin. I was in my office, minding my own business, working on Mrs. Mayer's bill, when I look up and there's Kenny. He's raving about me stealing from him. I don't know what the hell he's talking about. He's a fucking fruitcake. Then next thing he says he's gonna chop me up piece by piece until I tell him what he wants to know. Lucky for me I was wearing that bracelet, or I would have been learning how to write lefthanded. I started yelling, and Louie came in, and Kenny took off."

"I want some police protection," Spiro said. "Ms. Marvel here doesn't perform."

"I can have a blue-and-white drive you home tonight," Morelli said. "After that you're on your own." He passed his card to Spiro. "If there's a problem, you can give me a call. If you need someone fast, go to nine-one-one."

Spiro made a derisive sound and glared at me.

I smiled nicely and rocked back on my heels. "See you tomorrow?"

"Yeah," he said. "Tomorrow."

The wind had slacked off, and it was drizzling when we came out of the hospital.

"Warm front coming in," Morelli said. "Supposed to be nice weather behind the rain."

We climbed into Morelli's truck and sat, watching the hospital. Roman's squad car was parking in the driveway reserved for emergency vehicles. After about ten minutes Roman and his partner escorted Spiro into the squad car. We followed them to Demby and waited while they made sure Spiro's apartment was secure.

The cruiser rolled out of the lot, and we sat for a few minutes longer. Lights were on in Spiro's apartment, and I suspected they'd be burning all night.

"We should watch him," Morelli said. "Kenny's not thinking good. He's going to keep after Spiro until he gets what he wants."

"Wasted effort. Spiro doesn't have what Kenny wants."

Morelli was motionless, staring irresolutely through the rain-streaked windshield. "I need a different car. Kenny knows my truck."

It went unsaid that he knew my Buick. The whole world knew my Buick. "What about the tan cop car?"

"He's probably got that spotted, too. Besides, I need something that'll give me more cover. A van or a Bronco with tinted windows." He cranked the engine over and put the truck into gear. "You have any idea when Spiro opens in the morning?"

"He usually gets to work by nine."

Morelli knocked on my door at six-thirty, and I was way ahead of him. I'd already showered and dressed in what I'd come to think of as my work uniform. Jeans, warm shirt, shoes of the day. I'd cleaned Rex's cage and had Mr. Coffee cooking.

"This is the plan," Morelli said. "You follow Spiro, and I follow you."

I didn't think that sounded like much of a plan, but I didn't have anything better, so I didn't complain. I filled my thermos with coffee, packed two sandwiches and an apple into my little cooler, and turned my answering machine on.

It was still dark when I walked to my car. Sunday morning. No traffic. Neither of us was in a talkative mood. I didn't see Morelli's truck in the lot.

"What are you driving?" I asked.

"A black Explorer parked on the street, to the side of the building."

I unlocked the Buick and threw everything into the backseat, including a blanket, which it looked like I wouldn't need. It had stopped raining and the air felt much warmer. In the fifties, I guessed.

I wasn't sure if Spiro kept the same schedule on Sundays. The funeral home was open seven days a week, but I suspected weekend hours depended on bodies received. Spiro didn't seem like the sort to go to church. I crossed myself. I couldn't remember the last time I'd attended Mass.

"What was that all about?" Morelli asked. "What's with the sign of the cross?"

"It's Sunday, and I'm not in church . . . again."

Morelli put his hand on the top of my head. It felt steady and reassuring, and heat seeped into my scalp.

"God loves you anyway," he said.

His hand slid to the back of my head, he pulled me to him, and kissed me on the forehead. He gave me a hug, and then he was suddenly gone, striding across the lot, disappearing into the shadows.

I stuffed myself into the Buick, feeling warm and fuzzy, wondering if something was going on with Morelli and me. What did a kiss on the forehead mean, anyway? Nothing, I told myself. It didn't mean anything at all. It meant that sometimes Morelli could be a nice guy. Okay, so why was I smiling like an idiot? Because I was deprived. My love life was nonexistent. I shared an apartment with a hamster. Well, I thought, it could be worse. I could still be married to Dickie Orr, the horse's patoot.

The drive to Century Court was quiet. The sky had begun to lighten. Black layers of clouds and blue strips of sky. Spiro's apartment complex was dark, with the exception of Spiro's apartment. I parked and watched the rearview mirror for Morelli's headlights. No headlights appeared. I swiveled in my seat and scanned the lot. No Explorer.

No matter, I told myself. Morelli was out there, somewhere. Probably.

I had few illusions about my place in the scheme of things. I was the decoy, making myself clearly visible in the Buick, so Kenny wouldn't look too hard for a second man.

I poured coffee and settled in for the long wait. A band of orange appeared on the horizon. A light blinked on in the apartment next to Spiro. Another light appeared a few apartments down. The charcoal sky turned azure. Ta daaa! It was morning.

Spiro's shades were still drawn. There was no sign of life in his apartment. I was beginning to worry when his door opened and Spiro walked out. He tried his door to make sure it was locked and quickly walked to his car. He drove a navy blue Lincoln Town Car. The car of choice for all young undertakers. Undoubtedly leased and charged off to the business.

He was dressed more casually than usual. Stonewashed black jeans and running shoes. Bulky dark green sweater. A white bandage was wrapped around his thumb and peeked out from under his sweater sleeve.

He gunned the Lincoln out of the lot and turned onto Klockner. I'd expected some sort of acknowledgment, but Spiro barreled past without a sideways glance. Most likely he was concentrating on not messing his pants.

I followed at a leisurely pace. There weren't a lot of cars on the road, and I knew where Spiro was heading. I parked half a block from the funeral home, at an angle where I could see the front entrance, the side entrance, and also the small parking lot on the side with the walkway leading to the back door.

Spiro parked in the drive-through and entered through the side. The door stayed open while he punched in the security code. The door closed and a light flicked on in Spiro's office.

Ten minutes later Louie Moon showed up.

I poured more coffee and ate half a sandwich. No one else went in or out. At nine-thirty Louie Moon left in the hearse. He returned an hour later, and someone was rolled into the back of the house. I guessed this was why Louie and Spiro had to come in on a Sunday morning.

At eleven I used my cellular phone to call my mother and make sure Grandma Mazur was okay.

"She's out," my mother said. "I leave the house for ten minutes, and what happens? Your father lets your grandmother go off with Betty Greenburg."

Betty Greenburg was eighty-nine and was hell on wheels.

"Ever since that stroke in August Betty Greenburg can't remember anything," my mother said. "Last week she drove to Asbury Park. Said she meant to go to Kmart and made a wrong turn."

"How long has Grandma Mazur been gone?"

"Almost two hours. They were supposed to be going to the bakery. Maybe I should call the police."

There was the sound of a door slamming and a lot of shouting in the background.

"It's your grandmother," my mother said. "And she's got her hand all wrapped up."

"Let me talk to her."

Grandma Mazur came on the phone. "You won't believe this," she said, her voice trembling with anger and indignation. "The most terrible thing just happened. Betty and me were coming out of the bakery with a box full of fresh-made Italian cookies when none other than Kenny Mancuso himself walked out from behind a car, just as brazen as could be, and came right up to me.

"'Well, looky here,' he says, 'it's Grandma Mazur.'

"'Yeah, and I know who you are, too,' I said to him. 'You're that no-good Kenny Mancuso.'

"'That's right,' he says. 'And I'm gonna be your worst nightmare.'"

There was a pause, and I could hear her breathing, collecting herself.

"Mom said your hand was bandaged?" I asked, not wanting to push her but needing to know.

"Kenny stuck me. He took hold of my hand, and he stuck an ice pick into it," Grandma said, her voice unnaturally shrill, her words thick with the pain of the experience.

I pushed the big bench seat all the way back and put my head between my knees.

"Hello," Grandma said. "Are you still there?"

I took a deep breath. "So how are you now? Are you okay?"

"Sure I'm okay. They fixed me up good at the hospital. Gave me some of that Tylenol with codeine. You take some of that, and you could get run over by a truck and never feel a thing. And then on account of I was in a state, they gave me some relaxer pills.

"Doctors said I was lucky that the pick missed everything important. Just kind of slid between the bones and such. Went in real clean."

More deep breathing. "What happened to Kenny?"

"Took off like the yellow-bellied dog that he is. Said he'd be coming back. That this was just the beginning." Her voice broke. "Can you imagine?"

"Maybe it'd be best if you stay in the house for a while."

"That's what I think, too. I'm plain tired. I could use a cup of hot tea."

My mother came back on the line. "What's this world coming to?" she asked. "An old woman gets attacked in broad daylight, in her own neighborhood, coming out of a bakery!"

"I'm going to leave my cellular phone on. Keep Grandma in the house, and call me if anything else happens."

"What else could happen? Isn't this enough?"

I disconnected and plugged my cellular phone into the cigarette lighter. My heart was beating triple time, and my palms were slick with sweat. I told myself I had to think clearly, but my mind was clouded with emotion. I got out of the Buick and stood on the sidewalk, looking for Morelli. I waved my arms over my head in a here-I-am signal.

The cell phone chirped inside the Buick. It was Morelli, his voice laced with impatience or anxiety. Hard to tell which.

"What?" Morelli said.

I told him about Grandma Mazur and waited while the silence stretched taut between us. Finally there was an oath and a disgusted sigh. It had to be hard for him. Mancuso was family.

"I'm sorry," he said. "Is there anything I can do?"

"You can help me catch Mancuso."

"We'll catch him."

What was left unsaid was the mutual fear that we wouldn't catch him soon enough.

"You okay to follow the game plan?" Morelli asked.

"Until six. I'm going home for dinner tonight. I want to see Grandma Mazur."

There was no further activity until one o'clock, when the funeral home opened for afternoon viewings. I trained my binoculars on the front-room windows and caught a glimpse of Spiro in suit and tie. Obviously he kept a change of clothes on the premises. Cars were constantly coming and going in the parking lot, and I realized how easily Kenny could get lost in the traffic. He could paste on a beard or a mustache, wear a hat or a wig, and no one would notice one more pedestrian coming into the front door, side door, or back door.

I strolled across the street at two o'clock.

Spiro sucked in some air when he saw me, and instinctively brought his injured arm closer to his body. His movements were unnaturally abrupt, his expression dark, and I had a sense of a disorganized mind. He was the rat dropped into a maze, scrabbling over obstacles, scurrying down dead-end corridors, looking for the way out.

A man stood alone at the tea table. Fortyish, medium height, medium weight, upper body on the beefy side. He was wearing a sport coat and slacks. I'd seen him before. It took me a moment to figure it out. He'd been at the garage when they'd hauled Moogey out in a body bag. I'd assumed he was homicide, but maybe he was vice, or maybe he was a fed.

I approached the tea table and introduced myself.

He extended his hand. "Andy Roche."

"You work with Morelli."

He went immobile for a heartbeat while his regrouping reflex jerked into fast-forward. "Sometimes."

I took a winger. "Fed."

"Treasury."

"You going to stay inside?"

"As much as possible. We brought in a bogus body today. I'm the long-lost grieving brother."

"Very clever."

"This guy, Spiro, always piss in short jerks?"

"He had a bad day yesterday. Didn't get a lot of sleep last night."

CHAPTER
12

All right, so Morelli didn't tell me about Andy Roche. What's new. Morelli played his cards close to his vest. That was his style. He didn't show his whole hand to anyone. Not to his boss, not to his partners, and certainly not to me. Nothing personal. After all, the goal was to catch Kenny. I no longer cared how it was accomplished.

I backed off from Roche and had a few words with Spiro. Yes, Spiro wanted me to tuck him in. And no, he hadn't heard from Kenny.

I used the ladies' room and returned to the Buick. At five o'clock I packed it in, not able to shake the visions of Grandma Mazur getting stuck with an ice pick. I drove back to my apartment, threw some clothes in a laundry basket, added makeup, hair gel, and hair dryer, and dragged the basket out to the car. I went back and fetched Rex, set the answering machine, left the kitchen light burning, and locked the door behind me. The only way I knew to protect Grandma Mazur was to move back home.

"What's this?" my mother said when she saw the glass hamster cage.

"I'm moving in for a few days."

"You quit that job. Thank God! I always thought you could do better."

"I didn't quit my job. I just need a change."

"I have the sewing machine and the ironing board in your room. You said you'd never come home."

I had both arms wrapped around the hamster cage. "I was wrong. I'm home. I'll make do."

"Frank," my mother yelled. "Come help Stephanie, she's moving in with us again."

I nudged my way past her and started up the stairs. "Only for a few days. It's temporary."

"Stella Lombardi's daughter said that same thing, and three years later she's still living with them."

I felt a scream starting somewhere deep inside.

"If you'd given me some notice, I'd have cleaned," my mother said. "I'd have gotten a new bedspread."

I pushed the door open with my knee. "I don't need a new bedspread. This one is fine." I maneuvered around the clutter in the small room and set Rex on the bed while I cleaned off the top of the single dresser. "How's Grandma?"

"She's taking a nap."

"Not no more I'm not," Grandma said from inside her room. "There's enough noise out there to wake the dead. What's going on?"

"Stephanie's moving back home."

"Why'd she want to do a thing like that? It's damn boring here." Grandma peeked into my room. "You aren't pregnant, are you?"

Grandma Mazur got her hair curled once a week. In between sets she must have slept with her head hanging over the side of the bed because the tight little rolls lost some precision as the week marched on, but never seemed totally disturbed. Today she looked like she'd spray-starched her hair and been put through a wind tunnel. Her dress was rumpled from sleep, she was wearing pink velour bedroom slippers, and her left hand was encased in bandage.

"How's your hand?" I asked.

"Starting to throb. Think I must need some more of them pills."

Even with the ironing board and sewing machine occupying space, my room hadn't changed much in the past ten years. It was a small room with one window. The curtains were white with a rubberized backing. The first week in May they were exchanged for sheers. The walls were painted dusty rose. The trim was white. The double bed was covered with a quilted, pink-flowered bedspread, softened in texture and color by age and the spin cycle. I had a small closet, which was filled with seasonal clothes, a single maple dresser, and a maple nightstand with a milk-glass lamp. My high school graduation picture still hung on the wall. And a picture of me in my majorette uniform. I had never completely mastered the art of baton twirling, but I'd been perfection in boots when I'd strutted onto a football field. Once during a half-time show I'd lost control of my baton and flipped it into the trombone section. A shudder ripped through me at the memory.

I hauled the laundry basket up and stashed it in a corner, clothes and all. The house was filled with food smells and the clank of flatware being set. My father channel-surfed in the living room, raising the volume to compete with the kitchen activity.

"Shut it down," my mother shouted at my father. "You'll make us all deaf."

My father concentrated on the screen, pretending oblivion.

By the time I sat down to dinner my fillings were vibrating, and I'd developed a twitch in my left eye.

"Isn't this nice?" my mother said. "Everyone sitting down to dinner together. Too bad Valerie isn't here."

My sister, Valerie, had been married to the same man for a hundred years and had two children. Valerie was the normal daughter.

Grandma Mazur was directly across from me and was downright frightening, with her hair still uncombed and her eyes focused inward. As my father would put it, her lights were on, but there was no one home.

"How much of that codeine has Grandma taken so far?" I asked my mother.

"Just one pill that I know of," my mother said.

I felt my eye jump and put my finger to it. "She seems to be . . . disconnected."

My father stopped buttering his bread and looked up. His mouth opened to say something, but he thought better of it and went back to buttering his bread.

"Mom," my mother called out, "how many pills have you taken?"

Grandma's head rotated in my mother's direction. "Pills?"

"It's a terrible thing that an old lady can't be safe on the streets," my mother said. "You'd think we lived in Washington, D.C. Next thing we'll have drive-by shootings. The burg was never like this in the old days."

I didn't want to burst her bubble about the old days, but in the old days the burg had a Mafia staff car parked in every third driveway. Men were walked out of their homes, still in pajamas, and taken at gunpoint to the Meadowlands or the Camden landfill for ceremonial dispatch. Usually families and neighbors weren't at risk, but there'd always been the possibility that a stray bullet would embed itself in the wrong body.

And the burg was never safe from the Mancuso and Morelli men. Kenny was crazier and more brazen than most, but I suspected he wasn't the first of the Mancusos to leave a scar on a woman's body. To my knowledge none of them had ever ice-picked an old woman, but the Mancusos and Morellis were notorious for their violent, alcohol-fueled tempers and for their ability to sweet-talk a woman into an abusive relationship.

I knew some of this firsthand. When Morelli had charmed the pants off me fourteen years ago, he hadn't been abusive, but he hadn't been kind, either.

Grandma was sound asleep by seven o'clock, snoring like a drunken lumberjack.

I slipped into my jacket and grabbed my pocketbook.

"Where are you going?" my mother wanted to know.

"To Stiva's. He's hired me to help him close."

"Now that's a job," my mother said. "You could do a lot worse than to work for Stiva."

I closed the front door behind me, and took a deep, cleansing breath. The air felt cool on my face. My eye relaxed under the dark night sky.

I drove to Stiva's and parked in the lot. Inside, Andy Roche had reclaimed his position at the tea table.

"How's it going?" I asked.

"Some old lady just told me I looked like Harrison Ford."

I selected a cookie from the plate behind him. "Shouldn't you be with your brother?"

"We weren't all that close."

"Where's Morelli?"

Roche casually scanned the room. "No one ever knows the answer to that question."

I returned to my car and had just settled in when the phone rang.

"How's Grandma Mazur?" Morelli asked.

"She's sleeping."

"I hope this move to your parents' house is temporary. I had plans for those purple shoes."

This caught me by surprise. I'd expected Morelli to keep watching Spiro, but he'd followed me instead. And I hadn't spotted him. I pressed my lips together. I was a dismal bounty hunter. "I didn't see any other good alternatives. I'm worried about Grandma Mazur."

"You have a terrific family, but they'll have you on Valium in forty-eight hours."

"Plums don't do Valium. We mainline cheese-cake."

"Whatever works," Morelli said, and hung up.

At ten of ten I pulled into the mortuary drive-way and parked to one side, leaving room for Spiro to squeeze past. I locked the Buick and entered the funeral home through the side door.

Spiro was looking nervous, saying good-byes. Louie Moon was nowhere to be seen. And Andy had disappeared. I slipped into the kitchen and clipped a holster to my belt. I loaded the fifth round into my .38 and shoved the gun into the holster. I clipped on a second holster for my pepper spray, and a third for a flashlight. I figured at $100 a shot, Spiro deserved the full treatment.

I'd have heart palpitations if I had to use the gun, but that was my little secret.

I was wearing a hip-length jacket that for the most part hid my paraphernalia. Technically this meant I was carrying concealed, which was a legal no-no. Unfortunately, the alternative would generate instant phone calls all over the burg that I was packing at Stiva's. The threat of arrest seemed pale by comparison.

When the last of the mourners cleared the front porch I walked Spiro through the public areas on the top two floors of the house, securing windows and doors. Only two rooms were occupied. One by the bogus brother.

The silence was eerie, and my discomfort with death was enhanced by Spiro's presence. Spiro Stiva, Demonic Mortician. I had my hand on the butt of the little S & W, thinking it wouldn't have hurt to load up with silver bullets.

We paced through the kitchen, into the back hall. Spiro opened the door to the cellar.

"Hold it," I said. "Where are you going?"

"We need to check the cellar door."

"We?"

"Yeah, we. Like in me and my fucking bodyguard."

"I don't think so."

"You want to get paid?"

Not that bad. "Are there bodies down there?"

"Sorry, we're fresh out of bodies."

"So what's down there?"

"The furnace, for Chrissake!"

I unholstered my gun. "I'll be right behind you."

Spiro looked at the five-shot Smith & Wesson. "Cripes, that's a goddamn sissy gun."

"I bet you wouldn't say that if I shot you in the foot with it."

His obsidian eyes locked with mine. "I hear you killed a man with that gun."

Not something I wanted to rap about with Spiro. "Are we going downstairs, or what?"

The basement was basically one large room, and pretty much what you'd expect from a basement. With the possible exception of caskets stacked in one of the corners.

The outside door was just to the right at the foot of the stairs. I checked the door to make sure the bolt was thrown. "Nobody here," I said to Spiro, holstering my gun. I'm not sure whom I'd expected to shoot. Kenny, I suppose. Maybe Spiro. Maybe ghosts.

We returned to the first floor, and I waited in the hall while Spiro bumbled around in his office, finally emerging wearing a top coat, carrying a gym bag.

I followed him to the back door and held the door open, watching him activate the alarm and hit the light switch. The lights inside dimmed. The exterior lights remained on.

Spiro shut the door and pulled car keys from his coat pocket. "We'll take my car. You ride shotgun."

"How about you take your car, I take my car."

"No way. I pay a hundred bucks, I want my

gunny sitting next to me. You can take the car home with you and pick me up in the morning."

"That wasn't part of the deal."

"You were out there anyway. I saw you in the lot this morning, waiting for Kenny to make a move, so you could haul his ass back to jail. What's the big deal, so you drive me to work."

Spiro's Lincoln was parked close to the door. He aimed his remote at the car, and the alarm chirped off. He lit up when we were safely inside.

We were sitting in a pool of light on a deserted patch of driveway. Not a good spot to linger. Especially if Morelli wasn't in a position to see this part of the property.

"Put it in gear," I said to Spiro. "It's too easy for Kenny to get to us here."

He rolled the engine over, but he didn't move forward. "What would you do if all of a sudden Kenny jumped up alongside the car and pointed a gun at you?"

"I don't know. You never really know what you'll do in a situation like that until you do it."

Spiro thought about that for a moment. He took another drag on his cigarette and shifted to drive.

We stopped for a light at Hamilton and Gross. Spiro's head didn't move, but his eyes cut to Delio's Exxon. The pumps were lit, and there was a light on in the office. The bays were dark and closed. Several cars and a truck had been parked in front of the end bay. Drop-offs to be serviced first thing in the morning.

Spiro stared in silence, his face devoid of emotion, and I couldn't guess at his thoughts.

The light changed, and we motored through the intersection. We were halfway down the block when my brain kicked in. "Oh my God," I said. "Go back to the gas station."

Spiro braked and pulled to the side. "You didn't see Kenny, did you?"

"No. I saw a truck! A big white truck with black lettering on the side!"

"You're gonna have to do better than that."

"When I talked to the woman who managed the storage lockers she said she remembered seeing a white truck with black lettering make several passes in the area of your locker. It was too vague to mean anything at the time."

Spiro waited for a break in traffic and wheeled a U-turn. He parked at the edge of the macadam apron, behind the drop-offs. Chances of Sandeman still being at the station were slim, but I strained to see in the office all the same. I didn't want a confrontation with Sandeman if I could avoid it.

We got out and took a look at the truck. It belonged to Macko Furniture. I knew the store. It was a small family-owned business that had steadfastly stayed with a downtown location when others were moving to highway strip malls.

"This mean anything to you?" I asked.

He shook his head. "No. Don't know anybody at Macko Furniture."

"It's the right size for caskets."

"There must be fifty trucks in Trenton that fit this description."

"Yes, but this one is at the garage where Moogey worked. And Moogey knew about the caskets. He went down to Braddock and drove them back for you."

Dumb chick feeds information to slimy guy. Come on, slimy guy, I thought. Get careless. Give me some information in return.

"So you think Moogey was tight with someone from Macko Furniture, and they decided to steal my caskets," Spiro said.

"It's possible. Or maybe while the truck was being serviced, Moogey borrowed it."

"What would Moogey want with twenty-four caskets?"

"You tell me."

"Even with the hydraulic tailgate, you'd need at least two guys to move those caskets."

"Doesn't seem like a problem to me. You find some big oaf, pay him minimum wage. He helps you move caskets."

Spiro had his hands in his pockets. "I don't know," he said. "It's just hard to believe Moogey'd do something like that. There were two things you could always count on from Moogey. He was loyal, and he was dumb. Moogey was a big, dumb shit. Kenny and me let him hang out with us because he was good for laughs. He'd do anything we told him. We'd say, hey, Moogey, how about you run over your dick with a lawn mower. And he'd say, sure, you want me to get a hard-on first?"

"Maybe he wasn't as dumb as you thought."

Spiro didn't say anything for a couple beats, then he turned on his heel and walked back to the Lincoln. We kept quiet for the rest of the trip. When we reached Spiro's parking lot I couldn't resist another shot with the caskets.

"Kind of funny about you and Kenny and Moogey. Kenny thinks you've got something that belongs to him. And now we think maybe Moogey had something that belonged to you."

Spiro slid into a space, put the car in park, and swiveled his body in my direction. He draped his left arm over the wheel, his topcoat gaped, and I caught a glimpse of a gun butt and shoulder holster.

"What are you getting at?" Spiro asked.

"Nothing. Just thinking out loud. Thinking that you and Kenny have a lot in common."

Our eyes held, and cold fear ran the length of my spine and crawled through my stomach. Morelli was right about Spiro. He'd eat his young, and he wouldn't think twice about putting a bullet in my worthless brain. I hoped I hadn't pushed too hard.

"Maybe you should stop thinking out loud. Maybe you should stop thinking altogether," Spiro said.

"I'm going to raise my rates if you're going to get cranky."

"Christ," Spiro said, "you're already fucking overpaid. For a hundred dollars a night, the least you could do is throw in a blow job."

What I was going to throw in was a nice long time behind bars. It was a comforting thought, and it kept me going while I did my bodyguard thing in his apartment, flipping on lights, scoping out closets, counting dustballs under his bed, and gagging at the soap scum behind his shower curtain.

I gave his place a green light, drove the Lincoln back to the funeral home, and exchanged it for my Buick.

I caught Morelli in my rearview mirror half a block from my parents' house. He idled in front of the Smullenses' until I parked the Buick. When I stepped out of the car, he crept forward and parked behind me. I suppose I couldn't blame him for being cautious.

"What were you doing at Delio's?" Morelli wanted to know. "I assume you were baiting Spiro about the truck."

"You assume right."

"Anything come of it?"

"He said he didn't know anyone from Macko Furniture. And he discounted the possibility that Moogey might have taken the caskets. Apparently Moogey was the group idiot. I'm not even sure Moogey was involved."

"Moogey drove the caskets to New Jersey."

I leaned back against the Buick. "Maybe Kenny and Spiro didn't include Moogey in the master plan, but somewhere along the line Moogey found out and decided to cut himself in."

"And you think he borrowed the furniture truck to move the caskets."

"It would be one theory." I pushed off from the Buick and hitched my bag higher onto my shoulder. "I'm picking Spiro up at eight tomorrow to take him to work."

"I'll catch up with you in his lot."

I let myself into the darkened house and paused for a moment in the front hall. The house was always at its best when it was asleep. There was an air of satisfaction to the house at the end of the day. Maybe the day hadn't gone exactly right, but the day had been lived and the house had been there for its family.

I hung my jacket in the hall closet and tiptoed into the kitchen. Finding food in my kitchen was always hit or miss. Finding food in my mother's kitchen was a sure thing. I heard the stairs creak and knew from the tread that it was my mother.

"How did it go at Stiva's?" she asked.

"It went okay. I helped him lock up, and then I drove him home."

"I guess it's hard for him to drive with his wrist. I hear he got twenty-three stitches."

I pulled out some ham and provolone cheese.

"Here, let me," my mother said, taking the ham and cheese, reaching for the loaf of rye bread on the counter.

"I can do it," I said.

My mother took her good carving knife from the knife drawer. "You don't slice the ham thin enough."

When she'd made each of us a sandwich, she poured two glasses of milk and set it all on the kitchen table. "You could have invited him in for a sandwich," she said.

"Spiro?"

"Joe Morelli."

My mother never ceased to amaze me. "There was a time when you would have chased him out of the house with that carving knife."

"He's changed."

I tore into the sandwich. "So he tells me."

"I hear he's a good cop."

"A good cop is different from a good person."

I woke up disoriented, staring at a ceiling from a previous life. Grandma Mazur's voice snapped me back to the present.

"If I don't get into that bathroom there's gonna be a big mess in the hall," she yelled. "Last night's supper's going through me like goose grease."

I heard the door open. Heard my father mumble something indiscernible. My eye started to twitch, and I squinched it closed. I focused my other eye on the bedside clock. Seven-thirty. Damn. I'd wanted to get to Spiro's early. I jumped out of bed and rummaged through the laundry basket for clean jeans and a shirt. I ran a brush through my hair, grabbed my pocketbook, and rushed into the hall.

"Grandma," I hollered through the door. "Are you going to be long?"

"Is the Pope Catholic?" she yelled back.

All right, I could postpone the bathroom for half an hour. After all, if I'd gotten up at nine I wouldn't have used the bathroom for another hour and a half.

My mother caught me with my jacket in hand. "Where are you going?" she asked. "You haven't had breakfast."

"I told Spiro I'd pick him up."

"Spiro can wait. The dead people won't mind if he's fifteen minutes late. Come eat your breakfast."

"I don't have time for breakfast."

"I made some nice oatmeal. It's on the table. I poured your juice." She looked down at my shoes. "What kind of shoes are they?"

"They're Doc Martens."

"Your father wore shoes like that when he was in the army."

"These are great shoes," I said. "I love these shoes. Everyone wears shoes like this."

"Women interested in getting married to a nice man do not wear shoes like that. Women who like other women wear shoes like that. You don't have any funny ideas about women, do you?"

I clapped my hand over my eye.

"What's wrong with your eye?" my mother asked.

"It's twitching."

"You're too nervous. It's that job. Look at you rushing out of the house. And what's that on your belt?"

"Pepper spray."

"Your sister, Valerie, doesn't wear such things on her belt."

I looked at my watch. If I ate real fast, I could still get to Spiro by eight.

My father was at the table, reading his paper, drinking coffee. "How's the Buick?" he asked. "You giving it high-test?"

"The Buick's fine. No problems."

I chugged the juice and tried the oatmeal. It needed something. Chocolate, maybe. Or ice cream. I added three spoons of sugar and some milk.

Grandma Mazur took her seat at the table. "My hand feels better," she said, "but I got the devil of a headache."

"You should stay at home today," I said. "Take it easy."

"I'm going to take it easy at Clara's. I look a fright. Don't know how my hair got like this."

"No one will see you if you don't go out of the house," I argued.

"Suppose someone comes over? Suppose that good-looking Morelli boy comes to visit again? You think I want him seeing me like this? Besides, I got to go while I still got the bandage on and I'm big news. Not every day a person gets attacked at the bakery."

"I have things to do first thing this morning, but then I'll be back, and I'll take you to Clara's," I told Grandma. "Don't go without me!"

I wolfed down the rest of the oatmeal and had a fast half cup of coffee. I grabbed my jacket and pocketbook and took off. I had my hand on the door when the phone rang.

"It's for you," my mother said. "It's Vinnie."

"I don't want to talk to him. Tell him I've already left."

The cell phone rang just as I hit Hamilton.

"You should have talked to me at home," Vinnie said. "It would have been cheaper."

"You're breaking up . . . lousy connection."

"Don't give me that lousy connection crap."

I made some static sounds.

"And I'm not going to fall for that phony static, either. Make sure you get your keester in here this morning."

I didn't see Morelli lurking in Spiro's parking lot, but I assumed he was there. There were two vans and a truck with a cap. Both good possibilities.

I collected Spiro and headed for the funeral home. When I stopped for the light at Hamilton and Gross, we both turned our attention to the Exxon station.

"Maybe we should stop in and ask a few questions," Spiro said.

"What kind of questions?"

"Questions about the furniture truck. Just for the hell of it. I guess it would be interesting to see if Moogey was the one who took the caskets."

I figured I had a couple choices. I could torture him by saying, what's the point? Let's just get on with our lives. And then I'd drive right on by. Or I could play along to see how it goes. There was definitely some merit to torturing Spiro, but my best instincts told me to let him run with the ball and tag along.

The bays were open. Most likely Sandeman was there. Big deal. Compared to Kenny, Sandeman was starting to look small-time. Cubby Delio was working the office. Spiro and I ambled in together.

Cubby snapped to attention at the sight of Spiro. Little prick that he was, Spiro still represented Stiva's mortuary, and Stiva threw a lot of business to the station. All of Stiva's cars were serviced and gassed here.

"I heard about your arm," Cubby said to Spiro. "Damn shame. I know you and Kenny used to be friends. I guess he just went crazy. That's what everyone says."

Spiro passed it off with a wave of his hand that implied it was nothing more than an annoyance. He pivoted on his heel and looked out the office window at the truck, still parked in front of the bay. "I wanted to ask you about the Macko truck. Do you always service that truck? Does it come in regularly?"

"Yep. Macko has an account, just like you. They've got two trucks, and we do both of them."

"Who usually brings them in? Usually the same guy?"

"Usually it's Bucky or Biggy. They've been driving for Macko for a lot of years. Is there a problem? You looking to get some furniture?"

"Thinking about it," Spiro said.

"It's a good company. Family run. Keep their trucks in real good condition."

Spiro stuck his injured arm in his jacket. Small

man imitates Napoleon. "Looks like you haven't found a replacement for Moogey."

"Thought I had a guy, but he didn't work out. Hard to replace Moogey. When Moogey was running the station I hardly had to be here. Could take a day off once a week to go to the track. Even after he got shot in the knee, he was still reliable. Still came to work."

I suspected Spiro and I had parallel thoughts, and I was thinking that maybe Moogey borrowed the truck on one of those track days. Of course, if he borrowed the truck, someone else would have to be minding the store. Or someone else would have to be driving the truck.

"It's hard to get good help," Spiro said. "I have the same problem."

"I've got a good mechanic," Cubby said. "Sandeman's got his own ways, but he's a damn good mechanic. The rest of the people come and go. Don't need a rocket scientist to pump gas or change a tire. If I could find someone to work full-time in the office, I'd be set."

Spiro did some oily chitchat and oozed himself out of the office.

"You know any of the guys who work here?" he asked me.

"I've spoken to Sandeman. He has an attitude. Does a little recreational drug use."

"You tight with him?"

"I'm not his favorite person."

Spiro's gaze dropped to my feet. "Maybe it's the shoes."

I wrenched the car door open. "Anything else you want to comment on? Maybe you have a few words to say about my car?"

Spiro angled onto the seat. "Hell, the car is awesome. At least you know how to pick out a car."

I squired Spiro into the funeral parlor, where all security systems seemed intact. We did a superficial examination of his two customers and felt fairly certain no one had relieved them of any obvious body parts. I told Spiro I'd return for the night run and that he should beep me if he needed me sooner.

I would have liked to keep Spiro under surveillance. I figured he'd keep picking at the lead I'd given him, and who knows what he'd find? And even more important, if Spiro started moving around, maybe Kenny would move with him. Unfortunately, I couldn't conduct any meaningful surveillance in Big Blue. I'd have to find a different car if I wanted to tail Spiro.

The half cup of coffee I'd gulped at breakfast was working its way through my system, so I decided to go back to my parents' house, where I could use the bathroom. I could take a shower and give some thought to my car problem. At ten I'd chauffeur Grandma Mazur over to Clara's for an overhaul.

When I got home my father was in the bathroom, and my mother was in the kitchen, cutting vegetables for minestrone.

"I have to use the bathroom," I said. "Do you think Daddy will be long?"

My mother rolled her eyes. "I don't know what he does in there. Takes the paper in with him, and we don't see him for hours."

I snitched a chunk of carrot and a chunk of celery for Rex and hustled up the stairs.

I knocked on the bathroom door. "How much longer?" I yelled.

There was no answer.

I knocked louder. "Are you okay in there?"

"Christ," was the muttered reply. "A man can't even take a crap in this house . . ."

I went back to my room. My mother had made my bed and folded all my clothes. I told myself it was nice to be back home and have someone doing little favors for me. I should be grateful. I should enjoy the luxury.

"Isn't this fun?" I said to a sleeping Rex. "It's not every day we get to visit Grandmom and Grandpop." I lifted the lid to give him his breakfast, but my eye was twitching so badly I missed the cage entirely and dropped his carrot chunk on the floor.

By ten o'clock my father still hadn't come out of the bathroom, and I was dancing in the hall. "Hurry up," I said to Grandma Mazur. "I'm going to explode if I don't get to a bathroom soon."

"Clara has a nice bathroom. She keeps potpourri in it, and she's got a crocheted doll that sits on the extra roll of toilet paper. She'll let you use her bathroom."

"I know, I know. Get a move on, will you?"

She was wearing her blue wool coat and had a gray wool scarf wrapped around her head.

"You're going to be hot in that coat," I told her. "It's not very cold out."

"Haven't got anything else," she said. "Everything's gone to rags. I thought maybe after Clara's we could go shopping. I got my Social Security check."

"You sure your hand feels okay to go shopping?"

She held her hand in front of her face and stared at the bandage. "Feels okay so far. The hole wasn't real big. Tell you the truth, I didn't even know how deep it was until I got to the hospital. It happened so fast.

"I always thought I was pretty good at taking care of myself, but I don't know anymore. I don't move like I used to. I just stood there like a damn fool and let him stick me in the hand."

"I'm sure there wasn't anything you could do, Grandma. Kenny's a lot bigger than you, and you were unarmed."

Her eyes clouded behind a film of tears. "He made me feel like a silly old woman."

Morelli was slouched against the Buick when I came out of Clara's. "Whose idea was it to talk to Cubby Delio?"

"Spiro's. And I don't think he's going to stop with Delio. He needs to find those guns so he can get Kenny off his back."

"You learn anything interesting?"

I repeated the conversation for Morelli.

"I know Bucky and Biggy," he said. "They wouldn't get mixed up in something like this."

"Maybe we've jumped to the wrong conclusion about the furniture truck."

"I don't think so. I stopped by the Exxon station first thing this morning and took some pictures. Roberta says she thinks it's the same truck."

"I thought you were supposed to be following me! What if I was attacked? What if Kenny came after me with the ice pick?"

"I followed you part of the time. Anyway, Kenny likes to sleep in."

"That's no excuse! The least you could have done was let me know I was on my own!"

"What's the plan here?" Morelli wanted to know.

"Grandma will be done in an hour. I promised I'd take her shopping. And sometime today I have to stop in to see Vinnie."

"He going to yank you off the case?"

"No. I'll take Grandma Mazur with me. She'll straighten him out."

"I've been thinking about Sandeman . . ."

"Yeah," I said. "I've been thinking about Sandeman, too. Initially I thought he might be hiding Kenny. Maybe it's just the opposite. Maybe he screwed Kenny over."

"You think Moogey threw in with Sandeman?"

I shrugged. "It makes some sense. Whoever stole the guns had street contacts."

"You said Sandeman didn't show any signs of sudden wealth."

"I think Sandeman's wealth goes up his nose."

CHAPTER
13

"I feel much better now that my hair's back in shape," Grandma said, hoisting herself up onto the front seat of the Buick. "I even had her put a rinse in it. Can you tell the difference?"

She'd gone from gunmetal gray to apricot.

"It's more of a strawberry blond now," I said.

"Yeah, that's it. Strawberry blond. I always wanted to be one of those."

Vinnie's office was just down the street. I parked at the curb and pulled Grandma in after me.

"I've never been here before," Grandma said, taking it all in. "Isn't this something?"

"Vinnie's on the phone," Connie said. "He'll be with you in a minute."

Lula came over to get a closer look at Grandma. "So you're Stephanie's grandma," Lula said. "I've heard a lot about you."

Grandma's eyes brightened. "Oh yeah? What'd you hear?"

"For starters I heard you got stuck with an ice pick."

Grandma held her bandaged hand out for Lula to see. "It was this here hand, and it got stuck just about clean through."

Lula and Connie looked at the hand.

"And that isn't all that's happened," Grandma said. "The other night Stephanie got a man's part in Express Mail. Opened it up right in front of me. I saw the whole thing. It was stuck to a piece of foam with a hatpin."

"Get out," Lula said.

"That's just the way it came through the mail," Grandma said. "Sliced off like a chicken neck and stuck with a hatpin. Reminded me of my husband."

Lula leaned forward so she could whisper. "You talking about size? Was your man's part that big?"

"Heck no," Grandma said. "His part was that dead."

Vinnie stuck his head out of his office door, and swallowed hard when he saw Grandma. "Oh jeez," he said.

"I just picked Grandma up at the beauty parlor," I told him "And now we're going shopping. Thought I'd stop by to see what you wanted, since I was just down the street."

Vinnie's five-foot-nine frame hunched. His thinning black hair was slicked back and had the same level of shine as his pointy-toed black shoes.

"I want to know what's happening with Mancuso. This was supposed to be a simple pickup, and now I'm hanging out for a lot of money."

"I'm closing in," I said. "Sometimes these things take time."

"Time is money," Vinnie said. "My money."

Connie rolled her eyes.

And Lula said, "Say what?"

We all knew Vinnie's bond business was financed by an insurance company.

Vinnie balanced on his toes, hands loose at his sides. City boy. Slack-jointed. Tight-assed. "This case is out of your league. I'm giving it over to Mo Barnes."

"I don't know Mo Barnes from Adam's donkey," Grandma said to Vinnie. "But I know he can't hold a candle to my granddaughter. She's the best there is when it comes to bounty huntering, and you'd be a darn fool to take her off this Mancuso case. Especially now that I'm working with her. We're about to crack his case wide open."

"No offense," Vinnie said, "but you and your granddaughter couldn't crack a walnut with both hands, much less bring Mancuso in."

Grandma pulled herself up and edged her chin out a half inch.

"Uh-oh," Lula said.

"Bad things happen to people who take away from family," Grandma told Vinnie.

"What kinds of bad things?" Vinnie asked. "What's my hair gonna fall out? My teeth gonna rot in my head?"

"Maybe," Grandma said. "Maybe I'll put the evil eye on you. Or maybe I'll talk to your grandma Bella. Maybe I'll tell your grandma Bella how you talk fresh to an old woman."

Vinnie swayed foot to foot like a caged cat. He knew better than to displease Grandma Bella. Grandma Bella was even scarier than Grandma Mazur. Grandma Bella had on more than one occasion taken a grown man by the ear and brought him to his knees. Vinnie made a low sound behind clenched teeth and narrowed his eyes. He muttered something through tight lips, tipped backward into his office, and slammed his door shut.

"Well," Grandma said. "That's the Plum side of the family for you."

It was late afternoon when we finished shopping. My mother opened the door for us with a grim set to her mouth.

"I had nothing to do with the hair," I told her. "Grandma did that all by herself."

"This is my cross to bear," my mother said. She looked down at Grandma's shoes and genuflected.

Grandma Mazur was wearing Doc Martens. She was also wearing a new hip-length, down-filled ski jacket, jeans that she'd rolled and pegged, and a flannel shirt to match mine. We looked like *Tales from the Crypt* does the Bobbsey Twins.

"I'm going to take a nap before dinner," Grandma said. "Shopping wore me out."

"I could use help in the kitchen," my mother said to me.

This was bad news. My mother never needed help in the kitchen. The only time my mother requested help was when she had something on her mind and intended to browbeat some unfortunate soul into submission. Or when she wanted information. Have some chocolate pudding, she'd say to me. By the way, Mrs. Herrel saw you going into the Morellis' garage with Joseph Morelli. And why are your panties on inside out?

I dragged after her, into her lair, where potatoes boiled on the stove, steaming the air and fogging the window over the sink. My mother opened the oven door to check on the roast, and the smell of leg of lamb washed over me. I felt my eyes glaze and my mouth fall open in a stupor of expectation.

She moved from the oven to the refrigerator. "Some carrots would be nice with the lamb. You can peel the carrots," she said, handing me the bag and the paring knife. "By the way, why did someone send you a penis?"

I almost sliced off the tip of my finger. "Um . . ."

"The return address was New York, but the postmark was local," she said.

"I can't tell you about the penis. It's under police investigation."

"Thelma Biglo's son, Richie, told Thelma that the penis belonged to Joe Loosey. And that Kenny Mancuso cut it off while Loosey was getting dressed at Stiva's."

"Where did Richie Biglo hear this?"

"Richie tends bar at Pino's. Richie knows everything."

"I don't want to talk about the penis."

My mother took the paring knife out of my hand. "Look at these carrots you peeled. I can't serve these carrots. Some of the skins are left on."

"You shouldn't cut the skins off anyway. You should scrub them with a brush. All the vitamins are in the skin."

"Your father won't eat them with the skins on. You know how particular he is."

My father would eat cat shit if it was salted, fried, or frosted, but it took an act of Congress to get him to eat a vegetable.

"Seems to me Kenny Mancuso has it in for you," my mother said. "It's not a nice thing to send a penis to a woman. It's disrespectful."

I searched the kitchen for a new task, but I couldn't come up with anything.

"And I know what's going on with your grandmother, too," she said. "Kenny Mancuso is getting to you through your grandmother. That's why he attacked her at the bakery. That's why you're living here . . . so you can be close by if he attacks her again."

"He's crazy."

"Of course he's crazy. Everybody knows he's crazy. All the Mancuso men are crazy. His uncle Rocco hung himself. He liked little girls. Mrs. Ligatti caught him with her Tina. And then the next day Rocco hung himself. Good thing, too. If Al Ligatti had gotten hold of Rocco . . ." My mother shook her head. "I don't even want to think about it." She shut the heat off under the potatoes and turned to me. "How good are you at this bounty hunter business?"

"I'm learning."

"Are you good enough to catch Kenny Mancuso?"

"Yes." Maybe.

She lowered her voice. "I want you to catch that son of a bitch. I want you to get him off the streets. It's not right that a man like that is free to hurt old women."

"I'll do the best I can."

"Good." She took a can of cranberries from the pantry. "Now that we have things straight, you can set the table."

Morelli showed up at one minute to six.

I answered his knock and stood blocking the doorway, preventing him from slipping into the front hall. "What is it?"

Morelli leaned into me, forcing me to take a step back.

"I was driving by, doing a security check," Morelli said, "and I smelled leg of lamb."

"Who is it?" my mother called.

"It's Morelli. He was driving by, and he smelled the lamb. And he's leaving. RIGHT NOW!"

"She has no manners," my mother said to Morelli. "I don't know what happened. I didn't raise her like that. Stephanie, lay out an extra plate."

Morelli and I left the house at seven-thirty. He trailed after me in a tan panel van and parked in Stiva's lot when I pulled into the driveway.

I locked the Buick and walked over to Morelli. "You have anything to tell me?"

"I went through invoices from the garage. The truck was in for an oil change at the end of the month. Bucky brought it in around seven in the morning and picked it up the next day."

"Let me guess. Cubby Delio was gone that day. Moogey and Sandeman were working."

"Yeah. Sandeman signed off on the job. His name was on the invoice."

"Have you talked to Sandeman?"

"No. I got to the garage right after he left for the night. I checked his room and some bars, but I couldn't find him. Thought I'd make the rounds again later."

"Did you find anything interesting in his room?"

"His door was locked."

"You didn't look in through the window?"

"Thought I'd save that little adventure for you. I know how much you like to do that sort of thing."

In other words, Morelli didn't want to get caught on the fire escape. "You going to be here when I close up with Spiro?"

"Wild horses couldn't drag me away."

I crossed the lot and entered the funeral home through the side door. Word of Kenny Mancuso's bizarre behavior was obviously spreading because Joe Loosey, minus his penis, was laid out in the V.I.P. room and the crowd packed into the room rivaled the record-breaking viewing held for Silvestor Bergen, who died in the middle of his term as grand poo-bah of the VFW.

Spiro was holding court on the far side of the lobby, cradling the arm injured in the line of duty, making the most of his role as undertaker célèbre. People were clustered around him, listening intently as he told them God knows what.

A few people looked in my direction and whispered behind their memorial programs.

Spiro bowed out on his audience and signaled me to follow him into the kitchen. He grabbed the big silver cookie plate on his way, ignoring Roche, who was once again positioned at the tea table.

"Do you believe this bunch of losers?" Spiro said, emptying a bag of bulk-bought supermarket cookies onto the plate. "They're eating me out of house and home. I should be charging afterhours admission to see Loosey's stump."

"Anything new from Kenny?"

"Nothing. I think he's shot his wad. Which brings me to business at hand. I don't need you anymore."

"Why the sudden change of heart?"

"Things have quieted down."

"That's it?"

"Yeah. That's it." He swung out the kitchen door with the cookies and slapped them down on the table. "How're you doing?" he asked Roche. "I see your brother's getting some overflow from Loosey. Probably a bunch of people going in there wondering about your brother's state of affairs, if you know what I mean. You notice I gave him a half-casket viewing tonight so no one could try copping a feel."

Roche looked like he might choke. "Thanks," he said. "Glad you're thinking ahead."

I went back to Morelli and gave him the news. Morelli was lost in the shadows of the dark van. "Sudden."

"I think Kenny's got the guns. I think we gave Spiro a place to start looking, he passed it on to Kenny, and Kenny lucked out. And now the heat's off Spiro."

"It's possible."

I had my car keys in hand. "I'm going to check on Sandeman. See if he's come home yet."

I parked half a block from Sandeman's rooming house, on the opposite side of the street. Morelli parked directly behind me. We stood for a moment on the sidewalk, taking in the bulky house, black against blue night sky. Harsh light poured from a shadeless downstairs window. Upstairs two orange rectangles gave muted testimony to life within the front rooms.

"What kind of car does he drive?" I asked Morelli.

"He's got a hog and a Ford pickup."

We didn't see either on the street. We followed the driveway to the back of the house and found the Harley. No windows were lit in any of the rear rooms. No light in Sandeman's upstairs window. No one sat on the stoop. The back door was unlocked. The hall leading from the back door was dim, lit by a bare 40-watt bulb hanging from an overhead fixture in the front foyer. Television sounds escaped from one of the upstairs rooms.

Morelli stopped in the foyer for a moment, listening to the house, before continuing on to the second floor and then the third floor. The third floor was dark and quiet. Morelli listened at Sandeman's door. He shook his head no. No noise coming from Sandeman's room.

He went to the window, opened it, and looked out. "It would be unethical for me to break into his apartment," Morelli said.

As opposed to downright illegal for me.

Morelli glanced at the heavy-duty flashlight I held in my hand. "Of course a bounty hunter would have the authority to go in after her man."

"Only if she was convinced her man was in there."

Morelli looked at me expectantly.

I peeked out at the fire escape. "It's really rickety," I told him.

"Yeah," he said. "I noticed that. It might not hold me." He put a finger under my chin and gazed into my eyes. "I bet it would hold a dainty little thing like you."

I am many things. Dainty isn't one of them. I took a deep breath and angled myself out onto the fire escape. Iron joints groaned, and rusted metal shards flaked off underfoot and fell to the ground. I whispered an oath and inched toward Sandeman's window.

I cupped my hands to the glass and looked inside. The interior was blacker than black. I tried the window. It was unlocked. I gave the bottom window a shove, and it rose halfway and stuck.

"Can you get in?" Morelli whispered.

"No. The window's stuck." I squatted down, peered through the opening and worked the flashlight around the room. So far as I could see, nothing had changed. There was the same clutter, the same squalor, the stink of unwashed clothes and overflowing ashtrays. I saw no signs of struggle, flight, or affluence.

I thought I'd give one more try with the window. I braced my feet and pushed hard against the old wood frame. Masonry bolts tore loose from crumbling brick, and the slatted floor of the fire escape tipped to a 45-degree angle. Stairs slid out of place, railings ripped from their moorings, angle irons wrenched free, and I skidded feet first, ass second off into space. My hand connected with a crossbar, and in an act of blind panic and reflexive action, I held fast . . . for ten seconds. At the end of those ten seconds, the entire third-floor gridwork crashed onto the second-floor fire escape. There was a momentary pause. Long enough for me to whisper, "Oh shit."

Above me, Morelli leaned out the window. "Don't move!"

CHAAANG! The second-floor fire escape separated from the building and crumbled to the ground, carrying me with it. I landed flat on my back with a solid *whump*, which knocked the air out of my lungs.

I lay there stunned until Morelli's face once again loomed over me, just inches away.

"Fuck," he whispered. "Jesus, Stephanie, say something!"

I stared straight ahead, unable to talk, not yet able to breathe.

He felt for the pulse in my neck. Then his hands were on my feet, moving up my legs. "Can you move your toes?"

Not when his hand was feeling up the inside of my thigh like this. My skin felt scorched under his palm, and my toes were curled into a cramp. I heard myself make a sucking sound. "Your fingers go any higher up my leg, and I'm filing for sexual harassment."

Morelli rocked back on his heels and passed a hand over his eyes. "You just scared the hell out of me."

"What's going on out there?" A loud voice from one of the windows. "I'm calling the police. I'm not putting up with this shit. We got noise ordinances in this neighborhood."

I propped myself up on my elbow. "Get me out of here."

Morelli gently hoisted me to my feet. "You sure you're okay?"

"Nothing seems broken." I wrinkled my nose. "What is that smell? Oh God, I didn't mess myself, did I?"

Morelli turned me around. "Whoa!" he said. "Someone in this building has a big dog. A big, *sick* dog. And it looks like you hit ground zero."

I shrugged out of the jacket and held it at arm's length. "Am I okay now?"

"Some of it's splattered down the back of your jeans."

"Anyplace else?"

"Your hair."

This sent me into instant hysteria. "GET IT OUT! GET IT OUT!"

Morelli clapped a hand over my mouth. "Quiet!"

"Get it out of my hair!"

"I can't get it out of your hair. You're going to have to wash it out." He pulled me toward the street. "Can you walk?"

I staggered forward.

"That's good," Morelli said. "Keep doing that. Before you know it, you'll be to the van. And then we'll get you to a shower. After an hour or two of scrubbing you'll be good as new."

"Good as new." My ears were ringing, and my voice sounded far away . . . like a voice in a jar. "Good as new," I repeated.

When we got to the van Morelli opened the rear door. "You don't mind riding in back, do you?"

I stared at him blank-minded.

Morelli shone my flashlight in my eyes. "You sure you're okay?"

"What kind of dog do you think it was?"

"A big dog."

"What kind?"

"Rottweiler. Male. Old and overweight. Bad teeth. Ate a lot of tuna fish."

I started to cry.

"Oh jeez," Morelli said. "Don't cry. I hate when you cry."

"I've got rottweiler shit in my hair."

He used his thumb to wipe the tears from my

cheeks. "It's okay, honey. It's really not so bad. I was kidding about the tuna." He gave me a boost into the van. "Hold tight back here. I'll have you home before you know it."

He brought me to my apartment.

"I thought this was best," he said. "Didn't think you'd want your mother to see you in this condition." He searched through my pocketbook for the key and opened the door.

The apartment felt cool and neglected. Too quiet. No Rex spinning in his wheel. No light left burning to welcome me home.

The kitchen beckoned to my left. "I need a beer," I said to Morelli. I was in no rush for the shower. I'd lost my ability to smell. I'd accepted the condition of my hair.

I shuffled into the kitchen and tugged at the refrigerator door. The door swung wide, the fridge light went on, and I stared in dumb silence at a foot . . . a large, filthy, bloody foot, separated from the leg just above the ankle, placed next to a tub of margarine and a three-quarters-filled bottle of cranberry cocktail.

"There's a foot in my refrigerator," I said to Morelli. Bells clanged, lights flashed, my mouth went numb, and I crashed to the floor.

I struggled up from unconscious muck and opened my eyes. "Mom?"

"Not exactly," Morelli said.

"What happened?" I asked.

"You fainted."

"It was just too much," I said to Morelli. "The dog shit, the foot . . ."

"I understand," Morelli said.

I pushed myself up onto shaky legs.

"Why don't you go stand in the shower while I take care of things here?" Morelli said. He handed me a beer. "You can take your beer with you."

I looked at the beer. "Did this come from my refrigerator?"

"No," Morelli said. "It came from someplace else."

"Good. I couldn't drink it if it came from the refrigerator."

"I know," Morelli said, maneuvering me toward the bathroom. "Just go take a shower and drink your beer."

Two uniforms, a crime lab guy, and two guys in suits were in my kitchen when I got out of the shower.

"I've got an idea on the identity of that foot," I said to Morelli.

He was writing on a clipboard. "I've got the same idea." He turned the clipboard over to me. "Sign at the dotted line."

"What am I signing?"

"Preliminary report."

"How did Kenny get the foot into my refrigerator?"

"Broken bedroom window. You need an alarm system."

One of the uniforms left, carrying a large Styrofoam cooler.

I swallowed down a wave of revulsion. "Is that it?" I asked.

Morelli nodded. "I did a fast cleanup of your refrigerator. You'll probably want to do a more thorough job when you have time."

"Thanks. I appreciate the help."

"We went through the rest of the apartment," he said. "Didn't find anything."

The second uniform left, followed by the suits and the crime scene guy.

"Now what?" I asked Morelli. "Not much point in staking out Sandeman's place."

"Now we watch Spiro."

"What about Roche?"

"Roche will stay with the funeral home. We'll tag after Spiro."

We taped a big plastic garbage bag over the broken window, shut the lights off, and locked the apartment. There was a small crowd in the hall.

"Well?" Mr. Wolesky asked. "What was this about? Nobody'll tell us nothing."

"It was just a broken window," I said. "I thought it might have been something more serious, so I called the police."

"Were you robbed?"

I shook my head no. "Nothing was taken." So far as I knew, that was the truth.

Mrs. Boyd didn't look like she was buying any of it. "What about the ice chest? I saw a policeman carry an ice chest out to his car."

"Beer," Morelli said. "They were friends of mine. We're going to a party later."

We ducked down the stairs and trotted to the van. Morelli opened the driver-side door, and sick-dog odor poured out, forcing us to retreat.

"Should have left the windows open," I said to Morelli.

"We'll let it sit for a minute," he said. "It'll be fine."

After a few minutes we crept closer.

"It still smells bad," I said.

Morelli stood fists on hips. "I don't have time to scrub it down. We'll try riding around with the windows open. Maybe we can blow it out."

Five minutes later, the smell hadn't faded.

"That's it for me," Morelli said. "I can't take this smell anymore. I'm trading up."

"You going home for your truck?"

He made a left onto Skinner Street. "Can't. The guy I borrowed the van from has my truck."

"The undercover pig car?"

"Being fixed." He hooked onto Greenwood. "We'll use the Buick."

Suddenly I had a new appreciation for the Buick.

Morelli pulled up behind Big Blue, and I had the door open and my foot to the pavement while the van was still rolling. I stood outside in the crisp air, breathing deep, flapping my arms and shaking my head to rid myself of any residual stench.

We got into the Buick together and sat there for a moment appreciating the lack of odor.

I rolled the engine over. "It's eleven o'clock.

You want to go straight to Spiro's apartment, or do you want to try the funeral home?"

"Funeral home. I spoke to Roche just before you got out of the shower, and Spiro was still in his office."

The lot was empty when I got to Stiva's. There were several cars on the street. None looked occupied. "Where's Roche?"

"Apartment across the street. Over the deli."

"He can't see the back entrance from there."

"True, but the exterior lights work on motion sensors. If someone approaches the back door, the lights will go on."

"I imagine Spiro can disengage that."

Morelli slouched in his seat. "There's no good vantage point for watching the back door. If Roche was sitting in the parking lot, he still couldn't see the back door."

Spiro's Lincoln was parked in the drive-through. The light was on in Spiro's office.

I eased the Buick to the curb and cut the engine. "He's working late. Usually he's out of here by now."

"You have your cell phone with you?"

I gave him the phone, and he tapped in a number.

Someone responded on the other end, and Morelli asked if anyone was home. I didn't hear the response. Morelli ended the call and returned the phone.

"Spiro's still there. Roche hasn't seen anyone go in since the doors closed at ten."

We were parked on a side street, beyond the reach of the streetlight. The side street was lined with modest row houses. Most were dark. The burg was an early-to-bed, early-to-rise community.

Morelli and I sat there in comfortable silence for half an hour, watching the funeral home. Just a couple of old law enforcement partners doing their job.

Twelve o'clock rolled around. Nothing had changed, and I was feeling antsy. "There's something wrong with this," I said. "Spiro never stays this late. He likes money when it comes easy. He's not the conscientious type."

"Maybe he's waiting for someone."

I had my hand on the door handle. "I'm going to snoop around."

"NO!"

"I want to see if the back sensors are working."

"You'll screw everything up. You'll spook Kenny if he's out there."

"Maybe Spiro shut the sensors off, and Kenny's already in the house."

"He's not."

"How can you be so sure?"

Morelli shrugged. "Gut instinct."

I cracked my knuckles.

"You're lacking some critical attributes of a good bounty hunter," Morelli said.

"Like what?"

"Patience. Look at you. You're all tied up in knots."

He applied pressure at the base of my neck with

his thumb and inched his way up to my hairline. My eyes drooped closed, and my breathing slowed.

"Feel good?" Morelli asked.

"Mmmmm."

He worked my shoulders with both hands. "You need to relax."

"If I relax any more, I'll melt and slide off the seat."

His hands stilled. "I like the melting part."

I turned my face toward him, and our eyes held.

"No," I said.

"Why not?"

"Because I've already seen the movie, and I hate the ending."

"Maybe it'll have a different ending this time."

"Maybe it won't."

His thumb traced over the pulse in my neck, and when he spoke his voice was low and cat's-tongue rough. "How about the middle of the movie? Did you like the middle?"

The middle of the movie had smoked. "I've seen better middles."

Morelli's face creased into a wide grin. "Liar."

"Besides, we're supposed to be watching for Spiro and Kenny."

"Don't worry about it. Roche is watching. If he sees anything, he'll call my pager."

Was this what I wanted? Sex in a Buick with Joe Morelli? No! Maybe.

"I think I might be getting a cold," I said. "This might not be a good time."

Morelli made chicken sounds.

My eyes rolled to the top of my head. "That is so juvenile. That is just the response I'd expect from you."

"No it's not," Morelli said. "You expected action." He leaned forward and kissed me. "How's this? Is this a better response?"

"Umm . . ."

He kissed me again, and I thought, well, what the hell—if he wants to get a cold, that's his problem, right? And maybe I wasn't getting a cold, anyway. Maybe I had been mistaken.

Morelli pushed my shirt aside and slipped the straps of my bra over my shoulders.

I felt a shiver ripple through me and chose to believe the shiver was from the cool air . . . as opposed to a premonition of doom. "So you're sure Roche will page you if he sees Kenny?" I asked.

"Yeah," Morelli said, lowering his mouth to my breast. "Nothing to worry about."

Nothing to worry about! He had his hand in my pants, and he was telling me I had nothing to worry about!

My eyes rolled to the top of my head again. What was my problem? I was an adult. I had needs. What was so wrong about satisfying those needs once in a while? Here I had a chance for a real quality orgasm. And it wasn't as if I had false expectations. I wasn't some dumb sixteen-year-old expecting a marriage proposal. All I expected was a goddamn orgasm. And I sure as hell deserved one. I hadn't had a social orgasm since Reagan was president.

I did a fast check of the windows. Totally fogged. That was good. Okay, I said to myself. Go for it. I kicked my shoes off, and stripped of everything but my black string bikinis.

"Now you," I said to Morelli. "I want to see you."

It took less than ten seconds for him to get undressed, five seconds of which he used up on guns and cuffs.

I snapped my mouth closed and surreptitiously checked for drool. Morelli was even more amazing than I'd remembered. And I'd remembered him as being freaking outstanding.

He hooked a finger under my bikini string, and in one fluid movement removed my panties. He tried to mount me, and hit his head on the steering wheel. "Been a long time since I've done this in a car," he said.

We scrambled to the back and fell together, Morelli in an unbuttoned washed denim shirt and white sweat socks, and me in a fresh rush of uncertainty.

"Spiro could kill the lights, and Kenny could sneak in the back door," I said.

Morelli kissed my shoulder. "Roche would know if Kenny was in the house."

"How would Roche know?"

Morelli sighed. "Roche would know because he's wired the house."

I pushed away. "You didn't tell me! How long has the house been wired?"

"You aren't going to make a big deal of this, are you?"

"What else haven't you told me?"

"That's it. I swear."

I didn't believe it for a second. He was wearing his cop face. I thought back to dinner, and how he'd miraculously appeared. "How did you know my mother was cooking lamb?"

"I smelled it when you opened the door."

"Bullshit!" I grabbed my purse from the front seat and dumped the contents between us. Hairbrush, hair spray, lipstick, pepper spray, travel pack of tissues, stun gun, gum, sunglasses . . . black plastic transformer. Fuck.

I snatched at the bug. "You son of a bitch! You wired my pocketbook!"

"It was for your own good. I was worried about you."

"That's despicable! That's an invasion of privacy! How dare you do this without asking me first!" And it was also a lie. He was afraid I'd get a bead on Kenny and not cut him in. I rolled the window down and threw the transformer out into the street.

"Shit," Morelli said. "That thing's worth four hundred dollars." He opened the door and went out to retrieve it.

I pulled the door closed and locked it. Damn him anyway. I should have known better than to try to work with a Morelli. I climbed over the seat and slid behind the wheel.

Morelli tried the passenger-side door, but it was locked. All the doors were locked, and they were going to stay that way. He could freeze his stupid dick off for all I cared. Serve him right. I revved the engine and took off, leaving him standing in the middle of the street in his shirt and socks, with his woody hanging half-mast.

I got a block down Hamilton and reconsidered. Probably it wasn't a good idea to leave a cop standing naked in the middle of the street. What would happen if a bad guy came along? Morelli probably couldn't even run in his condition. Okay, I thought, I'll help him out. I made a U-turn and retraced to the side street. Morelli was right where I'd left him. Hands on hips, looking disgusted.

I slowed, rolled my window down, and tossed him his gun. "Just in case," I said. Then I floored it and roared away.

CHAPTER
14

I quietly crept up the stairs and breathed a long sigh of relief when I was safely locked in my bedroom. I didn't want to explain my I've-been-making-out-in-a-Buick-rat's-nest hair to my mother. Nor did I want her to glean through X-ray vision that my panties were stuffed into my jacket pocket. I undressed with the lights off, slunk into bed, and pulled the covers up to my chin.

I awoke with two regrets. The first was that I'd left the stakeout and had no idea if Kenny had been caught. The second was that I'd missed my window of opportunity to use the bathroom, and once again, I was last in line.

I lay in bed, listening to people shuffle in and out of the bathroom . . . first my mother, then my father, then my grandmother. When Grandma Mazur creaked down the stairs, I wrapped myself in the pink quilted robe I'd gotten for my sixteenth birthday and padded to the bathroom. The window over the tub was closed against the cold, and the air inside was thick with the scent of shaving cream and Listerine.

I took a fast shower, towel-dried my hair, and dressed in jeans and a Rutgers sweatshirt. I had no special plans for the day, other than to keep an eye on Grandma Mazur and to keep tabs on Spiro. Of course, that was working on the assumption that Kenny hadn't gotten himself caught last night.

I followed my nose to coffee brewing in the kitchen and found Morelli eating breakfast at the kitchen table. From the look of his plate he'd just finished bacon and eggs and toast. He slouched back at the sight of me, coffee cup in hand. His expression was speculative.

"Morning," he said, voice even, eyes not giving up any secrets.

I poured coffee into a mug. "Morning." Noncommittal. "What's new?"

"Nothing. Your paycheck is still out there."

"You come by to tell me that?"

"I came by to get my wallet. I think I left it in your car last night."

"Right." Along with various articles of clothing.

I took a slurp of coffee and set the cup on the counter. "I'll get your wallet."

Morelli stood. "Thank you for breakfast," he said to my mother. "It was wonderful."

My mother beamed. "Any time. Always nice to have Stephanie's friends here."

He followed me out and waited while I unlocked the car and scooped his clothes together.

"Were you telling the truth about Kenny?" I asked. "He didn't show up last night?"

"Spiro stayed until a little after two. Sounded like he was playing computer games. That was all Roche picked up on the bug. No phone calls. No Kenny."

"Spiro was waiting for something that never happened."

"Looks like it."

The tan wreck of a cop car was parked behind my Buick. "I see you got your car back," I said to Morelli. It had all the same dents and scrapes, and the bumper was still in the backseat. "I thought you said it was being fixed."

"It was," Morelli said. "They fixed the lights." He glanced over at the house and then back at me. "Your mother is standing at the door, watching us."

"Yep."

"If she wasn't standing there, I'd grab you and shake you until the fillings fell out of your teeth."

"Police brutality."

"It has nothing to do with being a cop. It has to do with being Italian."

I handed him his shoes. "I'd really like to be in on the takedown."

"I'll do the best I can to include you."

We locked eyes. Did I believe him? No.

Morelli fished car keys out of his pocket. "You'd better think of a good story to tell your mother.

She's going to want to know why my clothes were in your car."

"She won't think anything of it. I've got men's clothes in my car all the time."

Morelli grinned.

"What were those clothes?" my mother asked when I came into the house. "Pants and shoes?"

"You don't want to know."

"I want to know," Grandma Mazur said. "I bet it's a pip of a story."

"How's your hand?" I asked her. "Does it hurt?"

"Only hurts if I make a fist, and I can't do that with this big bandage on. I'd be in a pickle if it had been my right hand."

"Got any plans for today?"

"Not until tonight. Joe Loosey is still laid out. I only got to see his penis, you know, so I thought I'd like to go see the rest of him at the seven o'clock viewing."

My father was in the living room, reading his paper. "When I go, I want to be cremated," he said. "No viewing."

My mother turned from the stove. "Since when?"

"Since Loosey lost his Johnson. I don't want to take any chances. I want to go right from wherever I fall to the crematorium."

My mother set a plateful of scrambled eggs in front of me. She added a side of bacon, toast, and juice.

I ate my eggs and considered my options. I could sequester myself in the house and do my protective granddaughter thing, I could drag Grandma around with me while I did my protective grand-daughter thing, or I could go about my business and hope Grandma wasn't on Kenny's agenda today.

"More eggs?" my mother asked. "Another piece of toast?"

"I'm fine."

"You're all bones. You should eat more."

"I'm not all bones. I'm fat. I can't button the top snap on my jeans."

"You're thirty years old. You have to expect to spread when you hit thirty. What are you doing still wearing jeans, anyway? A person your age shouldn't be dressing like a kid." She leaned forward and studied my face. "What's wrong with your eye? It looks like it's twitching again."

All right, eliminate option number one.

"I need to keep some people under surveillance," I said to Grandma Mazur. "You want to tag along?"

"I guess I could do that. You think it'll get rough?"

"No. I think it'll be boring."

"Well, if I wanted to be bored I could sit home. Who are we looking for, anyway? Are we looking for that miserable Kenny Mancuso?"

Actually, I'd intended to hang tight to Morelli. In a roundabout way I suppose it amounted to the same thing. "Yeah, we're looking for Kenny Mancuso."

"Then I'm all for it. I have a score to settle with him."

Half an hour later she was ready to go, wearing her jeans and ski jacket and Doc Martens.

I spotted Morelli's car a block down from Stiva's on Hamilton. Didn't look like Morelli was in the car. Probably Morelli was with Roche, swapping war stories. I parked behind Morelli, being careful not to creep too close and knock out his lights, again. I could see the front and side door to the funeral home, and the front door to Roche's building.

"I know all about how to do this stakeout stuff," Grandma said. "They had some private eyes on television the other night, and they didn't leave out a thing." She stuck her head into the canvas tote bag she'd hauled along. "I got everything we need in here. I got magazines to pass the time. I got sandwiches and sodas. I even got a bottle."

"What kind of bottle?"

"Used to have olives in it." She showed me the bottle. "It's so we can pee on the job. All the private eyes said they did this."

"I can't pee in that bottle. Only men can pee in bottles."

"Darn," Grandma said. "Why didn't I think of that? I went and threw away all the olives, too."

We read the magazine and tore out a few recipes. We ate the sandwiches and drank the sodas.

After drinking the sodas we both needed to go to the bathroom, so we went back to my parents' house for a potty break. We returned to Hamilton, slid into the same parking place behind Morelli, and continued to wait.

"You're right," Grandma said after an hour. "This is boring."

We played hangman and counted cars and verbally trashed Joyce Barnhardt. We'd just started twenty questions when I glanced out the window at oncoming traffic and recognized Kenny Mancuso. He was driving a two-tone Chevy Suburban that looked to be as big as a bus. We exchanged surprised stares for the longest heartbeat in history.

"Shit!" I shouted, fumbling with the ignition key, swiveling in my seat to keep him in sight.

"Get this car moving," Grandma yelled. "Don't let that son of a skunk get away!"

I wrenched the gearshift into drive and was about to pull out when I realized Kenny had U-turned at the intersection and was closing ground between us. There were no cars parked behind me. I saw the Suburban swerve to the curb and told Grandma to brace herself.

The Suburban crashed into the back of the Buick, bouncing us forward into Morelli's car, which crashed into the car in front of him. Kenny backed the Suburban up, stepped on the gas, and rammed us again.

"Well, that takes it," Grandma said. "I'm too old for this kind of bouncing around. I got delicate bones at my age." She pulled a .45 long-barrel out of her tote bag, wrenched her door open, and scrambled out onto the sidewalk. "Guess this will show you something," she said, aiming the gun at the Suburban. She pulled the trigger, fire flashed from the barrel, and the kick knocked her on her ass.

Kenny floored the Suburban in reverse all the way to the intersection and took off.

"Did I get him?" Grandma wanted to know.

"No," I said, helping her to her feet.

"Did I come close?"

"Hard to say."

She had her hand to her forehead. "Hit myself in the head with the dang gun. Didn't expect that much of a kick."

We walked around the cars, surveying the damage. The Buick was virtually unscathed. A scratch in the chrome on the big back bumper. No damage that I could find in the front.

Morelli's car looked like an accordion. The hood and the trunk lid were crumpled, and all the lights were broken. The first car in line had been shoved a couple feet forward, but didn't look bashed. A small dent in the back bumper, which may or may not have been the result of this accident.

I looked up the street, expecting Morelli to come running, but Morelli didn't appear.

"Are you okay?" I asked Grandma Mazur.

"Sure," Grandma said. "I would have got that slimeball too if it wasn't for my injury. Had to shoot with one hand."

"Where'd you get the forty-five?"

"My friend Elsie loaned it to me," Grandma said. "She got it at a yard sale when she lived in Washington, D.C." She rolled her eyes up in her head. "Am I bleeding?"

"No, but you've got a notch in your forehead. Maybe we should take you home to rest."

"That might be a good idea," she said. "My knees feel sort of rubbery. Guess I'm not so tough as them television people. Shooting off guns never seems to take anything out of them."

I got Grandma in the car and clicked the seat belt across her chest. I took one last look at the damage and wondered about liability for the first car in line. The damage was minimal to none, but I left my business card under the windshield wiper in case he discovered the dent and wanted an explanation.

I assumed I didn't have to do this for Morelli, since I'd be the first person who came to mind.

"Probably it'd be best if we don't mention anything about the gun when we get home," I told Grandma. "You know how Mom is about guns."

"That's okay by me," Grandma said. "I'd just as leave forget the whole thing. Can't believe I missed that car. Didn't even blow out a tire."

My mother raised her eyebrows when she saw the two of us straggle in. "Now what?" my mother asked. She squinted at Grandma. "What happened to your head?"

"Hit myself with a soda can," Grandma said. "Freak accident."

Half an hour later Morelli came knocking at the door. "I want to see you . . . outside," he said, hooking his hand around my arm, jerking me forward.

"It wasn't my fault," I told him. "Grandma

and I were sitting in the Buick, minding our own business, when Kenny came up behind us and knocked us into your car."

"You want to run that by me again?"

"He was driving a two-tone Suburban. He saw Grandma and me parked on Hamilton. He made a U-turn and rammed us from behind. Twice. Then Grandma jumped out of the car and shot at him, and he drove away."

"That's the lamest story I've ever heard."

"It's true!"

Grandma stuck her head out the door. "What's going on out here?"

"He thinks I made up the story about Kenny hitting us with the Suburban."

Grandma snagged the tote bag from the hall table. She rummaged through it, came up with the .45-long barrel, and aimed it at Morelli.

"Jesus!" Morelli said, ducking out of the way, taking the gun from Grandma. "Where the hell did you get this cannon?"

"Borrowed it," Grandma said. "And I used it on your no-good cousin, but he got away."

Morelli studied his shoes for a beat before speaking. "I don't suppose this gun is registered?"

"What do you mean?" Grandma asked. "Registered where?"

"Get rid of it," Morelli said to me. "Get it out of my sight."

I shoved Grandma back inside with the gun and closed the door. "I'll take care of it," I said to Morelli. "I'll make sure it's returned to its owner."

"So this ridiculous story is true?"

"Where were you? Why didn't you see any of this?"

"I was relieving Roche. I was watching the funeral home. I wasn't watching my car." He glanced over at the Buick. "No damage?"

"Scratched the rear bumper."

"Does the army know about this car?"

I thought it was time to remind Morelli of my usefulness. "Did you run a check on Spiro's guns?"

"They all checked out. Registered nice and legal."

So much for usefulness.

"Stephanie," my mother called from inside. "Are you out there without a coat? You're going to catch your death."

"Speaking of death," Morelli said. "They found a body to go with your foot. It floated into one of the bridge supports this morning."

"Sandeman?"

"Yeah."

"You think Kenny is self-destructing, looking to get caught?"

"I think it's not that complicated. He's a squirrel. This started out as a clever way to make a lot of money. Something went wrong, the operation got fucked up, and Kenny couldn't handle it. Now he's wound up so tight his eyes are crossed, and he's looking for people to blame . . . Moogey, Spiro, you."

"He's lost it, hasn't he?"

"Big time."

"You think Spiro is as crazy as Kenny?"

"Spiro isn't crazy. Spiro is small."

It was true. Spiro was a pimple on the burg's butt. I glanced over at Morelli's car. It didn't look drivable. "You need a ride somewhere?"

"I can manage."

Stiva's lot was already filled at seven o'clock, and cars lined the curb for two blocks down Hamilton. I double-parked just short of the service driveway and told Grandma she should go in without me.

She'd changed into a dress and the big blue coat and looked very colorful marching up Stiva's front steps with her apricot hair. She had her black patent leather purse tucked into the crook of her arm, and her bandaged hand stood out like a white flag, proclaiming her as one of the walking wounded in the war against Kenny Mancuso.

I circled the block twice before finding a spot. I hustled to the funeral parlor, entered through the side door, and steeled myself against the claustrophobic hothouse heat and crowd murmur. When this was over I was never again going into a funeral parlor. I didn't care who died. I wasn't having any part of it. Could be my mother or my grandmother. They were going to have to manage on their own.

I sidled up to Roche at the tea table. "I see your brother's being buried tomorrow morning."

"Yeah. Boy, I sure am going to miss this place.

I'm going to miss these cheapskate, sawdust cookies. And I'm going to miss the tea. Yum, I sure do love tea." He looked around. "Hell, I don't know what I'm complaining about. I've had worse assignments. Last year I was on a stakeout, dressed up like a bag lady, and I got mugged. Got two broken ribs."

"Have you seen my grandmother?"

"Yeah. I saw her come in, but then I lost her in the crowd. I imagine she's trying to get a look at the guy that had his . . . um, thing, whacked off."

I put my head down and muscled my way into the room where Joe Loosey was laid out. I elbowed to the front until I reached the casket and the widow Loosey. I'd expected Grandma to have insinuated herself into the space reserved for the immediate family, her reasoning being that she'd seen Joe's penis and was now on intimate terms.

"I'm sorry for your loss," I said to Mrs. Loosey. "Have you seen Grandmother Mazur?"

She looked alarmed. "Edna is here?"

"I dropped her off about ten minutes ago. I expected she'd have come to pay her respects."

Mrs. Loosey put a protective hand on the casket. "I haven't seen her."

I pushed through the crowd and dropped in on Roche's fake brother. A handful of people were in the back of the room. From the level of animation I'd guess they were talking about the great penis scandal. I asked if anyone had seen Grandma Mazur. The answers were negative. I returned to the lobby. I checked the kitchen, the ladies' room, the porch to the side door. I questioned everyone in my path.

No one had seen a little old lady in a big blue coat.

Prickles of alarm had begun to dance along my spine. This was uncharacteristic of Grandma. She liked to be in the thick of things. I'd seen her walk through Stiva's front door, so I knew she was in the house . . . at least for a short time. I didn't think it likely she'd gone back outside. I hadn't seen her on the street while I was searching for a parking space. And I couldn't imagine her leaving without taking a peek at Loosey.

I walked upstairs and prowled through the second story rooms where caskets and files were stored. I cracked the door to the business office and flipped the light switch. The office was empty. The upstairs bathroom was empty. The walk-in linen closet that was filled with office supplies was empty.

I returned to the lobby and noticed Roche was no longer at the tea table. Spiro was alone at the front door, looking sour.

"I can't find Grandma Mazur," I said to him.

"Congratulations."

"Not funny. I'm worried about her."

"You should be. She's nuts."

"Have you seen her?"

"No. And it's the only decent thing that's happened to me in two days."

"I thought maybe I should check the back rooms."

"She's not in the back. I keep the doors locked during public hours."

"She can be sort of ingenious when she has her mind set on something."

"If she managed to get back there, she wouldn't stay long. Fred Dagusto is on table number one, and he's not a pretty sight. Three hundred and ten pounds of ugly flesh. Fat as far as the eye can see. Gonna have to grease him up to shoehorn him into a casket."

"I want to look at those rooms."

Spiro glanced at his watch. "You're going to have to wait until hours are over. I can't leave these ghouls unsupervised. You get a big crowd like this, and people start walking off with souvenirs. You don't watch the door, and you could lose the shirt off your back."

"I don't need a guide. Just give me the key."

"Forget it. I'm liable when there's a stiff on the table. I'm not taking any chances after Loosey."

"Where's Louie?"

"Has the day off."

I went out onto the front porch and stared across the street. The windows in the surveillance apartment were dark. Roche was probably there, listening and looking. Maybe Morelli was there, too. I was worried about Grandma Mazur, but I wasn't ready to drag Morelli into it. Better to let him watch the exterior of the building, for now.

I stepped off the porch and made my way to the side entrance. I scanned the parking lot and continued on to the garages at the rear, cupping my hands to see through the tinted hearse windows, examining the bed of the open-backed flower car, knocking on the trunk lid to Spiro's Lincoln.

The door to the cellar was locked, but the service door to the kitchen was open. I let myself in and did another run-through of the house, trying the door to the workrooms and finding it sealed tight, as promised.

I slipped into Spiro's office and used his phone to call home.

"Is Grandma Mazur there?" I asked my mother.

"Oh my God," my mother said. "You've lost your grandmother. Where are you?"

"I'm at the funeral parlor. I'm sure Grandma is here somewhere. It's just that there's a crush of people, and I'm having a hard time finding her."

"She isn't here."

"If she shows up, call me at Stiva's."

I dialed Ranger next and told him my problem, and that I might need help.

I went back to Spiro and told him if he didn't give me a tour of the embalming room I'd zing some electricity into his worthless hide. He thought about it for a moment, whirled on his heel, and stalked past the viewing rooms. He threw the hall door open with a crash and snapped back at me to make it fast.

As if I'd want to dawdle over Fred Dagusto.

"She isn't here," I said, returning to Spiro, who was straddling the doorjamb, keeping an eagle eye out for unusual bulges in overcoats that might indicate a mourner was absconding with a stolen roll of toilet paper.

"Yeah, right," he said. "Big surprise."

"The only place I haven't looked is the basement."

"She isn't in the basement. The door is locked. Just like this one was locked."

"I want to see."

"Listen," Spiro said. "She's probably gone off with some other old broad. She's probably at some diner, driving some poor waitress nuts."

"Let me into the cellar, and I swear I won't bother you anymore."

"That's a cheery thought."

An old man clapped a hand on Spiro's shoulder. "How's Con doing? He outta the hospital yet?"

"Yeah," Spiro said, brushing past. "He's out of the hospital. He'll be back to work next week. Monday."

"Bet you'll be happy to see him come back."

"Yeah, I'm jumping for joy just thinking about it."

Spiro crossed to the other side of the lobby, slithering between knots of people, ignoring some, toadying up to others. I followed him to the cellar door and waited impatiently while he fumbled with keys. My heart was skittering in my chest, fearful of what I might find at the foot of the stairs.

I wanted Spiro to be right. I wanted Grandma to be at a diner somewhere with one of her cronies, but I didn't think it was likely.

If she'd been forcibly removed from the house, Morelli or Roche would have acted. Unless she'd been taken out the back door. The back door was their blind spot. Still, they'd compensated for that by planting a bug. And if the bugs were working, Morelli and Roche would have heard me looking for Grandma and would be doing their thing . . . whatever that was.

I flipped the stairwell light switch and called out. "Grandma?"

The furnace roared in some far-off place, and there was the murmur of voices in the rooms behind me. A small circle of light brightened the cellar floor at the bottom of the stairs. I squinted to see beyond the light, strained to hear whatever small sound the cellar might offer up.

My stomach clenched at the silence. Someone was down there. I could feel it, just as surely as I could feel Spiro's breath on my neck.

The truth is, I'm not the heroic type. I'm afraid of spiders and extraterrestrials and sometimes feel the need to check under my bed for drooly guys with claws. If I ever found one, I'd run screaming out of my apartment and never come back.

"The meter's running," Spiro said. "You going down there, or what?"

I rummaged through my pocketbook for my .38 and descended the stairs with gun drawn. Stephanie Plum, chickenshit bounty hunter, takes stairs one at a time, practically blinded because her heart is beating in her throat so hard it's knocking her head back and forth, blurring her vision.

I steadied myself on the last step, reached left, and flipped the light switch. Nothing happened.

"Hey, Spiro," I called. "The lights won't go on."

He hunkered down at the top of the stairs. "Must be the circuit breaker."

"Where's the box?"

"To your right, behind the furnace."

Damn. Everything was black to my right. I reached for my flashlight, and before I could withdraw my hand from my pocketbook, Kenny sprang out of the shadows. He hit me from the side, and we both crashed to the floor, the impact knocking me breathless, the jolt sending my .38 skittering off into the dark, beyond my grasp. I scrambled to my feet and was slammed flat onto my chest. A knee jammed between my shoulder blades, and there was the prick of something very sharp pressed against the side of my neck.

"Don't fucking move," Kenny said. "You move an inch, and I'll shove this knife into your throat."

I heard the door close at the top of the stairs, heard Spiro hurry down. "Kenny? What the hell are you doing down here? How'd you get in?"

"I got in through the cellar door. I used the key you gave me. How the hell else would I get in."

"I didn't know you were coming back. I thought you got all the stuff stashed last night."

"Came back to check on things. Wanted to make sure everything was still here."

"What the hell's that supposed to mean?"

"It means you make me nervous," Kenny said.

"I make *you* nervous? That's good. You're the

one who's fucking squirrelly, and I make *you* nervous."

"Better watch who you're calling fucking squirrelly."

"Let me tell you the difference between you and me," Spiro said. "This is all business for me. I act like a professional. Somebody stole the caskets, so I hired an expert to find them. I didn't go around shooting my partner in the knee because I was pissed. And I wasn't so stupid that I used a fucking stolen gun to shoot him with and then got myself caught by an off-duty cop. I wasn't so fucking nuts that I thought my partners were plotting against me. I didn't think this was some fucking coup.

"And I didn't go wacko over sweetie pie here. You know what your problem is, Kenny? You get on an idea, and you can't get off. You get obsessed with shit, and then you can't see anything else. And you always have to be the fucking show-off. You could have gotten rid of Sandeman nice and quiet, but no, you had to hack off his fucking foot."

Kenny chuckled. "And I'll tell you what *your* problem is, Spiro. You don't know how to have fun. Always the serious undertaker. You should try sticking that big-bore needle into something alive for a change."

"You're sick."

"Yeah, you're not so healthy yourself. You've spent enough time watching me work my magic."

I could hear Spiro shift behind me. "You're talking too much."

"Doesn't matter. Sweetie pie isn't going to tell anyone. She and her granny are going to disappear."

"Fine by me. Just don't do it here. I don't want to be involved." Spiro crossed the room, flipped the circuit breaker, and the lights flashed on.

Five crated caskets lined one wall, the furnace and water heater sat in the middle of the room, and a jumble of crates and boxes had been stacked next to the back door. It didn't take a genius to guess the contents of the crates and boxes.

"I don't get it," I said. "Why did you bring the stuff here? Con is coming back to work on Monday. How will you keep this from him?"

"It'll be gone by Monday," Spiro said. "We brought everything in yesterday, so we could take inventory. Sandeman was carrying the whole shitload around in his pickup, doing fucking tailgate sales. Lucky for us you saw the furniture truck in Delio's. Another couple of weeks with Sandeman running loose and nothing would have been left."

"I don't know how you got it in, but you'll never get it out," I said. "Morelli is watching the house."

Kenny snorted. "It goes out the same way it came in. In the meat wagon."

"For Christ's sake," Spiro said. "It's not a meat wagon."

"Oh yeah, I forgot. It's a slumber coach." Kenny stood up and yanked me to my feet. "The cops watch Spiro, and they watch the house. They don't watch the slumber coach and Louie Moon. Or at least who they think is Louie Moon. You could put a hat on Bonzo the chimp and put him behind those tinted windows, and the cops would think it was Louie Moon. And good old Louie is real cooperative. You just give Louie a hose and tell him to clean things up, and Louie is busy for hours. He don't know who's driving around in his goddamn slumber coach."

Not bad. They dressed Kenny up to look like Louie Moon, brought the guns and ammo to the funeral home in the hearse, parked the hearse in the garage, and then all they had to do was run the boxes between the garage and the back door to the cellar. And Morelli and Roche couldn't see the back door to the cellar. They probably couldn't hear anything in the cellar either. I didn't think it likely Roche would have bugged the cellar.

"So what's with the old lady?" Spiro asked Kenny.

"She was in the kitchen looking for a teabag, and she saw me cutting across the lawn."

Spiro's face tightened. "Did she tell anybody?"

"No. She came barreling out of the house, yelling at me for stabbing her in the hand. Telling me I needed to learn respect for old people."

So far as I could see, Grandma wasn't in the cellar. I hoped it meant Kenny had her locked in the garage. If she was in the garage, she might still be alive, and she might be unhurt. If she was tucked away somewhere in the cellar, beyond my view, she was much too quiet.

I didn't want to consider the reasons for too quiet, preferring to squash the panic clawing at my stomach and replace it with some more constructive emotion. How about cool reasoning? Nope. I didn't have any of that available. How about cunning? Sorry, low on cunning. How about anger? Did I have any anger? Fucking A. I had so much anger my skin could hardly contain it all. Anger for Grandma, anger for all the women Mancuso'd abused, anger for the cops who were killed with the stolen ammo. I pulled the anger in until it was hard and razor sharp.

"Now what?" I said to Kenny. "Where do we go from here?"

"Now we put you on ice for a while. Until the house empties out. Then I'll see what kind of a mood I'm in. We have a bunch of options being that we're in a funeral parlor. Hell, we could strap you to the table and embalm you while you're still alive. That would be fun." He pressed the tip of the knife blade to the back of my neck. "Walk."

"Where?"

He jerked his head. "Over to the corner."

The crated caskets were stacked in the corner. "To the caskets?"

He smiled and prodded me forward. "The caskets come later."

I squinted into the corner shadows and realized the caskets weren't flush to the wall. Tucked behind the caskets was a refrigeration unit with two body drawers. The drawers were closed, the metal trays locked behind heavy metal doors.

"Gonna be nice and dark in there," Kenny said. "Give you time to think."

Fear slid down my spine and sickened my stomach. "Grandma Mazur . . ."

"Turning into a Popsicle, even as we speak."

"NO! Let her out! Open the drawer, I'll do whatever you want!"

"You'll do whatever I want anyway," Kenny said. "You're not going to be moving too fast after an hour in there."

Tears were pouring down my cheeks and sweat prickled under my arms. "She's old. She's no threat to you. Let her go."

"No threat? Are you kidding? That old lady is criminally insane. You know what it took to get her in that drawer?"

"She's probably dead by now, anyway," Spiro said.

Kenny looked at him. "You think so?"

"How long she been in there?"

Kenny checked his watch. "Maybe ten minutes."

Spiro stuffed his hands into his pockets. "You lower the temperature?"

"No," Kenny said. "I just shoved her in."

"We don't keep the drawers cold if they're un-occupied," Spiro explained. "Saves on electricity. Probably it's only around room temperature."

"Yeah, but she could have died from fright. What do you think?" Kenny asked me. "You think she's dead?"

A sob stuck in my chest.

"Sweetie pie is speechless," Kenny said. "Maybe

we should open the drawer and see if the old bag's breathing?"

Spiro released the latch and yanked the door open. He grabbed the end of the stainless steel tray and slowly rolled it toward him, so that the first thing I saw was Grandma Mazur's shoes pointing toes up, then Grandma's bony shin, her big blue coat, arms rigidly at her sides, hands hidden under the folds of the coat.

I felt myself sway under a wave of grief. I forced air into my lungs and blinked to clear my vision.

The tray reached its full extension and clicked into place. Grandma stared unflinching at the ceiling, eyes open, mouth set, still as stone.

We all gaped at her in silence for several moments.

Kenny was the first to speak. "She looks dead all right," he said. "Roll her back in."

The whisper of a sound stuck in the corner. A hiss. We all pricked our ears and concentrated. I saw the very slightest tightening around Grandma's eye. The hiss again. Louder this time. Grandma sucking air through her dentures!

"Hmmm," Kenny said. "Maybe she's not dead yet."

"You should have cranked the unit down," Spiro offered. "This baby'll go down to zero. She wouldn't have lasted ten minutes if you'd had it at zero."

Grandma made some feeble movements on the tray.

"What's she doing?" Spiro asked.

"She's trying to sit up," Kenny said. "But she's too old. Can't get those old bones to cooperate, huh, Granny?"

"Old," she whispered. "I'll show you old."

"Shove the drawer back in," Kenny said to Spiro. "And fix the freezer setting."

Spiro started to roll the tray in, but Grandma kicked out with her feet, stopping the slide. She had her knees bent, and she was pounding against the steel with her feet, clawing and knocking inside the drawer.

Spiro grunted and rammed the tray home, but the tray was inches short of clicking into place, and the door wouldn't close.

"Something's stuck," Spiro said. "This won't go in all the way."

"Open it up," Kenny said, "and see what's wrong."

Spiro eased the tray back.

Grandma's chin appeared, her nose, her eyes. Her arms were extended over her head.

"You making problems, Granny?" Kenny asked. "You jamming the drawer with something?"

Grandma didn't say anything, but I could see her mouth working, her dentures grinding against each other.

"Get your arms down at your sides," Kenny told her. "Stop fucking with me. I'm gonna lose my patience."

Grandma struggled to get her arms out, and finally her bandaged hand popped free. The other hand followed, and in that hand was the .45 long-barrel. She swung her arm straight from the shoulder and squeezed off a round.

We all hit the floor, and she fired again.

Silence followed the second shot. No one moved but Grandma. She elbowed herself to a sitting position, and took a moment to settle.

"I know what you're thinking," Grandma said into the silence. "Do I have any more bullets in this here gun? Well, with all the confusion, what with being locked up in a refrigerator, I plum forgot what was in here to start with. But being that this is a forty-five Magnum, the most powerful handgun in existence, and it could blow your head clean off, you just got to ask yourself one question. Do you feel lucky today? Well, do you, punk?"

"Christ," Spiro whispered. "She thinks she's fucking Clint Eastwood."

BAM! Grandma fired and knocked out a light.

"Dang," she said, "must be something wrong with this sight."

Kenny scrambled to the ammo cases to get a gun, Spiro ran for the stairs, and I inched toward Grandma on my belly.

BAM! She got another shot off. It missed Kenny, but it tore into one of the cases. There was an instant explosion, and a fireball rose to the basement ceiling.

I jumped to my feet and dragged Grandma off the tray.

Another case exploded. Fire crackled across

the floor and traced along the wooden casket casings. I didn't know what was exploding, but I thought we were lucky not to have been hit by flying fragments. Smoke roiled from the burning boxes, cutting into the light, stinging my eyes.

I yanked Grandma to the back door and shoved her out into the yard.

"Are you okay?" I yelled at her.

"He was going to kill me," she said. "He was going to kill you too."

"Yes."

"It's terrible what happens to people. That they lose respect for life."

"Yes."

Grandma looked back at the house. "Good thing not everyone's like Kenny. Good thing some human beings are decent."

"Like us," I said.

"Well, I suppose, but I was thinking more of Dirty Harry."

"That was some speech you gave."

"Always wanted to give that speech. Guess there's a silver lining to everything."

"Can you walk around to the front of the building? Can you find Morelli and tell him I'm back here?"

Grandma lurched toward the driveway. "If he's there, I'll find him."

Kenny had been on the opposite side of the cellar when we rushed to get out. Either he'd gone up the stairs, or he was still inside, making his way close to the floor, trying to get to the back door.

I was putting my money on the latter. Too many people at the top of the stairs.

I was standing about twenty feet from the door, and I wasn't sure what I'd do if Kenny appeared. I didn't have a gun or a defense spray. I didn't even have a flashlight. Probably I should get the hell out of there and forget about Kenny. The money's not worth it, I said to myself.

Who was I kidding? This wasn't about money. This was about Grandma.

There was another small explosion, and flames flared through the kitchen windows. People shouted from the street, and I could hear sirens in the distance. Smoke poured through the cellar door and swirled around a human form. A hellish creature, backlit by fire. Kenny.

He bent at the waist and coughed and took in some air. His hands hung loose at his sides. Didn't look like he'd been able to find a gun. That was a break. I saw him glance side to side and then come straight toward me. My heart almost jumped out of my chest, until I realized he didn't see me. I was standing, lost in shadow, in his line of escape. He was going to skirt the garage and disappear into the back alleys of the burg.

He moved stealthily forward, silent against the roar of the fire. He was less than five feet away when he saw me. He stopped short, startled, and our eyes locked. My first thought was that he would bolt and run, but he lunged at me on an oath, and we both went down, kicking and clawing. I gave him a good shot with my knee and stuck my thumb in his eye.

Kenny howled and pushed off, rising to a crouch. I grabbed for his foot, and he went down again, hard on his knees. We did more rolling on the ground. More kicking and clawing and swearing.

He was bigger and stronger than me, and probably crazier. Although some might argue that last point. What I had on my side was anger. Kenny was desperate, but I was freaked-out enraged.

I didn't just want to stop him . . . I wanted to hurt him. Not a nice thing to have to admit. I'd never thought of myself as a mean and vengeful person, but there it was.

I squeezed my hand tight in a fist and swung into him backhand, landing a blow that sent shock waves up my arm. There'd been a crunch and a gasp, and I saw him flail out in the darkness, arms wide open.

I grabbed hold of his shirt and shouted for help.

His hands clamped onto my neck, his breath hot on my face. His voice was thick. "Die."

Maybe, but he'd go down with me. I had his shirt in a death grip. The only way he was going to get away was to take the damn thing off. If he strangled me unconscious, I'd still have my fingers dug into his shirt.

I was so focused on the shirt it took me a while to realize the pack had enlarged to three.

"Jesus," Morelli was yelling in my ear. "Let go of his shirt!"

"He'll get away!"

"He won't get away," Morelli shouted. "I've got him."

I looked beyond Morelli and saw Ranger and Roche round the corner of the house with two uniforms.

"Get her off me," Kenny screeched. "Jesus! These Plum bitches are goddamn animals!"

There was another crunch in the darkness, and I suspected Morelli had accidentally broken something belonging to Kenny. Like his nose, maybe.

CHAPTER

15

I had Rex's cage wrapped in a big blue blanket so he wouldn't get a chill while I transported him. I eased him off the Buick's front seat and pushed the door closed with my butt. It was nice to be moving back to my apartment. And it was nice to feel safe. Kenny was locked up without bail, and I expected he'd be locked up for a good long time. Hopefully for life.

Rex and I took the elevator. The doors slid open on the second floor, and I stepped out feeling good inside. I loved my hallway, and I loved Mr. Wolesky, and I loved Mrs. Bestler. It was nine o'clock in the morning, and I was going to take a shower in my very own bathroom. I loved my bathroom.

I balanced Rex on my hip while I unlocked my door. Later today I'd stop by the office and pick up my recovery fee. Then I'd go shopping. Maybe I'd buy a new refrigerator.

I set Rex on the table by the couch and opened the curtains. I loved my curtains. I stood there for a while, admiring my view of the parking lot, thinking that I also loved the parking lot.

"Home," I said. Nice and quiet. Private.

There was a knock at the door.

I squinted through the peephole. It was Morelli.

"Thought you'd want to get filled in on some details," Morelli said.

I opened the door to him and stepped back. "Kenny talked?"

Morelli moved into the foyer. His posture was relaxed, but his eyes ticked off the details of his surroundings. Always the cop. "Enough to piece things together," he said. "Turns out there were three conspirators, just as we thought . . . Kenny, Moogey, and Spiro. And they each had a key to the storage locker."

"One for all, and all for one."

"More like nobody trusted anybody else. Kenny was the brains behind it all. He planned the theft, and he had an overseas buyer for the stolen ammo."

"The phone numbers to Mexico and El Salvador."

"Yeah. He also got a nice advance . . ."

"Which he spent ahead of time."

"Yep. Then he went to the locker to get the stuff ready for shipment, and guess what?"

"No stuff."

"Yep again," Morelli said. "Why are you wearing your jacket?"

"I just got in." I looked wistfully toward the bathroom. "I was about to take a shower."

"Hmmm," Morelli said.

"No hmmm. Tell me about Sandeman. Where does Sandeman figure in?"

"Sandeman heard some conversations between Moogey and Spiro and got curious. So he tapped into one of the many skills he acquired during a life of petty crime, duped the locker key off Moogey's key ring, and by process of lengthy elimination, found the locker."

"Who killed Moogey?"

"Sandeman. He got nervous. Thought Moogey might have eventually figured out about the borrowed furniture truck."

"And Sandeman told all of this to Kenny?"

"Kenny can be very persuasive."

There was no doubt in my mind.

Morelli played with the zipper on my jacket. "About that shower . . ."

I pointed with straight arm and extended finger to my door. "Out."

"Don't you want to know about Spiro?"

"What about Spiro?"

"We haven't caught him yet."

"He's probably gone underground."

Morelli winced.

"That's undertaker humor," I told him.

"One more thing. Kenny had an interesting spin on how the fire got started."

"Lies. All lies."

"You could have avoided a lot of terror if you'd just left that bug in your pocketbook."

I narrowed my eyes and crossed my arms over my chest. "This is a subject best forgotten."

"You left me standing bare-assed in the middle of the street!"

"I gave you your gun, didn't I?"

Morelli grinned. "You're going to give me more than that, Cupcake."

"Forget it."

"Not likely," Morelli said. "You owe me."

"I owe you nothing! If anyone is owed, it's me! I caught your cousin for you!"

"And in the process burned down Stiva's Mortuary and destroyed thousands of dollars' worth of government property."

"Well, if you're going to be picky about it . . ."

"Picky? Sweetie pie, you are the worst bounty hunter in the history of the world."

"That does it. I have better things to do than to stand here and take your insults."

I pushed him out of my foyer, into the hall, slammed the door closed, and threw the bolt. I pressed my nose to the door and looked through the peephole.

Morelli grinned at me.

"This is war," I yelled through the door.

"Lucky for me," Morelli said. "I give good war."

ABOUT THE AUTHOR

Janet Evanovich is the #1 *New York Times* best-selling author of the Stephanie Plum series and the coauthor of the Lizzy and Diesel series, the Knight and Moon series, the Alexandra Barnaby novels, the Fox and O'Hare series, the *Troublemaker* graphic novel, and *How I Write: Secrets of a Bestselling Author*.

Stephanie Plum returns in
Janet Evanovich's

FORTUNE AND GLORY

Tantalizing Twenty-Seven

Turn the page for a sneak peek.

CHAPTER

1

My name is Stephanie Plum and I'm a fugitive apprehension agent in Trenton, New Jersey. I'm not especially brave, so you would think I'd pretty much stay out of trouble. Unfortunately, I occasionally ignore the obvious signs of danger and stumble into something ugly with the potential for disaster. This was one of those times. I was in a tunnel under a strip club, and I was with my coworker, Lula.

"This is a bad idea," Lula said to me. "My nipples are all shrunk up and trying to hide inside my body. It's like what men's gonads do when someone comes at them with a butcher knife. Those suckers abandon ship and there's nothing left but an empty nut sack. Not that I know firsthand. I'm just sayin' what I hear."

Aside from being a bounty hunter, I think I'm pretty normal. I have shoulder-length curly

brown hair that's usually pulled back into a ponytail, blue eyes from my mother's Hungarian an-
cestors, and a bunch of rude hand gestures from
my father's Italian side of the family. My nipples
aren't as smart or nearly as big as Lula's. They
were currently snug inside my sports bra, going
along for the ride, and not paying attention to
much of anything.

"Not only that, but I think my hair's standing
on end," Lula said. "Look at it. Is it standing on
end? It feels like it. My scalp is all tingly. That's a
for-sure sign that something horrible is going to
happen to us."

Lula's hair is always a surprise. Some days it's
lavender. Some days it's braided. Some days it
isn't even Lula's real hair. Today it was a massive
puffball of chemically induced black ringlets shot
through with hot pink highlights and sprinkled
with glittery tiny pink stars. It was awesome. The
rest of Lula is equally awesome, as her bounty
runneth over in booty and boob and everything
else. Today she was packed into a yellow spandex
mini bandage dress that was sized for a much,
much smaller woman. I was in my usual uniform
of sneakers, jeans, and girly T-shirt.

Lula and I were playing hooky from bounty
hunting to track down Lou Salgusta, a mob guy
who specializes in information extraction and
revenge by barbecuing various body parts of his
victims. He's one of six hit men who, years ago,
bought a strip club called the Mole Hole. It's located in downtown Trenton, and it's famous for

its cheap drinks, outstanding burgers, and mob-occupied back room. It was common knowledge that the six club owners each had a personal La-Z-Boy recliner in the back room, and the possession of one of those recliners was as good as, if not better than, being made.

Recently, Salgusta and one of his La-Z-Boy pals, Charlie Shine, decided my grandmother had the key to a treasure. They kidnapped Grandma and me, and while we endured some terrifying moments, we were able to escape with minimum damage. Problem is, Shine and Salgusta still want the key to the treasure, and we saw them murder a man in cold blood while we were captive. So, there's incentive for Salgusta and Shine to capture us again, persuade Grandma to give them the key, and then kill us.

"I know it's a righteous undertaking to protect your granny," Lula said, "but we aren't exactly that *Die Hard* guy."

"John McClane?"

"No, Bruce Willis. I'm guessing you don't even have a gun. I'm guessing your gun is home in your brown bear cookie jar."

She was right about the gun, and she was right about us not being Bruce Willis. Unfortunately, I can't let any of that stop me, because I love my grandma, and I will do whatever it takes to protect her. And as I see it, the only way to protect her is to track down Salgusta and Shine and get them behind bars.

Twenty minutes ago, I got a call from my mom,

who'd gotten a call from Margie Wisneski, who'd gotten a call from her alcoholic brother that he was having his midmorning pick-me-up at the Mole Hole, and that Lou Salgusta had just walked in and gone straight to the back room.

Lula and I rushed to the scene, but the back room was empty when we arrived. Margie's brother was still at the bar and swore that Salgusta went into the back room and didn't come out.

"There's gotta be a secret way out of that room," Lula said. "That's the way it always is in the gangster movies. You've got to have a way to sneak out when the bulls show up. That's what they used to call the police. I know all about this because I got the classics movie channel on my TV package."

We returned to the back room and looked around. Six La-Z-Boy chairs. A monster safe. A card table with four folding chairs. Big-screen TV. No windows or doors other than the door opening to the barroom.

After several minutes of searching, we found a trapdoor hidden under a rug. We opened the door, climbed down a ladder, and stood squinting in the dim light of an escape tunnel that was approximately six feet high and three feet wide. It was encased in concrete and lit by a single bulb that was about thirty feet in front of the ladder.

Lula and I were now standing under that bulb. The tunnel changed from concrete to dirt at this point. It was supported by wood posts at regular intervals and it narrowed slightly.

"I'm going back," Lula said. "No way in hell am I going to squeeze myself into that dirt tunnel. First off, it's going to smudge up my dress. And second, it's the tunnel to death and doom."

"I imagine you got the death-and-doom message from your nipples?"

"Don't underestimate my nipples. I got nipple radar. When they talk, I listen."

Lula turned and huffed back to the ladder. She climbed the ladder and stopped at the top.

"This here door's closed," she said.

"You followed me down. Did you close the door?"

"Yeah. I didn't want anyone to know we were down here. I didn't count on it being so hard to get open again."

"Maybe there's a latch somewhere. A button to push," I said.

"I'm feeling all around and I don't see no button."

"Are you sure you can't push the door open?"

"Would I be standing here on this freaking ladder if I could get the freaking door open?" Lula said.

I replaced Lula on the ladder and tried the door. No luck. I climbed down the ladder and pulled my cell phone out of my pocket. No bars. I looked down the corridor at the dark, dirt tunnel of death and doom.

"Guess what?" I said.

"I don't like 'guess what.' And I don't like the way this place smells," Lula said, following me to the end of the concrete.

"It smells like dirt."

"Exactly," Lula said. "There's no other smells besides dirt, and that would indicate that we're underground with no windows or anything. Like we're in a tomb. You see what I'm saying?"

"We aren't in a tomb. We're in a tunnel that Lou Salgusta just used so it has to go somewhere."

Okay, truth is, I was every bit as creeped out as Lula. I didn't like being underground. It was claustrophobic. The air was heavy with dirt and damp, and I had to keep reminding myself that I wasn't suffocating. Even worse was the thought that Lou Salgusta might be waiting at the other end. I wanted to capture him, but I wasn't confident that I could do it under these circumstances.

I tapped my phone's flashlight app. "Stay close behind me and don't use your phone," I said to Lula. "We should save your battery."

"Do you want my gun, being that you're first in line?"

"Sure."

I took the gun from her not so much for self-defense as to make sure Lula didn't panic and accidentally shoot me in the back.

We walked a short distance and the tunnel curved. The single lightbulb disappeared from view and there was only blackness in front of us and behind us.

"I can't see what I'm walking on," Lula said. "It feels squishy and I hear water dripping."

Water was dripping from the top of the tunnel

and the dirt underfoot was muddy. I could see men's footprints in the mud. Salgusta, I thought. Maybe someone else. Hard to tell in the dark. The tunnel came to a T-intersection. I flashed the light in both directions and saw nothing but endless dark tunnel. I went right, following the footprints.

"There's something dropped on my neck," Lula said. "I can feel it crawling. It's one of them big tarantulas. Lord help me, I got them all over me!"

I turned and flashed the light on Lula. "I don't see anything. I think you're just getting dripped on."

"It was on me and then it jumped off."

I directed the light to the ground and a small rat scurried away.

"Holy hell," Lula said.

I bit into my lip to keep from screaming and moved forward.

"I bet there's snakes up ahead," Lula said. "That's the way it is with Indiana Jones. First the tarantulas and rats and then the snakes. Where's the end of this freaking tunnel? I want to see the light. Where the heck is the light?"

"Hang on," I said. "I'm following footprints."

"I think we must be coming to the end because I smell something different," Lula said. "It doesn't smell like just dirt anymore. It smells like kerosene or gasoline or something."

I'd noticed the smell when we turned the corner a while back. I didn't think it was a good sign since we were following a man whose best friend was an acetylene torch.

"What's those red dots in front of us?" Lula asked.

I flashed the light at the dots. "Rats," I said.

"Shoot them!"

I wasn't going to waste bullets on rats. I was saving them for whatever more horrible, more ferocious creatures might be lurking in the dark. Alligators or a slimy mud monster or Lou Salgusta.

I saw a flicker of light far down the tunnel. Another flicker eerily illuminated a smiling face, and WHOOOSH, the face disappeared behind a curtain of fire. Flames licked at the ground in front of a monstrous fireball and raced toward us.

I turned and shoved Lula. "Run!"

We ran blind in the dark, my flashlight beam bouncing around. A swarm of rats were also running for their lives, squealing beside us. I stepped on one and kicked another out of the way. Lula was huffing and puffing in front of me.

"Run faster!" I yelled. "I've got a wall of fire behind me."

We reached the intersection, made the turn, and the fire roared past us. We were bent over, catching our breath and I thought I heard footsteps, far off in one of the tunnels.

"We need to get to the trapdoor," I said to Lula. "Get moving."

"What happens when we get to the trapdoor?" Lula asked.

"We open it."

The dirt was dry underfoot in this part of the

tunnel and the single bulb was visible in front of us. We passed under the light and I stared up at the wood door.

"Stand back," I said to Lula.

I emptied the clip into the door where I thought the latch was located. The door was pocked with rounds, and I could see through a couple of holes I'd drilled in the wood. I climbed the ladder and pushed, but the door didn't budge. I heard the scuff of shoes and muffled speech. I banged on the door and yelled for help.

The trapdoor was wrenched open and a young guy in a black Mole Hole T-shirt looked down at me. "What the heck?" he said, taking my hand, helping me out.

Lula was right behind. "No kidding, what the heck," she said. "You gotta fix that door. Bad enough you got a creep-ass tunnel down there, but your door don't even work when you want to get out. I got ruined Via Spigas, and I gotta take this dress to the cleaners. You know how much they charge to clean a dress? And on top of that, there's fireballs and rats down there, and I'm pretty sure I got the rat cooties on me." She tugged her skirt down over her ass and looked at the guy who helped me out. "You're the bartender, right? I want one of them man-eater burgers with extra fries and a chardonnay."

"Not a good idea," I said. "There might be someone following us, and I'm out of bullets."

"Yeah, but I really need a burger," Lula said. "I'm about having a heart attack. I need something to calm myself. I need meat and grease and cheese."

I could identify. My blood pressure was just a couple of notches below stroke level, but a burger wasn't going to do it for me. I wanted to get out of the Mole Hole. I needed air. I needed distance from the smiling face of Lou Salgusta.

"We can get a burger on the way to the office," I said. I looked at the bartender. "Thanks for the help. We appreciate it."

"Yeah, no problem. I wouldn't have heard the gunshots, but the music shut off between sets." He looked down at the open trapdoor. "I didn't know there was a tunnel."

I turned to go and almost bumped into a woman who was standing behind me. She was my height and about my age. She was exotically pretty, with long brown hair and large almond-shaped eyes. She was dressed in black. Black Louboutin combat boots with signature spikes covering the toes. Black skinny jeans. Black tank top with a black, Loro Piana Traveller jacket. Her lipstick was perfectly outlined just like her eyes.

"Did I hear you say there was a tunnel?" she asked.

"This here is the tunnel from hell," Lula said.

The woman moved closer and studied the ladder. "What's down there?"

"Mostly mud and rats," I said.

"Interesting," she said. "A tunnel under a strip club. If you'll excuse me, I think I'll investigate."

"And fire," I said. "Did I mention the fire?"

She was already halfway down the ladder.

"Hey!" I yelled at her. "The tunnel is dangerous. You shouldn't be exploring down there."

She disappeared from view, her boots echoing on the concrete for a short time, and then there was silence.

"Do you know her?" I asked the bartender.

"Never saw her before," he said.

"She's not from Jersey," Lula said. "She doesn't talk right. She sounds like Eliza Doolittle. And she's a crazy lady, but she got good taste in purses. She had a Fendi mini backpack hanging from her shoulder. I always wanted one of them."

Lula and I were splattered with mud and smelled of gasoline. We left the back room, walked through the dimly lit barroom, and went out the door. We stood blinking in the bright sunlight.

"I need to get out of these clothes before I got spontaneous combustion going on," Lula said.

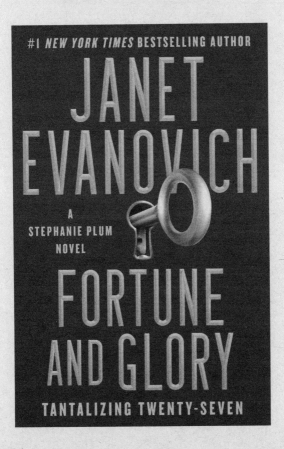